Oranges
for
Christmas

MARGARITA MORRIS

This novel is a work of fiction and, except in the case of historical fact, any resemblance to actual persons, living or dead, is purely coincidental.

Margarita Morris asserts the moral right to be identified as the author of this work.

Published by Margarita Morris at CreateSpace

Cover
By L1Graphics

ISBN: 0-9927489-2-0
ISBN-13: 978-0-9927489-2-0

For Steve

CONTENTS

ACKNOWLEDGMENTS

I first visited Berlin in 1987 on a travel grant from Jesus College, Oxford, and for that I am extremely grateful. I am also indebted to my friend, Kristin, who showed me around and took me to East Berlin.

Here is a list of the most useful books I consulted during my research:

The Wall – The People's Story by Christopher Hilton (2001)
Stasiland – Stories from Behind the Berlin Wall by Anna Funder (2003)
The Lost World of Communism – An Oral History of Daily Life Behind the Iron Curtain by Peter Molloy (2009)
1989 The Berlin Wall – My Part in its Downfall by Peter Millar (2009)
Der Tunnel in die Freiheit – Berlin, Bernauer Strasse by Ellen Sesta (2001)
East Berlin by Dr. Eckart D. Stratenschulte, translated by Shiel Ross (1988)
The File – A Personal History by Timothy Garton Ash (1997)

I would like to thank my children for having the patience and maturity to visit lots of Berlin Wall sites during their summer holiday. But most of all I would like to thank my husband, Steve, for his unwavering support, dedication as a first reader, insightful and constructive comments, help with technology and willingness to rough it in youth hostels.

PREFACE

After the end of World War II, Germany was divided into four Occupied Zones: British, American, French and Soviet. Berlin, which was geographically in the Soviet Zone, was divided into four Occupied Sectors: British, American, French and Soviet. But the Berliners continued to live and work there as if it was one city, which it was. Until the unthinkable happened...

1 SUNDAY 13 AUGUST 1961

Sabine

I open my eyes and see a head hanging upside down. Grinning at me.

Brigitta springs down from the top bunk, lithe as a cat, and whips the blanket off me.

"*Komm, Sabine. Steh auf!*" Come on, Sabine. Get up. She is excited. We both are.

We haven't seen our older brother Dieter in – how long has it been? – Six weeks? More like two months now I think about it. Yes – it was the middle of June, before school ended. Now that he lives and works in West Berlin we don't get to see him so often. During the week we're at school and most weekends he works long hours at the *Hotel Zoo*. But not today.

Brigitta takes hold of my hands and pulls me out of bed.

"Okay, okay. I'm getting up."

The linoleum is cool under my feet. It is still early. I glance at the alarm clock that sits on top of the old chest of drawers. Half past six. But already, through the gap in the curtains, I catch a bright glint of sunlight. Another hot day; perfect weather for sunbathing and picnicking.

"What shall I wear?" I ask Brigitta, who has already put on her blue summer skirt and is pulling on her white blouse.

I pull open the wardrobe door which creaks in protest and consider my options. They are not many. It has to be either the blue dress with the tiny white polka dots or the yellow one, bright as a sunflower.

"Wear the yellow dress," says Brigitta. "It's a happy colour for a happy day."

I slide the dress off its hanger. "Back in a minute." I tiptoe down the corridor to the bathroom so as not to wake Mother.

The plan is for Brigitta and I to take the *S-bahn* train to the *Hauptbahnhof* in West Berlin, meet up with Dieter and then go on to the lake at *Wannsee*. Dieter said he would bring the picnic because you can buy better food in West Berlin – oranges and things like that. Besides, it's best not to carry too much when travelling from the East to the West – it rouses the suspicions of the border guards. People with suitcases are hauled off trains and interrogated. They think anyone carrying more than a handbag is trying to leaving the East for good. A picnic hamper would be sure to raise eyebrows.

I turn the tap and water sputters out. The plumbing in the apartment is temperamental. I don't want to risk waking Mother with the banging that comes from the pipes if you wait for hot water to come through, so I quickly splash cold water over myself at the sink and pat myself dry. Then I put on the yellow dress and join Brigitta in the kitchen.

She is standing on a chair so she can reach the half loaf of *Schwarzbrot* that is left in the cupboard. She passes it down to me and I cut two slices of the dense, dark brown bread. There's no butter to put on it. I went to the shop yesterday but Frau Maier said they had run out of butter and, no, she didn't know when the next delivery would be. We eat the bread as it is, gazing out of the window at the empty street five storeys below.

Out of habit I reach for the dial on the radio. I like to listen to RIAS, *Radio in the American Sector*, even though, strictly speaking, it's illegal to do so in East Berlin. But then I think of Mother, of how tired she looked when she came home from the factory last night, and I leave the radio switched off. Mother needs her rest. Last night she told us to enjoy ourselves and that she sends her love to Dieter. She hopes he'll have time to visit us soon.

Brigitta clears away the breakfast things while I fetch our *Personalausweise*, the personal identity cards that every citizen is required to carry with them at all times.

"*Fertig?*" asks Brigitta when I reappear. Ready?

I nod. "Let's go." She opens the door to the apartment and we slip outside onto the dark landing.

Dieter

Spread out on the kitchen table it looks like a feast. I go over everything one last time to make sure I haven't forgotten anything.

Six bread rolls, still warm from the baker's. Emmental cheese. Eight slices of smoked ham. *Apfelstrudel*. Bananas and oranges – a rare treat for Brigitta and Sabine. Lemonade. And

Schokoladenkuchen – chocolate cake which I baked myself. Sabine will be impressed at my new found culinary skills. You can't even buy proper chocolate in East Berlin. And as for bananas and oranges, well, most people have probably forgotten what they look like.

I start packing the food into the picnic hamper, wrapping the bread rolls in a clean tea-towel to keep them fresh. I wonder what Sabine and Brigitta are doing right now. I bet they're already on their way. Brigitta always did wake up at the crack of dawn and she won't want to miss a minute of today. I lay the rolls at the bottom of the hamper and place the ham and Emmental on top. Just wait until they see this food. They'll have to take some back for Mother – she loves fresh oranges. And a slice of chocolate cake.

Thinking of Mother, I feel a little guilty. It's my first Sunday off in ages and I should really be visiting my family in East Berlin. But Sabine and Brigitta so wanted to go to the lake at *Wannsee* and we should do it whilst the good weather holds. Of course, Mother could come too, but Sabine said she would want to rest after a hard week at the factory. I reach across the table for the bananas, slotting them into a corner of the hamper. I tell myself I'll visit Mother in East Berlin in September. And, of course, at Christmas.

I place the chocolate cake carefully into the hamper and arrange the oranges around the edge. My resolution to visit Mother in September has assuaged my feelings of guilt and once more I feel excited that Sabine and Brigitta are visiting me today and not the other way around. The truth is, when I think of my old home in East Berlin, it's like a different country, a different world, even though it's only the other half of the city in which I still live. But there's no way I'd go back there. The Communists in the East talk of building a better future for everyone – housing, education and all that, but really they just want to control people's lives. No one is allowed to criticise the Party. If you do, you'll be locked up. They spy on their own citizens all the time. Who can live in a place like that? They call themselves democratic, but that's a joke. I mean, how can it be a democratic country when there's only one Party? The other parties are just there for show – puppets of the Communists. Over here in the West, we don't just have real democracy and the freedom to say what we think, we have shops, restaurants, bars and nightclubs on the *Ku'damm* that most East Berliners couldn't imagine in their wildest dreams.

I go over all these arguments in my head every time I think about my decision to move west, justifying my actions to myself. But, I do have one regret and that's that I didn't try harder to persuade Mother, Sabine and Brigitta to come with me. But I was impatient to get going and Mother…well let's just say Mother doesn't like change. Sabine, I know, is torn, but she tends to take Mother's side saying Mother doesn't want to leave her home and her work, that she still likes to visit Father's grave, all the old arguments. But I can see which way the wind is blowing. There's no future for them over there in the East.

I close the lid on the hamper and pull the leather straps through the metal buckles. As I pull the straps tight I decide once and for all that they must leave East Berlin and come and live in the West. I will not take "no" for an answer.

I check my watch. It's still early, only seven

o'clock. I've got plenty of time before I need to catch the train from *Anhalter Bahnhof.* I make myself a black coffee and switch on the radio, tuning in to RIAS. As I'm carrying the coffee over to the table, the announcer says something so shocking and unexpected that I come to a sudden standstill, jolting the mug. I yelp in pain as hot coffee scalds my right hand.

Sabine

The stairwell is gloomy, even in the middle of the day.

I don't believe in ghosts but the smell of frying cabbage and stale tobacco which rises up to our landing from Herr Schiller's apartment on the floor below evokes a memory so strong, I feel as if Father is here right now.

The pungent smell catches my nostrils and I am taken back eight years to the age of nine, one year older than Brigitta is now. Brigitta is a baby in our mother's arms. We are standing at the door to the apartment. Dieter is on Mother's right and I am on her left. Father is on the landing. Mother is asking him not to do something, almost pleading with him. I don't understand what they're talking about. Something about *construction workers* and a *general strike.* Mother says it will be *too dangerous.* I can hear the fear in her voice and I move closer to her. Father says *not to worry.* Everything will be *different now Stalin is dead.* Father says we must *stand up for what we believe in* and he looks down at Dieter and me and smiles. I catch the sense of his words and feel proud of him. I want him to be proud of me too. He kisses Mother on the cheek, pecks Brigitta on the forehead, then bends down to Dieter and me. He ruffles Dieter's hair and strokes the side of my face, planting a kiss on the tip of my nose. Dieter asks if he can go with Father, but Father says, *no, not this time.* He promises he'll be *back in time for dinner.* We never see him again.

I know now that Father was going to a demonstration at *Alexanderplatz.* People were demanding political change and workers' rights. They didn't get either. Instead what they got were Soviet tanks that rolled in and quashed the demonstration. Hundreds were arrested or injured. Dozens killed. One of them was Father.

I try to dispel the memory by pressing the light switch. The fluorescent lights flicker reluctantly into life and the timer starts to tick, like a bomb about to explode.

"Race you to the bottom," I say.

"You're on," laughs Brigitta. We have this thing about making it to the ground floor before the light times out. Before we are plunged into darkness.

It's a long way down. We live in a two-bedroom apartment on the top floor, the fourth to be precise, of an old nineteenth-century apartment block in the *Prenzlauer Berg* district. As we run down the stairs, I can't help noticing how shabby the building has become. The olive green paint is peeling off the walls and the linoleum on the stairs is wearing thin. My hand brushes lightly over the wooden banister which has long since lost its sheen.

Brigitta is already ahead of me. She always wins this game.

We pass Herr Schiller's door on the third floor where the smell of tobacco is at its strongest. It mingles with the aroma of frying potato and cabbage. I smile to myself. Herr Schiller likes his food, and it shows in his substantial girth. His size matches his larger than life personality and generous spirit. He's a good neighbour to have. I can hear the crackle of his radio but I can't make out the words.

Brigitta speeds up past Frau Lange's door on the second floor, so I do too. Brigitta insists that Frau Lange is really a witch waiting to toss little children into her *Kachelofen*, the large, round coal burning oven that takes centre stage in traditional German living rooms. I fear Brigitta may have read *Hänsel und Gretel* a few too many times. I don't know what Frau Lange does exactly, but I think she has some senior role working for the authorities. Anyway, there's something unnerving about her. She is Herr Schiller's opposite in every way imaginable. Whilst he is round and fat, she is thin and angular, where he is jovial and generous, she is dour and mean, where he is kind and friendly, she exudes an aura of hostility. So it makes sense to try and avoid unnecessary encounters with her.

From the apartment on the first floor the sounds of small children are clearly audible; running, laughing and shrieking. The Mann family have a four year old boy called Olaf and a six year old girl called Michaela. They often play in the *Hinterhof*, or courtyard, out the back of the building, but today they are cooped up inside. I think I hear a woman crying, but it's difficult to be sure over the noise of the children.

"I win," shouts Brigitta who makes it to the bottom just as the lights click off.

"Well done," I say, pausing a moment to catch my breath.

We walk past the post boxes lined up on the wall like a row of metal bird houses and push open the heavy wooden doors that lead out onto our street,

Stargarder Strasse.

"Which way?" asks Brigitta.

I think for a moment. "Let's walk to *Alexanderplatz*," I say, "then we can take the *S-bahn* train to the *Hauptbahnhof* via *Friedrichstrasse* without having to change." *Friedrichstrasse* is the last stop in East Berlin before the line crosses the sector border into the West.

We set off at a brisk pace. *Stargarder Strasse* is empty at this time on a Sunday morning. The shutters at Frau Maier's food shop are pulled down and the *Kneipe* on the street corner where the locals like to go for a drink is in darkness. We turn into *Prenzlauer Allee*, the main road that leads to *Alexanderplatz*. A tram trundles past, otherwise the road is quiet.

We walk past bombed out plots and bullet damaged buildings. This part of Berlin still bears the scars of the Second World War. The Americans and British are helping to rebuild West Berlin, but here the Soviets are letting everything fall apart. I know Dieter will try again to persuade us to leave East Berlin and join him in the West. The last time I saw him, in June, we talked about the large numbers of East Germans who are fleeing Communism simply by crossing the border into West Berlin. They go to the refugee centre at *Marienfelde* where they are given food and identification papers. "You should do it," Dieter said. "Before it's too late." I know he's right. We should have done it months ago. This time I'll make Mother see sense. I'll insist that she...

"Watch out!" Brigitta grabs my arm.

I was so lost in my thoughts that I hadn't seen the car chugging along the road. It's a *Trabant*, a square box on wheels that everyone calls a *Trabi*. The two-stroke engine is causing the exhaust to spew out a haze of noxious fumes. We both cover our mouths as the car limps past. What a joke. I've seen cars in West Berlin and they're so much better than what we have here. Besides, you can't just buy a car in East Berlin, you have to apply for one and then it takes about ten years to acquire it. That vehicle is probably the driver's most prized possession and it looks as if it was made out of cardboard and sticky tape.

We arrive at the concrete expanse of *Alexanderplatz* without further mishap. The huge square is empty save for a handful of people milling about outside the *Rotes Rathaus*, the nineteenth-century red-brick Town Hall. I never want to linger at *Alexanderplatz*, knowing it was here that Father was mown down by a Soviet tank, so we head straight to the *S-bahn*, buy our tickets and make our way to the platform.

We're in luck. A train arrives within seconds and we jump on. As it clanks its way westwards we talk about how much we're looking forward to seeing Dieter again.

"Will he remember to bring oranges?" asks Brigitta.

"I hope so."

"And chocolate cake?"

"He better do."

"If not I'll push him into the lake with all his clothes on." We both laugh.

The train stops at *Friedrichstrasse* before crossing the border into West Berlin. I peer out of the window at the empty platform, impatient for the train to start moving again, but nothing happens.

"Why aren't we moving?" asks Brigitta after a moment.

"I don't know."

We look up and down the carriage. Other people are also clearly confused. Then there's an announcement over the loudspeaker on the platform.

"The train at platform B is terminating," says a crackly voice.

I look out of the window and see that we're on platform B.

"All passengers must leave the train on platform B," says the crackly voice. That's odd. I don't know what's happening, but this train clearly isn't going anywhere.

"Look," says Brigitta, pointing through the train window. Two soldiers armed with machine guns are marching, side-by-side along the platform. The sight of them gives me a queer feeling in the pit of my stomach. Brigitta looks at me with wide eyes, her eyebrows raised.

"*Komm*," I say, jumping to my feet. "Let's find out what's going on."

We leave the train along with the other dozen or so passengers. They are as confused as we are. A man says something about a radio announcement this morning but I don't catch exactly what. We head towards the exit. A large crowd has already gathered in the station concourse. Everyone is talking and shouting at once. I hold onto Brigitta's hand because I don't want to lose her in the crowd. We squeeze our way to the front. I see a uniformed *S-bahn* employee trying to make himself heard above the noise of the crowd, and gesticulating with his hands. I make my way towards him, dragging Brigitta in my wake. I have a bad feeling about this but I don't want to say anything to Brigitta until I'm sure. When we are close enough I hear the *S-bahn* employee telling people to go and buy a newspaper if they want to know what's going on. Some people have already done so and are waving copies of *Neues Deutschland* around, crying and shouting. I go cold all over when I hear what they are saying.

"*Die Grenze ist geschlossen!*" shouts a man. The border is closed!

"*Mit Stacheldraht!*" cries a woman, tears streaming down her face. With barbed wire!

Dieter

The coffee has gone cold.

I push it to one side and bring my fist down, hard, on the table.

"*Verdammt!*" Damn! My voice sounds unnaturally loud in the empty kitchen.

There is only one thing on the radio today. The thing I feared most has happened; the border between East and West Berlin has been closed. With barbed wire. And not just barbed wire through the middle of the city but all the way around West Berlin making it impossible for East Berliners and East Germans alike to access West Berlin. According to the radio, armed guards are manning the checkpoints between East and West and armed Factory Fighters, those East German workers trained for combat, are guarding the barbed wire. The Communist Party didn't like the fact that so many people were leaving for the West, so they have plugged the hole which was West Berlin. The border is now closed. No one can cross it, in either direction.

But what I don't understand is, *how the hell did they manage to pull off a stunt like that?* Nobody had any idea, although maybe we should have guessed something like this might happen.

I think of Sabine and Brigitta getting up this morning, looking forward to the picnic. Will they have heard the news on the radio? Or are they at this very moment at the border, being refused entry to West Berlin? If they don't know about the barbed wire then they could be on the train heading towards *Friedrichstrasse* right now. The radio announcer said that no trains are allowed to cross the border.

I'm so angry I think I might explode if I sit here any longer. I throw the cold coffee down the sink and grab my jacket from a hook on the kitchen door. Bernd, my flatmate, is still asleep in bed. I don't bother waking him, but go out slamming the apartment door behind me.

Outside, the streets of *Kreuzberg* are just waking up. Bleary-eyed students blinking in the bright morning sun; old men shuffling on their way to the kiosk to buy the morning paper and their daily supply of tobacco. The debris of Saturday night - beer bottles and cigarette stubs - litters the streets. When I returned home late yesterday evening, the streets were packed with the usual throngs of students, drinking and partying. Bernd was going out and tried to persuade me to join him, but I knew I had to be up early to meet Sabine and Brigitta, so I went to bed.

I head up to *Zimmerstrasse* which runs along the border between East and West Berlin, and stare in disbelief at the sight in front of me. Yesterday, this was an ordinary street. Now there are huge tangled coils of barbed wire, at least a metre high, running down the middle of the road. On the other side of the wire armed Factory Fighters are standing guard.

I follow the path of the barbed wire, around

Potsdamer Platz and along the edge of the *Tiergarten* until I reach the *Brandenburger Tor*, the old city gate. With its enormous six stone columns crowned with the statue of Victory riding her chariot, the *Brandenburger Tor* is Berlin's most famous landmark. It lies at the western edge of the huge park, the *Tiergarten*. The park is in the British sector of Berlin, the gate is in the Soviet sector, hence on the other side of the border. Today East German soldiers are standing in a line in front of the gate, rifles at the ready. The message is clear: Keep away!

Crowds of angry men and women have gathered on the Western side. They are shouting abuse at the East German guards across the border.

I try to see past the soldiers into *Pariser Platz* on the eastern side of the gate. I can just make out handfuls of East Berliners over there. Are Sabine and Brigitta amongst them? It's impossible to say from this distance.

It feels as if the world has gone mad. Berlin is *one* city. You can't just divide a city in two by rolling out barbed wire, can you? Some small part of me hopes that the East Germans are just trying to make a point, a symbolic gesture, trying to assert their sovereignty. Maybe, it's partly our fault for not taking them more seriously; for buying up all their cheap petrol until they run dry; for going to the East for a haircut that costs peanuts; for laughing at their crappy cars. But even so, this is going too far and they need to be told enough is enough.

So I join in with the angry crowds for a while, shouting abuse and throwing stones, even though I know that sort of behaviour never really does any good. And then the West Berlin police arrive to try and calm things down. I don't want to be arrested so I distance myself from the crowds and wander disconsolately back towards *Potsdamer Platz*, wishing more than anything I could crush the barbed wire flat.

Sabine

Barbed wire – *Stacheldraht* - the word has always filled me with horror. Ever since I was six, and Dieter was nine. We were spending the summer with Tante Bettina and Onkel Thomas on their farm in the countryside south west of Berlin. Every morning Tante Bettina sent us outside with a basket to collect the eggs. The chicken run was surrounded by barbed wire to keep the foxes out. The grass was left to grow long around the edge of the chicken run, obscuring the barbed wire, but it was there all the same and you had to be careful not to scratch yourself on it. We let ourselves into the chicken run through a small wooden gate that Onkel Thomas had built himself. One morning as we were about to enter the chicken run, I caught a movement in the long grass out of the corner of my eye. Curious, I went to see what it was and sprang back in horror. A rabbit was caught on the barbed wire, its fur matted with blood. It was feebly kicking its hind legs, trying to free itself. I dropped the basket and ran to find Onkel Thomas. We must free the rabbit and save its life. Big, kind Onkel Thomas would know what to do. I had visions of myself nursing the injured rabbit back to health, maybe even keeping it as a pet. But when I told Onkel Thomas what I'd found, he fetched a gun from the shed and shot the rabbit between the eyes. The sound startled all the chickens who squawked with fright and ran for shelter into their hut. The rabbit lay lifeless on the ground. That night Tante Bettina served rabbit stew for dinner. I refused to eat a thing.

I see that rabbit in my mind's eye as we head towards the station exit, and I imagine people caught on the wire, bleeding to death, like so many defenceless rabbits, waiting to be shot in the head. I feel dizzy at the thought.

"Where are we going?" asks Brigitta.

"I want to see what's going on," I say. Despite my horror of barbed wire, I have to see this for myself.

As we climb the stairs, Brigitta is bursting with questions.

"What does it mean?" she asks. "Why are those people" – she points back towards the crowds in the station – "saying there is barbed wire at the border?"

"They're saying that the border between East and West Berlin is closed," I say. "We can't travel to West Berlin. We can't go to the British, French or American sectors. We can't leave the Soviet sector."

"Just today?" asks Brigitta, frowning in puzzlement. "Or forever?"

"I don't know."

"But what about Dieter? Can he come here?"

"I don't know that either."

I don't know anything right at the moment. I can't think straight. The idea of the border being closed like that, overnight, is bewildering. Yesterday we could have travelled to West Berlin and today we can't. A line has been drawn through the middle of the city and we are not permitted to cross it. Our brother is on the other side of that line. They can't just separate us like that can they? There are lots of families who live between both halves of the city; parents in the East, grown up children in the West; grandparents in the West, grandchildren in the East.

Berlin is, after all, one city. At least it was until this morning.

We leave the station and set off towards the nearest border point, the *Brandenburger Tor*.

Walking west down the broad avenue of *Unter den Linden* I look up at the stone figure of Victory on top of the gate. She is driving her chariot pulled by four galloping horses and in her right hand she is brandishing the Iron Cross of Victory. *If only she were real,* I think, *she would ride roughshod over any barbed wire.* On the other side of the gate, through the archways, is the British Sector of West Berlin; so close and yet so far.

We stop some way from the gate. We daren't go any closer because there are tanks and rows of Factory Fighters with rifles slung over their shoulders. The men are lined up in front of the gate ready to shoot anyone who tries to break through their defences.

We can't see through the archways of the gate with all the soldiers and tanks in the way, but we can just make out the shouts of people on the western side. They're not frightened of protesting over there, in West Berlin. I wonder if Dieter is amongst them.

We walk on, hand in hand, towards *Potsdamer Platz* and all we can see is miles and miles of barbed wire, great tangled coils of it snaking through the city. Where has it all come from? How could all this barbed wire be kept hidden until it was rolled out last night? There's just so much of it, and it's far too high and wide to climb over. Besides, armed men are patrolling along its path so it would be suicidal to try.

At *Potsdamer Platz* we are closer to the wire than we were at the *Brandenburger Tor*. We do our best to ignore the armed soldiers standing in front of it.

Suddenly a voice calls our names.

"Sabine! Brigitta!"

We turn at the sound, startled, but also excited because we'd know that voice anywhere. It's Dieter. He's on the other side of the wire, frantically waving at us.

Before I can stop her, Brigitta's hand slips out of mine and she runs towards him, runs towards the barbed wire.

"Stop!" A harsh voice shouts at Brigitta.

A guard leaps forward and stands in front of her, aiming his rifle at her chest. I scream and run towards her.

"*Bitte!* Don't shoot! For God's sake please don't shoot!"

Brigitta is frozen to the spot, turning her head wildly to look for me. She is terrified beyond anything I've ever seen.

"No closer to the barbed wire!" shouts the guard. He has a thick Berlin accent and an angry looking face. She is about ten metres from the barbed wire. I catch up to her and throw my arms around her.

"She's not trying to escape!" I shout at the guard, my voice cracking. "She just saw a…a friend over there." I don't want to admit to this man that we have a brother living in West Berlin.

The guard shrugs his shoulders as if to say, why should he care about our friends. "You must not approach the anti-fascist protective barrier." He sounds like he's reciting a phrase learnt in school and his language strikes me as ridiculous. Is that what they're calling the barbed wire? An anti-fascist protective barrier? I would laugh if the situation wasn't so serious.

It's no laughing matter for the guard who keeps

his rifle pointed at Brigitta. I look past him and see Dieter standing on the other side of the wire. His face is a picture of terror at the sight of the rifle being aimed at his little sister.

I take Brigitta's hand in mine. "*Komm*," I say pulling her aside. The guard mutters under his breath. I stare helplessly at Dieter. More than anything I want to run to him. If I could I would lift Brigitta over the wire and tell Dieter to take her to safety, but the guard is still watching us. I shake my head at Dieter to tell him we can't come any closer. He nods his understanding. I think he's crying.

Brigitta and I wave to Dieter across the barbed wire. There is nothing else we can do. Brigitta starts to cry and I hold her close to me. I give Dieter one final wave, then I turn and lead Brigitta away. Twice I turn around. Dieter is still there watching us go. He looks bereft.

It breaks my heart to leave Dieter, but I must take Brigitta home and check on Mother. If she has heard the news, she will be worrying about us. We catch the train back to *Alexanderplatz* and hurry up *Prenzlauer Allee*. By the time we reach *Stargarder Strasse* we are hot and out of breath.

The street is livelier than it was when we left it this morning. People must have heard the news and come outside to talk about it. They are gathered in clusters, arms folded, shaking their heads. The grocer, Frau Maier, is standing outside her shop, talking to her neighbours. I want to stop and tell her what happened to us at *Friedrichstrasse* and *Potsdamer Platz*, but I also want to get home, so we carry on.

At our building, the Mann children from the first floor have been sent outside to play in the *Hinterhof* at the back of the building, but they are standing still, looking confused. They know something bad has happened but they don't understand what.

Brigitta presses the light switch on the ground floor and runs to the stairs. We climb the stairs even faster than we descended them this morning. There is crying coming from the Mann apartment on the first floor. We don't even give Frau Lange a thought as we dash past her door on the second floor. By the time we reach Herr Schiller's door on the third floor I have fallen behind. Brigitta is running ahead of me, like a bird flying effortlessly to the top of the building. When I catch up and enter our apartment, she is already standing there with her arms around Mother who is sitting at the kitchen table, listening to the radio, her head in her hands.

I sit down opposite Mother. She looks frail and much older than her forty-one years. Her hair, which is streaked with grey, is falling limply around her face. There are dark rings under her eyes as if she has not slept well. She pulls her brown cardigan close around her. I know she must be reproaching herself for not listening to Dieter and leaving East Berlin when we had the chance. I lean across the table and take hold of her hand.

She looks at me with red, swollen eyes. "What will we do now?"

The question hangs in the air. I don't know the answer. I don't think there is one. But I want to stay positive because hope is the only thing we have left.

"The Western Allies won't let them get away with this," I say doing my best to sound confident. "The British, Americans and French will put a stop to it. They must."

Mother shakes her head. "And where were the Americans, British and French when the Soviets crushed the uprising in '53? I don't recall them rushing to our assistance." Her voice sounds harsh and resentful. It is unusual for her to speak so bitterly of Father's death.

"But Berlin is a single city," I say. "You can't just build a wall through the middle of a city. It's absurd."

"I'm afraid that is exactly what's going to happen," says Mother. "We've left it too late. We are prisoners here now."

A single tear runs down her face and lands on the table.

Dieter

I wipe the tears from my face, staring at the spot where Sabine and Brigitta were. I don't know how long I stand there. I want to run after them but I can't get through the barbed wire. And anyway, who would cross from West to East? Only an idiot. No, the only thing to do is to escape from the East, but how?

I still can't believe that I saw them, Sabine and Brigitta. They were so close, no more than twenty metres away. Sabine was wearing her bright yellow dress, as if she wanted to enjoy herself today. I can only assume that they didn't know anything about the barbed wire when they set off from home this morning.

And Brigitta – I couldn't believe how much she's grown since I last saw her. She likes me to pick her up and swing her around in the air as if she's flying. But when she ran towards me today that monster shouted and pointed his rifle at her and I couldn't hear anything except the blood pounding in my ears and all I could see were Brigitta's eyes, wide with fear. I will never forget that look on her face as long as I live. The guard is standing with his back to me now, rifle at the ready, watching the East Berliners who are gathering on the other side of the wire. I feel such a raw hatred for him, I swear if I had a gun at my disposal, I'd shoot him here and now in cold blood.

"*Arschloch!*" I shout at him. Arsehole! He doesn't respond. I turn away in disgust, not wanting to spend another moment anywhere near him.

I turn down *Stresemannstrasse* and aimlessly follow the line of the barbed wire as it turns left into *Niederkirchnerstrasse* and on into *Zimmerstrasse*. I come to Checkpoint Charlie, the border crossing point for foreigners, including West Germans, going in and out of East Berlin.

An American patrol car has pulled up at the checkpoint. The border guards are trying to turn it away. The American in the passenger seat winds down his window, leans out and announces in a booming voice, "We have the right to cross this border."

"No one can cross the border," says a German soldier.

The American is having none of it. A crowd gathers on the west side and watches the altercation with a growing sense of alarm. If the Soviets and East Germans start arguing with the Americans, who knows where it could lead? World War Three?

I turn away and start making my way back through the streets of *Kreuzberg*. I've seen enough barbed wire this morning to last me a lifetime. The city has been torn in two but the barbed wire has also torn a hole in my family and right now I don't know if it can ever be mended.

Sabine

A knock at the door startles us out of the silence and despondency into which we have sunk.

I get up from the kitchen table and go to answer it. It's our neighbour from the third floor, Herr Schiller. His huge frame fills the doorway and in front of his oversize belly he is carrying a large, lidded earthenware dish from which the rich, warm smell of cooking is rising. I realise, suddenly, that I'm very hungry.

"*Guten Tag,* Fräulein Neumann," he says making a small bow. Herr Schiller is always unfailingly polite.

"*Guten Tag,* Herr Schiller. What a pleasant surprise."

"I have made a large quantity of fried potato and cabbage," he says, looking down at the dish in his great paw like hands, "and thought you, your mother and sister might like to share it with me."

"That sounds wonderful," I say inviting him into our apartment.

It is a kind gesture, typical of Herr Schiller who is always so generous towards us. At Christmas he brings us a goose or a turkey (we never ask him where he finds these treats, suspecting that his methods may be not entirely legal). During the winter months he helps us carry coal up from the cellar, and when it snows he fetches his shovel and clears the pavement outside the building. In 1942 he was away at the front when his wife was killed by a bomb that destroyed the building she was in. They didn't have any children.

He follows me into the kitchen and his entrance has an immediate effect on our sombre mood. Brigitta jumps up from the table and runs to Herr

Schiller giving him a big hug. He is like a substitute father for her.

"Careful," he laughs, "this dish is very hot." He sets the dish down in the middle of the table.

"Herr Schiller has brought us some food to share," I say.

Mother manages to rouse herself and thanks him for his generosity. She busies herself fetching plates from the cupboard whilst I open a tin of meat and cut it into slices. The business of preparing lunch makes us forget, for a moment, the new situation in Berlin. Herr Schiller spoons out generous portions of his potato and cabbage mixture and we sit down to our meal.

We eat for a few moments in silence. Fried cabbage and potato is simple, comforting food and never tasted so good. Then Herr Schiller asks, "You have heard the news?"

"We've more than heard it," I say. "This morning Brigitta and I experienced it first hand."

As we eat, Brigitta and I take it in turns to describe the events of the morning - the confusion at *Friedrichstrasse* station, the *S-Bahn* employee telling everyone to go and buy a newspaper, the guards at the *Brandenburger Tor*, the barbed wire at *Potsdamer Platz* and Dieter on the other side of the wire.

"He was just standing there," says Brigitta, her mouth full of fried potato, "and I ran towards him and…"

I kick her ankle under the table and give an infinitesimal shake of my head. I don't want her worrying Mother with the story of how the guard pointed his rifle at her. That would be too much for Mother to take, especially after what happened to Father.

"…and we waved to him," she finishes by

saying.

Mother is busy dishing out more potato and cabbage and hasn't noticed anything. But Herr Schiller looks from me to Brigitta as if he knows there is more to our story than we are letting on. He heard the news on the radio this morning and is appalled by what has happened.

"As a young man," he says, waving his fork in the air, "I believed in the principles of a Communist state – equality and sharing. But what we have now is oppression and dictatorship. They are trying to keep people here by force and that is unforgivable."

When we have finished eating, Mother clears away the plates and asks Herr Schiller if he would like some tea. There's no coffee in East Berlin at the moment.

Herr Schiller wipes his mouth with the back of his hand and lumbers to his feet. "Thank you, but no. I have…things I need to do." We wait for him to explain, but he is silent. Then he says, "I will come and see you all in a few days." He inclines his head to each of us in turn. "Please don't trouble yourself, Fräulein Neumann, I can see myself out." He picks up the empty earthenware dish and leaves.

With the departure of Herr Schiller a gloom settles on our little household once more. Mother says she has a headache and is going to lie down. Brigitta takes her book of fairy stories from the living room and disappears with it to the bedroom, wanting to escape the events of the morning in tales of captured princesses and evil witches. No one will miss me for a couple of hours so I decide to go out rather than hang around the apartment, worrying about the future.

This time I am unable to avoid Frau Lange who is on her way up the stairs just as I am going down. I see her stick-like figure and the top of her grey head before she sees me.

As always I do my best to be polite. "*Guten Tag,* Frau Lange."

I have no idea if she was ever married but, like all German women of a certain age, she is known as *Frau* whereas I sometimes feel as if I will always be an unmarried *Fräulein.* I think she must be in her fifties. She has a thin, pinched face. I wonder if Herr Schiller ever offers her his fried cabbage and potato. She looks like a woman who needs feeding up.

At the sound of my voice she looks up and raises her eyebrows, taking in at one glance the yellow dress I'm wearing. No doubt she considers it a sign of western frivolity. She doesn't approve of Dieter moving to West Berlin and has told me so to my face on a number of previous occasions. Unlike Herr Schiller, she is never friendly. So I am taken aback when her normal stern look dissolves into something approaching a smile.

"Have you heard the news?" she asks.

"Of course," I say, keen to be on my way before the light times out.

She gives a sigh of satisfaction and nods her head. "*Endlich!*" she says. At last!

I stare at her in astonishment. It's well known she is a dedicated member of the Communist Party, but can she really approve of the government splitting the city in half? Her next words leave me in no doubt as to her true feelings.

"At last they are starting to build the Wall between East and West Berlin. Now we will be able to develop our socialist society without interference from *over there.*" She means the people in West Berlin with their capitalist economy and their valuable *Deutschmarks,* compared to which our *Ostmarks* are not worth the paper they're printed on.

I wouldn't normally prolong a conversation with Frau Lange, but her comments have riled me.

"But they can't just split the city in two," I say. "What about the people who live here? Who have relatives across the border?"

Frau Lange shrugs. "One has to make sacrifices for what one believes in."

I want to say that I don't believe in this Communist country, that I don't think it's the right way to go, but I bite my tongue, not wishing to provoke an argument.

Frau Lange takes her front door key from her pocket and puts it into the lock. "I too have made sacrifices in the past," she says. Then she disappears inside and closes the door behind her.

I don't know what she means and I'm not sure I want to find out. The light times out and I am plunged into darkness. I run my hand over the wall until I find the switch, then hurry down the rest of the stairs before I encounter anyone else.

Outside it's hot. The sun is high in the sky and I think with bitterness how Brigitta and I should have been bathing in the lake at *Wannsee* by now. I wonder for a moment about going to see my friend Astrid because she always manages to cheer me up when I'm feeling down, but then I remember she's away camping, so instead I walk a short distance down *Stargarder Strasse* until I reach a building similar to my own. From a panel of six buzzers I press the one named Fischer and wait. There's a crackle then a voice.

"*Ja?*"

"*Hans, ich bin's.*" Hans, it's me.

The door clicks open, I step into the dark lobby of the apartment building and climb the stairs to the third floor. My oldest friend in the whole world is waiting for me.

Dieter

I walk past a busy restaurant on the street corner and the smell of frying *Bratwurst* suddenly makes me feel hungry. I look at my watch and realise that I've been walking in a daze for hours; it's nearly two o'clock. I head back to the apartment. Everything is as I left it this morning, yet the world has changed. The abandoned picnic hamper is still on the kitchen table. I guess I'll share the food later with Bernd, but it won't taste as good. I don't want to look at it now, a reminder of what today should have been. I put the basket on the floor and turn on the radio. It seems the Americans did finally get through Checkpoint Charlie.

The door opens and Bernd shambles into the kitchen in his pyjamas, his hair sticking up, rubbing his eyes and yawning. Typical.

"*Was passiert?*" he asks, going to the sink and running himself a glass of water. What's happening?

He asks that question every morning. It's not that he has any interest in the outside world, it's just his way of saying, *Hi, how's it going?*

I don't answer him but just turn up the radio. The announcer is saying that the East Germans started rolling the barbed wire out at half past one in the morning. *Half past one in the morning!* You have to hand it to them, they're bloody organised, but that's what's so frightening about this. If they can do this, what else can they do?

As Bernd wakes up and takes in what the announcer is saying, all the colour drains from his face. For once the answer to his question, *What's happening?* is not *Nothing.*

Sabine

I've known Hans since we were at *Kindergarten* together, aged six. He's like another brother to me. On my first day at *Kindergarten* I clung to Mother's legs, not wanting her to go. But Hans came over and invited me to play a game with him. I went with him and didn't notice when Mother left. When she came to collect me later that day, I cried again because I didn't want to go home.

Ever since Father died, Dieter and I have had to be the strong ones at home. And since Dieter left to go and live in West Berlin that role has fallen increasingly on my shoulders. But with Hans, I don't have to pretend to be strong. I can be myself with him. He stands in the doorway, regarding me with his bright blue eyes.

"Come here," he says, taking my hand and leading me into the apartment. His hair is wet as if he has just stepped out of the shower and he smells of fresh soap. I find I'm crying as I tell him about my journey to *Friedrichstrasse* station this morning.

"We were supposed to be meeting Dieter at the *Hauptbahnhof*," I sob, "and then going onto the lake at *Wannsee.*"

Hans takes me into the living room where his mother, Frau Fischer, is sitting reading today's copy of *Neues Deutschland.* A few years older than Mother, Frau Fischer is a good looking woman with well-cut auburn hair who bears her sorrows with patience and fortitude. She keeps the apartment immaculate and it always smells of beeswax. On seeing me enter she puts down the newspaper and takes off her reading glasses, setting them down on a small table in front of two framed photographs; one of Hans taken a couple of months ago on his seventeenth birthday and one of her husband who was killed in Russia during the war. Hans never knew his father.

"Sit down, dear," says Frau Fischer gesturing to a chair. She doesn't have to ask me what the matter is. "Would you like some tea?"

I dry my eyes and shake my head. "No, thank you."

"Actually, you're lucky to catch me here," says Hans. "I was about to go out."

Frau Fischer bites her lip and frowns.

"Where to?" I ask.

Hans makes an impatient gesture with his hands. "Look, we can't just sit here whilst the government rolls out barbed wire. We need to do something. Take action. The people in West Berlin are protesting. If we take this lying down, they'll think we want a wall through the middle of Berlin. If we let the authorities get away with this, Berlin will be split forever."

That's just like Hans, to want to fight back. I smile at his fervour.

Frau Fischer looks worried. "You need to be careful Hans. The fact is, some people do want there to be a wall. You don't want to get yourself into trouble with the Party." Her eyes flick towards me. She knows what happened to Father when he joined the protests in '53. With her own husband dead, Hans is all she has left.

"But don't you see?" says Hans. "The Communists have acted completely unreasonably. This time the Americans and British will be on our side. They won't let the East Germans get away with building a wall. But why should they fight on our behalf if we can't even be bothered to stand up for ourselves?"

I think to myself, *that wasn't Mother's opinion*, but I don't say anything because I so much want Hans to be right.

"I'll come with you," I say, looking up at him. I turn to Frau Fischer. "Don't worry, I'll make sure he doesn't do anything stupid."

Her face relaxes a little. "All right."

Once we're outside Hans sets off towards *Alexanderplatz*. I walk quickly to keep up. As we head down *Prenzlauer Allee* I ask Hans how he first heard the news that the border was closed.

"On the radio, of course. I guess you didn't turn the radio on this morning?"

I shake my head. "Mother was asleep and I didn't want to wake her."

He nods his understanding.

When we arrive at *Alexanderplatz*, it's unrecognisable from how it was this morning. Back then, which feels like a lifetime ago, the huge concrete square was empty apart from a few people outside the *Rotes Rathaus*. Now that the news has spread, the square is swarming with people. They have gathered together, as people do at such times – when war breaks out, when peace is announced and when freedoms are taken away. Seeing so many people at *Alexanderplatz* makes me nervous, knowing what happened here in '53, so I clutch hold of his arm, something I've never done before.

He puts his hand over mine and gives it a squeeze. "Stay close," he says in my ear. I intend to do just that.

We weave our way towards the centre of the square. There are all sorts of people here: men, women, children. Like the passengers I saw this morning at *Friedrichstrasse* station, they are disbelieving, angry, confused. Middle-aged women, probably war widows, stand in tight-knit groups talking, clutching handkerchiefs, wringing their hands, pointing towards the west. Maybe they have children or elderly parents over there. There are chants of *Freiheit*, Freedom, from younger groups. Hans watches them closely and I notice a keen glint in his eyes. It is protesters like that who will be arrested first if the authorities step in, so I try and steer Hans in the opposite direction, mindful of the promise I made to Frau Fischer to keep him safe.

But more and more people are thronging into the square and as the crowd presses in around us I start to feel uneasy. Crowds can be volatile, a single word or action igniting a spark that can turn into an inferno at any moment. People are shouting, angry at the barbed wire that has been rolled out at the border, but after a while I discern other voices in the crowd - not everyone here is opposed to the closure of the border. There are anti-western chants of *Imperialism is evil*, and *Death to the Fascist pigs*.

Hans has noticed them too. "Stasi," he says nodding in the direction of one man who is proclaiming power to the socialist state. "I bet you these people have been planted by the Party."

At the word *Stasi* a shiver runs through me. Short for *Ministerium für Staatssicherheit*, Ministry of State Security, the Stasi are feared by ordinary people. They do not wear uniforms, so they look like regular citizens, but they keep a close watch over everyone, always on the lookout for any signs of dissent against the Party. They also employ large numbers of unofficial informers, *Inoffizielle Mitarbeiter*, known as IMs for short, ordinary people who spy on friends, neighbours, colleagues, even family members, and report back to their controlling officers. Of course no one admits to being an informer, otherwise people would stop speaking to them and then they'd have nothing to report. The whole system relies on secrecy and a willingness amongst some people to betray their friends for the sake of…what? The state? Or is it personal gain? I've never been sure.

Maybe it's just paranoia but suddenly I have the feeling that we're being watched. I feel overdressed and conspicuous in my yellow dress amongst this crowd of people who are mostly wearing greys and browns, the colours of ordinary life. I look like I'm dressed for a party. I imagine myself identified in a Stasi report – *the girl in the yellow dress.*

I wish we could leave but it becomes more difficult to move as the crowds increase. I look towards the edge of the square and my heart misses a beat. In front of the *Rotes Rathaus*, Factory Fighters stand in a line, their feet planted squarely, guns and rifles at the ready.

"Look," I say pointing towards the *Rathaus*. "I think we should go."

But the crowd is surging forward, towards the Fighters, and we are being dragged along with it. There is nothing we can do. Someone must have given a signal because the Fighters start to move, in formation, towards the crowd. *Please don't shoot*, I think. If they start firing now there will be a massacre.

By now we are near the front of the crowd. A young man shouts that the barbed wire "is illegal" and "a gross infringement of his liberties." He is behaving peacefully and his words are thoughtful and articulate, but nevertheless three Factory

Fighters immediately move in on him. Two of them take hold of his arms and the third jabs his rifle into the man's back. The young man struggles in vain to break free as the fighters march him away at gunpoint and shove him into the back of a windowless van. There are a number of such vans parked around the edge of the square. I see lots of hot-headed protesters taken out in this way, mainly young men. I think, *they will be locked up and interrogated; the Stasi will have them on file, forever; their families may never hear of them again.* One hears of such stories.

"We should get out of here," says Hans. I couldn't agree more.

But just then a new group of protesters surges forward. Either they aren't aware of what the Factory Fighters are doing or they don't care. A particularly loud member of the group, an angry man with long hair, shouts at the Factory Fighters, "You're all stooges of the Communist Party! Cowards! You're no better than concentration camp guards!" He punches the air with his fist. His companions eagerly join in the shouting. We are standing too close to them. Whilst I share their sentiments, I don't want to be arrested. Six Factory Fighters start running towards us. If we don't move now we'll be arrested along with the whole group. I spot a gap in the crowd and pull Hans towards it. We push our way past dozens of people and suddenly find ourselves on the edge, free of the crowds.

I collapse forward, hands on knees, and try to catch my breath. My heart is hammering in my chest. Hans puts his hand on my back.

"Are you all right?"

I straighten up, nodding. "Yeah, I'm fine."

But Hans isn't looking at me. He's watching the Factory Fighters as they arrest the angry man and his friends. His eyes narrow.

"I have to get out of this country," he says, under his breath. "I can't stay here. Not now."

I know how he feels, but I don't know how we can leave with the barbed wire in place and security so tight.

We walk back to *Stargarder Strasse* in silence, no longer holding onto each other. The events of this morning and what I've just seen at *Alexanderplatz* have left me feeling stunned. As we walk, I remember all those times when Dieter tried to persuade us to follow him to the West and the excuses we gave – I only have a couple more years left at school, Brigitta will miss her friends, Mother wants to be near where Father and Oma Klara, our grandmother, are buried, we're lucky to have an apartment and a good neighbour. Now I realise how short-sighted we were not to have gone when we had the chance. But how were we to know? Our leader, Walter Ulbricht, said no-one had any intention of building a wall. I know now we were wrong to believe him. I make a decision, there and then, not to trust anything I'm told by any Party official in the future but only to trust what I see with my own eyes and feel in my own heart.

When we reach Hans' building we stop. He looks at me as if he's about to say something. He reaches forward with his hand, then stops himself and thrusts his hands into his pockets. He clears his throat. "Well...I should go and let Mother know I'm still alive." He smiles weakly at his attempt at humour.

"Sure."

He doesn't move, so I say, "Will you tell her

what we saw? About people being arrested?"

"Absolutely," he says nodding his head. His light-heartedness has vanished and he looks deadly serious. "Everyone needs to understand what is happening to this country."

"Of course." I turn to go. I won't be able to tell Mother what we saw, it would worry her too much. "I'll see you around."

I walk back to our building and climb the stairs. There's no sign of Frau Lange this time. Herr Schiller's apartment is also quiet when I walk past.

We spend the evening quietly, no one wanting to talk about the events of the day. At bedtime I unzip the yellow dress and let it slide onto the floor. I return it to its hanger in the wardrobe and climb into bed. Brigitta is already in the top bunk. I lie down on the bottom bunk and listen to her turning over. I can tell she's thinking about something.

"Sabine?"

"*Ja?*"

"I think Herr Schiller is going to help us leave East Berlin."

I wasn't expecting her to say anything like that. "What makes you think so?"

"Oh, it was just the way he looked at us as he was leaving. I'm sure he's got a plan."

I think she's been reading too many fairy tales in which the brave prince rescues the imprisoned princess, but I just say, "Goodnight, Brigitta. Try and get some sleep."

I spend most of the night lying awake, thinking of Dieter on the other side of the barbed wire, wondering if he's thinking of us.

2 FORBIDDEN TERRITORY

Sabine

The next day Mother has already gone to work when Brigitta and I get up. We go into the kitchen for breakfast. As we eat the last of the *Schwarzbrot*, I turn on the radio, hoping to hear that the barbed wire has miraculously disappeared, that the Western Allies have ordered its removal, that it was all a bad dream. But I am disappointed. Restrictions are tighter than ever. Thousands of East Berliners who work in West Berlin are not being allowed across the border. They are being told to find a job in East Berlin.

I switch the radio off. I don't want to hear any more at the moment. Right now, there is nothing we can do but try and get on with our lives.

We are almost out of food so after breakfast I tell Brigitta we are going shopping. I remove the shopping bag from the hook on the kitchen door and prise the lid off the biscuit tin where we keep our *Ostmarks*. We have twenty Marks left until

41

Mother is paid at the end of the month. At least food is cheap in East Berlin, if you can find any to buy that is.

We make our way to the corner shop with the worn wooden sign that reads *Lebensmittel* – Food. The shop used to be named after its owners – Herr and Frau Maier – a couple of old Berliners, stalwarts who have lived in this neighbourhood all their lives and know everything that is going on. People would say, *I'm popping down to Maiers' to get a few things* when they just wanted to catch up on the local gossip. But the Communists did away with traditional shop names and replaced them with functional ones so now the shop is optimistically called *Lebensmittel* in the expectation that it might sell something edible.

Brigitta collects a basket at the door and we wander around the shop looking for things to buy. In the tiny fruit and vegetable section Brigitta picks up some potatoes, but soon puts them back. They are speckled with black dots and are already sprouting green shoots.

"Those ones at the back are not so bad," I say. She chooses four potatoes which are less blemished than their comrades and puts them in the basket.

The carrots are covered in a white film so I leave them.

"How about an onion?" asks Brigitta. She picks one up but it squashes in her hand, leaving a trail of white pus on her fingertips. I wonder where Herr Schiller finds decent vegetables for his fry ups. I choose the least mangy looking white cabbage on offer and put it in the basket. There is no fruit of any kind. I can't remember the last time I tasted an orange.

We move on to the shelves of tinned food and stock up on imported Polish meat. Finally we go to the shelves filled with identical green and brown bottles. Some of them contain beer and others contain tomato juice. It's impossible to tell them apart without reading the faded labels. I select one that claims to be tomato juice and we make our way to the check-out. Then I have an idea.

Herr and Frau Maier are the only people I know who have a telephone. It's in the office at the back of the shop and they are happy to let people use it for a few *Pfennig*. I could try ringing Dieter at the hotel. He doesn't have a phone in his apartment, but the hotel does. He gave me the number once, so that I could contact him in case of an emergency. I have it written down in a leather-bound notebook I keep in the chest of drawers in our bedroom. The notebook was a present from Oma on my sixteenth birthday. I wish now I'd thought to bring it with me, but it won't take long to go home and fetch it. The thought of speaking to Dieter cheers me up.

I recognise the woman in front of us in the queue. She works in the hairdresser's on *Pappelallee*. She doesn't know me but I think her name is Frau Klein. She lifts her basket with both hands and puts it down by the till. It is laden with tins of meat and speckled potatoes.

"*Guten Tag,* Frau Klein," says Frau Maier as she taps the prices into the till. "How are you today?"

Frau Klein runs a hand over her tightly permed hair and sighs. She leans close to Frau Maier and drops her voice.

"To tell you the truth, I'm worried about what will happen to the business. We get a lot of customers from West Berlin, but they won't be able to come *now.*" She gives Frau Maier a meaningful look.

Frau Maier understands her. She shakes her head

and makes a tutting noise with her tongue.

"I tried to phone my sister this morning," continues Frau Klein as she loads the potatoes into her shopping bag. "You know, the one who lives in *Spandau*?"

I don't mean to eavesdrop, but I'm standing so close I can't help overhearing. My ears prick at the mention of *Spandau*. It's an outlying district of West Berlin.

"But I couldn't get through," says Frau Klein. She glances around the shop as if she expects the Stasi to have planted listening devices in the cabbages, then continues in an even lower voice. "The phone lines to West Berlin have been cut."

I feel the blood draining from my face. The lines have been cut? If that's true then there's no way I can contact Dieter. I look at Frau Maier, hoping that she will contradict what Frau Klein has just said, but Frau Maier nods her head. "I know. I tried the phone myself this morning. I couldn't get through either."

So that's that then. There's no point me asking Frau Maier if I can use her phone.

Frau Klein finishes loading her shopping into her bag and takes out her purse to pay.

"I'll have to write to her I suppose," she says as she hands over some crumpled *Ostmarks*.

Frau Maier puts the notes into the till and counts out the change. "Just be careful what you write," she says dropping the coins into Frau Klein's hand. "The Stasi open all letters between East and West Berlin. They read everything."

Frau Klein nods. "Don't worry, I will." Then she lifts her shopping bag off the counter and walks out, taking with her any hope I had of contacting Dieter.

Dieter

I walk into the hotel kitchen early on Monday morning, straight into a heated row between the hotel manager Herr Pohl, a short, rotund man prone to angry outbursts, and the chef, a fiery Italian called Signor Settino.

"There are guests who have been waiting over half an hour for their morning coffee," shouts Herr Pohl, turning beetroot.

"Is not my problem!" exclaims Signor Settino, throwing his hands into the air. "Eh, I ava no staff. Da waiters can-not get to work. Dey live in East Berlin. Dey can-not cross de border."

Signor Settino catches sight of me. "Ah, Dieter, please take dis coffee upstairs." He indicates a tray of silver coffee pots with a wave of his hand. "Now, *scusi* Herr Pohl, I ava work to do." He turns away from the hotel manager who looks flustered and bewildered.

I do as I am told. We won't just be missing waiters today. There are chamber maids, reception staff, porters, who all live in East Berlin. None of them will be able to get to work. All over West Berlin there must be shops, offices and hotels missing half their employees. The *Grenzganger*, those who live in the East and work in the West, will have to find jobs in East Berlin. Instead of working in a smart western hotel or shop, they will probably end up in some rundown *Trabant* factory.

I'm busy all morning, serving in the restaurant, helping to carry guests' luggage and taking kitchen deliveries. Herr Pohl has shut himself in his office where he is drawing up plans to recruit new members of staff to replace those he has lost.

At one o'clock I slip away from the kitchen

where I've been peeling potatoes for the last hour and go to the hotel lobby where the receptionist, Kerstin, is checking the bookings register.

"*Guten Tag,* Kerstin."

She looks up from the register and gives me a shy smile. "Dieter, how are you?"

"Fine. I was just wondering, my sister Sabine hasn't phoned has she? I thought she might try to get in touch, because..." My voice trails away.

Kerstin tilts her head to one side and looks at me sympathetically. "I'm sorry, haven't you heard?"

"Heard what?"

"The lines to East Berlin are dead. We can't phone them and they can't phone us."

Verdammt! Damn!

I clench my fists. I can feel the anger welling up inside me. Not only have the Communists imprisoned their people, they've cut off all lines of communication. I could write to Sabine but the Stasi would be sure to open the letter and read it. I need to find another way of contacting Sabine but at the moment I've no idea what that is.

Sabine

Over the next few days we follow the situation on the radio. As Mother predicted, America, Britain and France have done nothing to force the removal of the barbed wire. In places, teams of Factory Fighters have started building a solid Wall out of concrete blocks and the rubble from bombed buildings. And we still don't know where Herr Schiller has gone. We haven't seen him since he brought us the fried cabbage and potato to share. I listen out for him whenever I pass by his door and once or twice I've knocked, but there's no response. Brigitta still believes he's plotting an escape plan for us all. I wish I shared her optimism, but I don't.

I go for walks, drawn to the border like a moth to a flame. I see what this Wall is doing to ordinary people. A mother in West Berlin holds her newborn son up to the barbed wire so that an older woman, probably his grandmother, can kiss his tiny, wrinkled forehead. A young bride in a satin knee length dress and holding a bouquet of flowers, stands with her new husband in West Berlin and waves at a middle-aged couple (her parents?) in East Berlin who are leaning from a third floor window.

One day I go to *Bernauer Strasse*. I've heard about this street from snippets of conversation in the shop. On one side the houses are in the West and on the other they are in the East. The road itself and the pavements, on both sides, belong in the West. Before the border was closed, people living on the East side only had to step outside their front doors to find themselves in West Berlin. Now those doors are locked and guarded and the ground floor windows bricked up.

I approach *Bernauer Strasse* from one of the side roads. There's a small group of men and women standing nearby, talking. I stop not far away and look towards the border. I can't access *Bernauer Strasse* itself because the side road is barricaded with barbed wire. They haven't yet started building a wall here. Three border guards with rifles slung over their shoulders are patrolling the wire. On the west side, protesters are shouting at the guards, calling them *concentration camp guards*.

There's nothing unusual in any of this. I'm about to leave when a noise in a nearby side street attracts the attention of the guards. Two of them go to see what the disturbance is about, whilst the third guard stays by the barbed wire. But there's something odd about him.

He's a tall, slim young man, wearing the full soldier's uniform complete with knee-length boots and metal helmet, but he doesn't hold himself rigid the way his comrades do. If anything, he appears nervous. He goes up to the wire, touches it with his bare hands, and then walks away again. He repeats this a couple of times. One of the guards who went to examine the disturbance shouts, "What are you doing?"

"Just inspecting the wire," says the young soldier. "It's starting to rust already."

"Forget it," replies the other guard, "It'll be replaced by concrete tomorrow."

The young guard steps away from the wire, but half a minute later he's back and this time I see quite clearly what he is doing. He is pressing the wire down with his hand, lowering the height of it. The other two haven't noticed.

The young guard walks away from the wire once more, looks around and suddenly makes a run for it, sprinting towards the wire, then leaping into the air and launching himself over the top, his arms outstretched for balance. His rifle dangles from his right shoulder. For a moment he seems suspended in mid-air. A camera flashes in the West. He lands on his feet. There are shouts of joy from the protesters on the other side. He is ushered into a police van and driven away. Safe.

The other border guards suddenly wake up and run back to the barbed wire, rifles at the ready. But they are too late. The young soldier has gone. In a single leap, he has risked his life in a bid for freedom, and he has won.

My heart is pounding at what I have just seen, at the idea that it is possible to escape, if you have the courage and take your chance wherever you find it.

I head for home, keen to tell Mother and Brigitta what I have just seen. As I enter the apartment I am met by a familiar smell of tobacco and fried cabbage. I rush into the kitchen and find that we have a guest. Herr Schiller has returned.

He must have just arrived because Mother is busy making a mug of tea for him which she sets down on the table. She is frowning and her lips are tightly drawn. I wonder what the matter is. Brigitta, however, gives me a smile and a wink as if she knows some special secret.

"Sit down," says Brigitta to me. "Herr Schiller has some exciting news for us."

I join Herr Schiller and Brigitta at the table. Mother takes the fourth chair, her hands clasped so tight that the knuckles of her fingers show white.

Herr Schiller drinks down his tea in big, slurping mouthfuls. He is wearing an old check shirt stained with oil. His hair is a mess and his hands are covered with scratches. He has a bandage on the thumb of his left hand. I wonder what on earth he's been doing to end up in that state.

When he has finished the tea he puts the mug down on the table, wipes his mouth with the back of his hand and looks at each of us in turn. "I think I can get us to West Berlin," he says in a hushed voice. "That is, if you want to come with me."

Brigitta jumps up in her seat. "Yes, we do, don't we Mother? Sabine? We want to be with Dieter." Her cheeks are flushed with excitement.

I'm so surprised I don't know what to say for a moment.

Mother looks pale. "Will it be safe?"

I think of the guard I saw today jumping over the wire. He was lucky he wasn't shot and killed. Everywhere I've been in Berlin, the barbed wire is guarded by armed men.

"Will we escape through the sewers?" asks Brigitta, her eyes wide. "Michaela Mann said she heard her parents talking about people escaping through the sewers."

Mother gasps in horror, her hand flying to her mouth.

Herr Schiller looks bemused. "*Nein, nein, mein Liebchen,*" he says patting Brigitta on the hand, "we won't have to go underground." Mother sighs out.

"So what then?" I ask.

Herr Schiller taps his nose with his finger. "There are still one or two things I need to sort out before I'm sure it will work, so I won't go into the details now. But if all is well, I will come for you tomorrow at nine o'clock in the evening. Can you be ready?"

I look across the table at Mother and raise my eyebrows in a question. She has always been reluctant to leave behind familiar surroundings, the apartment, her job. But things are different now. Her son is on the other side of the Wall. He can't come here, and we can't go there. If we don't take this chance now, we may never see him again. Mother looks at me as if she wants me to give her reassurance. I think back to what I saw at *Alexanderplatz* and what Hans said about needing to get out of East Berlin. I turn to Herr Schiller.

"Is there room for two more people in your plan?"

He shakes his head. "Unfortunately not. There will be a severe limit on space, I'm afraid. That means you can bring no more than one small bag with you."

This is hard to take, to think that we have a chance to escape but that I will have to leave my friend and his mother behind. But what can I do? My first duty is to my family. I look back at Mother. "We should try," I say. "It might be our only chance."

She gives an imperceptible nod.

"*Gut*," says Herr Schiller, standing up. "Remember, tomorrow, at nine. I will come for you."

Dieter

"*Das ist Scheiss!*" That's bullshit.

I can hear the exasperation in my voice. Bernd just doesn't get it. So I try to explain it one more time. "Listen, if the Americans were going to do something about it they'd have done it by now. It's already way too late. They rolled the barbed wire out five days ago, for goodness' sake. They're already turning it into a solid wall. The East Germans and the Soviets are saying, *Up yours, Kennedy!* and the Americans aren't going to do a sodding thing about it because they're frightened that if they do, World War Three will break out."

Bernd doesn't know what to say. He doesn't know anyone over there, on the other side of the barbed wire. We're sitting in a *Kneipe* in *Kreuzberg* drinking beers. It's a bohemian place, the sort of bar that attracts artists, students and political agitators. Old copies of the weeks' newspapers litter the tables and benches.

"May I?" I say to the guy at the next table, leaning over to pick up a newspaper he is no longer reading. He pushes the paper in my direction and takes a swig of his whisky. It's Wednesday's edition of *Bildzeitung.*

"Look at this," I say to Bernd, thrusting the newspaper in front of him.

> *Der Osten handelt – Was tut der Westen?*
> *Der Westen tut NICHTS!*

> The East acts – what does the West do?
> The West does NOTHING!

Whilst Bernd reads the *Bildzeitung* article, the guy with the whisky passes me a copy of *Die Welt.* The picture on the front page is amazing.

"Hey Bernd," I say. "See this." Bernd lays the *Bildzeitung* to one side and looks at this new picture. I study it too.

The grainy photo shows a soldier leaping over the barbed wire at one of the side streets off *Bernauer Strasse.* The camera has captured him poised in mid-air, right foot just touching the top of the wire, left foot following behind. His arms are outstretched for balance, his right hand holding onto the strap of the rifle that is dangling on his shoulder. It's a real action shot – the sort of thing that will go round the world and make headlines. In the background a group of East Berliners stand chatting. They clearly weren't expecting to see such a sight or they might have been paying more attention. I look more closely at the group in the background. They are out of focus, but one of them looks remarkably like Sabine.

"What about that then?" I say. "Even their own guards are escaping if they can. At least the ones with half a brain."

"True," says Bernd. "It's a terrible situation, but surely someone will do something about it. What about the British? Or the French?" He takes a gulp of his beer.

I snort with derision. "Are you kidding? The French haven't got the stomach or the resources for a fight with East Germany, and the British won't do anything without the Americans to hold their hands. No, if we want to help our fellow Berliners in the East then we're going to have to do it ourselves."

Bernd chokes on his beer. "What are you suggesting?" he splutters. "What can ordinary people do if the American and British armies don't want to get involved?"

"Well I don't know off the top of my head, but it must be possible to do something."

I feel rattled. The truth is, I don't know what I can do to help people in the East. I just feel I should be doing something.

Bernd shakes his head at me. "If the East Germans catch anyone helping their citizens escape, they'll put them in prison for sure."

I ignore his comment. I know he has a point, but it's my family who are imprisoned behind the Wall. I have to try and do something.

I catch the eye of the man sitting at the next table, the one who passed me the newspaper. He's watching me. *My God*, I think, *I hope he's not a Stasi spy*. I realise I may have spoken rashly in a public place. But somehow I don't think he's a spy; he looks too individual with his fair hair flopping over his eyes and his fashionable western clothes teamed with an ex-military greatcoat. The Stasi are all robots.

"It's getting late," says Bernd looking at his watch. He stands to leave.

"Hang on," I say, picking up my beer. I've been arguing so much, I haven't had a chance to drink it yet. Bernd walks towards the door whilst I swallow the last of my beer. I stand up to follow him and the man at the next table stands up too.

"*Warten Sie, bitte*," he says. Wait. He's speaking German but there's something else in his accent. Dutch? American? I turn to face him and he holds out his hand in greeting.

"Harry," he says in a voice that I now think is more American than Dutch.

I take his hand. "Dieter." I'm not used to strangers introducing themselves like this and I look at him warily. He shakes my hand firmly and laughs.

"I'm sorry," he says, "but I couldn't help overhearing your conversation just now." He has rugged good looks and the sort of charm all the girls seem to fall for. He pushes his hair back off his forehead and regards me with steady, deep brown eyes.

I sense that he's not dangerous and start to relax a little.

I shrug. "No matter."

He reaches into his coat pocket and pulls out a piece of paper. "Listen, if you really want to do something to help get people out of East Berlin, come to a meeting on Friday." He passes me the piece of paper with an address and a time scrawled on it. *Jakobstrasse 51, Friday, 8pm.* "We need people like you," he says. Then he turns and walks out without waiting for a reply.

I stare at the piece of paper. Then I fold it and put it in my pocket. By the time I join Bernd outside, the address is already seared onto my memory.

Sabine

Before we make our bid for freedom, Mother wants to visit the graves of Father and Oma one last time. They are both buried in the *Invaliden* Cemetery in East Berlin. If our escape to West Berlin is successful then we will never be able to pay our respects again.

We dress in sombre clothes befitting the occasion, Brigitta in her best navy skirt and Mother in her black coat which she's had since before the war. I have on a dark blue dress which I keep for visiting the cemetery.

Brigitta wanted to bring some flowers but the florist has run out.

Brigitta never knew Father. She was born a month before he died. But I remember him clearly as a man of strong principles who stood up for what he believed in, which was why he was out on the streets that fateful day when the Soviets used tanks to quash the workers' rebellion.

The shock of Father's death coming so soon after the birth of a new baby plunged Mother into a depression from which she has never fully recovered. Our grandmother, Oma Klara, moved to Berlin from the countryside to help look after us. She brought her book of fairy stories with her. But to me, her own life was more fraught with drama than any fairy story. She lost her brother in the Somme in the First World War, she hid Jews in the attic of her house during the Second World War, she lost her husband in a Soviet labour camp and she worked as one of Berlin's *Trümmerfrauen* (rubble women), after the war, clearing the rubble of the bombed buildings stone by stone. But Oma Klara never complained, because she was a survivor. As we approach the cemetery I ask myself what she would want us to do, and I know she would want us to try and escape.

Oma Klara passed away last winter after a bout of influenza. We buried her next to Father, on the far side of the cemetery, close to the *Schifffahrtskanal*, one of the canals between East and West Berlin.

As we make our way across the cemetery, I can't help noticing that it is empty. There is no one tending the graves of their loved ones, or standing in silent contemplation beside a headstone. Our footsteps seem unnaturally loud in the silence.

"Stop!"

The man's voice shatters the silence like gunfire.

I look around, trying to locate the source of the voice. Brigitta whimpers and Mother turns pale and starts to tremble. Two helmeted border guards are marching towards us, both of them carrying rifles. One is older than the other, with a protruding beer belly and a sagging jaw. He positions himself right in front of us, whilst the younger guard, who looks barely more than a teenager, stands to the side, trying to look menacing.

"Where are you going?" barks the older man. "Don't you know this part of the cemetery is out of bounds?"

Mother takes a sharp intake of breath. Brigitta moves half behind me, clutching hold of my left hand. This is all too reminiscent of the events at *Potsdamer Platz*. The guard looks at Mother but when she offers no explanation, he turns to me.

"We are going to visit the graves of our father and grandmother," I say. "We come here every month to pay our respects."

"That is no longer possible," he says. "This part of the cemetery is close to the border and you are forbidden from entering it. You must not come within one hundred metres of the border. It is strictly forbidden." At these words he stands up extra tall and thrusts his stomach out so that the buttons on his shirt look as if they are about to pop.

This is crazy. Not come within one hundred metres of the border? What does he think we are going to do? Swim across the canal? In our mourning clothes?

I glance across at the younger guard. He nods his agreement and purses his lips at us, defying us to challenge the authority of his more senior colleague. Out of sight of his superior, he glares at me and tilts his rifle in our direction.

"But..." begins Mother in a quavery voice. I lay a hand on her arm.

"It's no good arguing," I say. "We must leave."

The older guard nods, pleased that I have understood his message. The younger one looks disappointed that this isn't going to end in a shoot out.

I slip my right hand through Mother's arm. Then I lead Mother and Brigitta back the way we came. I keep my head high, determined not to show the guards how scared I am.

It is only when we are back outside the cemetery gates that I start to shake. Mother and Brigitta are both sobbing, but for the moment I am too stunned to cry. *How dare they*, I want to shout. *How dare they stop us visiting the graves of our loved ones. These people have no heart.*

I feel as if Father and Oma have died a second time. Their graves lie in forbidden territory and we cannot visit them. We must return home and wait for Herr Schiller. He promised he would come for us tonight.

Dieter

Herr Pohl is still struggling to find enough new staff to fill the vacancies at the hotel so I'm run off my feet all day, fetching, carrying, clearing, peeling. But at the same time, I keep thinking about last night's meeting with Harry and his idea of helping people escape from East Berlin. I'd do anything to get Sabine, Brigitta and Mother out of the East. I won't know until tomorrow night what Harry has in mind.

At six o'clock I've just finished cleaning one of the bedrooms when I see Herr Pohl at the end of the corridor, heading in my direction. I've been on my feet for ten hours and I'm blowed if I'm doing any more. I pretend not to notice him and disappear at a run down the emergency stairs. I grab my jacket from the staff cloakroom and head outside.

I buy myself a filled bread roll from a kiosk and eat it wandering around the streets. I don't want to go home and listen to more depressing reports on the radio so on an impulse I head down to the *S-bahn* platform at *Anhalter Bahnhof* and wait for the next train heading north to *Oranienburg*. I'm curious to see what will happen. The S-1 line starts and finishes in West Berlin, but there's a section in the middle where it passes through East Berlin. Kerstin, the receptionist, said you can still travel on the S-1 line, you just can't get off at the stations in the East anymore.

The *Oranienburg* train pulls into the station and I jump on board, sitting down in an empty seat by the window. There aren't many people in the carriage, just an old woman with her shopping bags and a dozen or so bored-looking office workers on their way home. The doors close and the train starts to move forwards.

The first station is *Potsdamer Platz* which is in East Berlin. As we approach the platform the train slows to a crawl but does not actually stop. No one else seems bothered by this. Presumably they've done this journey loads of times and are used to it. But this is the first time I've taken this *S-bahn* line since the Wall went up, and I sit with my forehead pressed against the window, both fascinated and disturbed by the sight of the dimly-lit, deserted platform. Devoid of passengers, the station has a dead feel to it. Two armed border guards are patrolling the platform.

We leave the station and the train speeds up. Then it slows down once more and crawls through a deserted *Unter den Linden* without stopping. At *Friedrichstrasse* the train does actually stop but no one gets on or off; only West Germans and foreigners can go to East Berlin now. One or two people exchange nervous glances, as if stopping here makes them uneasy. But we soon move on, there being no reason to linger at *Friedrichstrasse*. It's the same at *Oranienburger Strasse* and *Nordbahnhof* as it was at *Potsdamer Platz* and *Unter den Linden*: deserted ghost stations with armed border guards on the platform. Who do they think they might need to shoot? East Berliners cannot access these stations and the passengers on the train are hardly likely to try and jump off.

The train speeds up once more and a few minutes later comes to a stop at *Humboldthain*. We're back in West Berlin and the platform is reassuringly packed with commuters. I feel the muscles in my shoulders relax. I jump up from my seat and get off the train.

I realise I'm quite close to *Bernauer Strasse* where

the East German guard jumped over the wire. His picture has been in all the papers and he's become something of a hero in West Berlin, so I start to walk in the direction of this now famous street, wondering if I'll see any other daring escapes.

The ground floor windows of the buildings on the East side of *Bernauer Strasse* have all been bricked up. The sight of these grand old buildings with their windows blanked out is as depressing as the ghost stations I just travelled through. It seems crazy to me that I can walk up and down this street quite freely, but inside those buildings are people who can no longer access the pavement outside their front doors. Then I realise people *are* trying to escape from the houses, just not via the front door or the ground floor windows. They are jumping from the upper storeys.

At various points along the street firemen are holding aloft safety blankets and people are jumping onto them.

I join a group of spectators outside one such building. We watch in nail-biting silence as a white-haired old lady in a black dress dangles precariously from a first floor window ledge, her feet about four metres from the ground. A man in the building is trying to pull her back inside, back into East Berlin. But a younger man, standing on the window ledge directly below hers takes hold of her right ankle. Another man leaps up onto the neighbouring window ledge and grabs hold of her left ankle. The Fire Brigade waits patiently below with a blanket to catch her.

The crowd holds its breath.

For what feels like an age, the old woman hangs suspended in mid-air, pulled between two opposing political systems. But in the end gravity comes to her rescue, and she slips out of the grasp of the man in the building and tumbles down onto the blanket. The crowd lets out its collective breath, and roars in triumph.

I take the train back to *Anhalter Bahnhof*, passing through the ghost stations once more. This time they don't bother me so much. I feel buoyed up by the bravery of the old woman who was prepared to risk her neck jumping to freedom. I hope Mother will be as brave if the time comes.

Sabine

Back home in *Stargarder Strasse* the minutes tick past. Mother has withdrawn into herself and is making no effort to prepare for tonight's escape. The events in the cemetery and the idea of escaping with Herr Schiller are clearly more than she can handle. She sits at the kitchen table staring at a photograph of Father taken in 1950 on a rare day out in the countryside north of Berlin. I leave her there and try to focus on what I need to do before Herr Schiller comes. I wish I could go and say good-bye to Hans but I feel too guilty at having to abandon him. If only he and his mother could come with us, but Herr Schiller was clear there wouldn't be space and my first priority is to get Mother and Brigitta out of East Berlin and to re-unite us all with Dieter.

Herr Schiller said we could only bring one small bag. Escaping to the West means leaving most of our belongings behind, not that there are many of those. I find a canvas rucksack and wonder what to put in it. We should take as many clothes as we can manage but they won't all fit into the bag. To save space I come up with the idea that we should all wear extra pairs of underwear and three pairs of socks or tights. Brigitta puts two cardigans on over her blouse. I reach out to touch my yellow dress hanging in the wardrobe, feeling its soft cotton between my finger and thumb. I wish I could take it with me but there just isn't space. I tell myself there will be plenty more dresses to buy in West Berlin and close the wardrobe door.

Brigitta insists that we take Oma's book of fairy tales. I fetch my leather notebook from the chest of drawers in the bedroom and put it in the rucksack. Everything else we must leave behind.

At seven o'clock I prepare a simple meal of bread, cold tinned meat and boiled cabbage. I encourage Brigitta to eat, even though I have no appetite myself. Mother pushes her food around the plate, barely eating a thing. In the end I give up on the meal and clear the plates away, throwing most of the food into the bin. Such a waste.

Brigitta curls up in the armchair in the sitting room and pretends to read her book but I notice that she doesn't turn the page for more than half an hour. I look in on Mother who is still sitting immobile at the kitchen table, in a kind of stupor. I hope we're not going to have a problem getting her out of the apartment when the time comes. I leave her and wander back into the sitting room. I don't want to sit down. I am on edge, listening for the sound of footsteps on the stairs and jumping every time a car passes in the street.

As nine o'clock approaches I begin to wonder if this is all a dream. Nothing seems real anymore. I'm about to leave, forever, the only home I've ever known and I can't quite take it in. The living room clock ticks loudly. Then at a minute past nine o'clock I hear the unmistakable thump of Herr Schiller's heavy tread on the stairs. There's a knock at the door.

Brigitta closes her book and looks at me with huge round eyes. *This is it*, I think - *the start of an unknown adventure which, if it succeeds, will take us to freedom in West Berlin but, if it fails*...but I don't want to think about that now. I pull myself together and go to answer the door.

The bear-like figure of Herr Schiller stands on the landing. In his hands he is carrying a bottle of *Sekt* which rather takes me by surprise. I feel it's a little premature to be celebrating.

He walks into the apartment and I close the door behind him. He sees me looking at the champagne bottle and smiles.

"If anyone asks," he says holding up the bottle, "then we are going to visit my brother to celebrate his birthday."

"Ah, I see."

He follows me into the sitting room where Brigitta and Mother are waiting for us. Mother is wearing her best black coat, the one she wore to the cemetery this morning. She looks overdressed, but I bite my tongue.

"All ready?" he asks.

I nod.

"*Gut*," he says. I lift the rucksack onto my shoulders. It feels bulky and heavy despite our economical packing. I take one last look at the home in which I grew up – the old chairs with the worn upholstery, the *Kachelofen* in the corner, the wallpaper that is starting to peel in places. Then we step out onto the landing. Mother locks the door and slips the key into an inside pocket of her coat.

We follow Herr Schiller down the stairs. I pray

that we won't meet any of our neighbours in case they ask awkward questions. But to my dismay, as we descend to the second floor, we see Frau Lange coming up the stairs. I think, *this could ruin everything.*

Frau Lange pauses on the landing outside her apartment, clearly surprised to find so many of her neighbours all going out at the same time. She looks at each of us in turn with narrowed eyes. I hover at the back, aware that the rucksack I am carrying could give us away more than anything. Herr Schiller breaks the icy silence that has descended.

"My dear Frau Lange, how good to see you." He sounds as if he's addressing a long lost friend. He spreads his arms wide as if he's about to embrace her, the bottle of champagne clearly visible in his hand. "We are on our way to celebrate my brother's birthday. Would you like to join us?"

I think, *is he mad? This could risk the whole operation.* I hold my breath, waiting for her to speak.

She looks at him as if she is seriously considering the invitation, then slowly shakes her head. "That is very kind of you Herr Schiller, but I'm afraid I have things I must do this evening."

To my ears her words don't ring true. Is she just being polite? Does she suspect us of trying to escape? I'm sure she must do. And when she says she has things to do, does she mean she will go and report us to the Stasi?

But Herr Schiller shows no sign of suspecting her meaning. "*Ach*, it is a shame you are unable to join us."

"Good evening to you Herr Schiller," says Frau Lange as she opens the door to her apartment and disappears inside. I breathe a sigh of relief that she's gone.

We make it down the rest of the stairs without

meeting anyone else. Outside it is already dark.

I walk in front with Herr Schiller. Mother and Brigitta follow behind.

"Where does your brother live?" I ask Herr Schiller, not even sure if he actually has a brother.

"In the district of *Treptow*," he replies without batting an eyelid. "We will need to take the *S-bahn* to *Baumschulenweg*." Maybe he does have a brother.

Treptow is south of here. It's a quieter area than *Prenzlauer Berg*, less built up and with more green spaces. To the west of *Treptow* is the district of *Neukölln* which is in the American sector and therefore in West Berlin. Between *Treptow* and *Neukölln* lies the *Teltow* Canal. As we walk, I ponder these facts, wondering what Herr Schiller has in mind.

Just before we reach the *S-bahn* station I can't help asking Herr Schiller, "Why did you ask Frau Lange to join us? Weren't you worried she might accept?"

Herr Schiller shakes his head. "I asked her because it seemed polite to do so, but I knew she was unlikely to accept. Frau Lange has too much of a cross to bear."

I want to ask him what he means but we have arrived at the station and there's no more time.

We board the *S-bahn* train at *Prenzlauer Allee* and sit in silence as we head south. I don't ask Herr Schiller any more questions. I'm too afraid of being overheard by the Stasi or their informers.

At *Baumschulenweg* Herr Schiller stands up, still clutching his bottle of champagne, and we follow him onto the platform and out of the station.

He leads the way down *Baumschulenstrasse*, a typical Berlin street of tall tenement buildings dotted here and there with shops on the ground floor. At this time of night the shops are shut and there is hardly anyone about. We pass a *Kneipe* on the street corner from where there is a smell of beer and chatter of voices. Otherwise the street is empty.

Eventually we turn off the main street into an even quieter area with detached houses and small gardens. The road narrows and we come to a rusted iron gate leading to some allotments. The allotments are shrouded in darkness. Herr Schiller reaches into his breast pocket and produces a small torch which he passes to me.

"Put it on when we're away from the road," he whispers, "and keep it pointing down." Then he pushes open the gate which squeaks on its hinges and we follow him into the allotments.

After we've gone about thirty metres I switch on the torch and, as Herr Schiller instructed, shine it on the ground just ahead of us. We follow a narrow path between the gardening plots. Each plot has its own wooden shed. In the pool of light from the torch I can make out rows of neatly tended potatoes, runner beans and cabbages. I suspect this is where Herr Schiller obtains his supplies of vegetables. We reach what must be the middle of the allotments, and Herr Schiller whispers at us to stop. Mother, Brigitta and I stand very close to one another, our breathing sounding loud in the empty night.

Herr Schiller goes up to an old wooden shed and taps lightly on the door.

"Horst," he calls in a voice that's barely audible. "*Ich bin's.*" It's me.

The shed door creaks open and Horst appears. He is unmistakably a younger version of Herr Schiller with the same laughing eyes and enormous build. He acknowledges us with a nod of his head.

So the *brother* part of Herr Schiller's story at least is true.

"Is everything ready?" asks Herr Schiller.

"*Ja.*"

They disappear into the shed and reappear a moment later carrying a huge square object which only just fits through the shed door.

"What is it?" I ask, stepping forward to help them.

"A raft," says Herr Schiller quite calmly as if this was the sort of thing everyone kept in their garden sheds.

A raft? I almost laugh out loud at the ingenuity of it. We are going to sail to the West like survivors from a shipwreck. But Mother gasps in horror and I realise just getting her on board will be a challenge.

The brothers lean the raft against the shed and Horst goes back inside, returning with two oars which look as if they have been newly carved out of planks of wood.

Herr Schiller looks at us as if deciding the best way to proceed. "Give the torch to Brigitta," he tells me. "She can light the way and you and Frau Neumann can each take a corner of the raft at the back. Horst and I will carry the front end and an oar each." Herr Schiller speaks quietly, but with some authority, and to my relief Mother seems willing to co-operate.

I pass the torch to Brigitta whilst Herr Schiller and his brother lay the raft down flat. Then they each pick up an oar and position themselves at the front of the raft. Mother and I stand at the back.

"Ready?" asks Herr Schiller.

"Yes," I say.

The four of us bend down, grab hold of our respective corners and lift the raft off the ground.

It's not as heavy as it looks, but the wood is thick and rough to hold and I feel a splinter pressing into my palm.

"That way," says Herr Schiller to Brigitta, nodding his head in the direction he wants her to go.

We set off at a crawl, slowed down by this large, cumbersome object. In the dim light I can see that the raft is constructed out of four empty oil barrels tied to half a dozen planks of wood which have been crudely hammered together with a couple of cross planks. There are ropes at either end to keep hold of it when it is lowered into the water. The raft isn't heavy to carry, just awkward and bulky.

I realise now the allotments must extend as far as the *Teltow* Canal. I'm grateful that Herr Schiller didn't tell us his plan in advance because I'm sure that Mother would have refused to come if she had known what it entailed. She isn't the strongest swimmer and the thought of escaping over water would have terrified her.

As we make our slow, plodding progress, I wonder how Herr Schiller and his brother managed to build the raft without anyone noticing and reporting them to the Stasi. This is what he must have been doing when we didn't see him for days.

Eventually we reach the edge of the allotments. In front of us is a low fence, then a road which is quiet at this time of night, then the canal. The canal is the actual border between East and West Berlin. There is no barbed wire here. They probably thought the water was enough of a barrier, but it is inconceivable that the area isn't being guarded.

Herr Schiller indicates with a wave of his hand that Brigitta should turn off the light. She does so and we are plunged into darkness. We crouch down low behind the fence and listen.

Silence.

Our eyes slowly adjust to the dark and we start to discern the outline of things. A cloud moves to one side, revealing a half moon which is reflected in the black water of the canal. I try to gauge the width of the canal. I guess it's about twenty-five metres. In the far distance are the lights of houses in the American sector. There is no sign of any border guards.

"*Jetzt,*" whispers Horst to his brother. Now.

As silently as we can we lift the raft over the fence and carry it to the edge of the water. We lower it down gently, keeping hold of the ropes. It looks much smaller now that it's in the water and I wonder if it's big enough to carry us all. I can see why Herr Schiller said there wouldn't be room for anyone else.

Herr Schiller leans close to whisper. "Horst and I are the heaviest so we will climb aboard first to stabilise it. Then each of you get on and we'll be off."

I hold the ropes tight whilst Herr Schiller and Horst kneel down and clamber aboard on all fours. The raft lurches under their combined weight, which is not inconsiderable, and for a moment it looks as if they are going to topple into the water.

Mother lets out a small cry.

"*Shhh!*" I say, aware of how her voice carries in the still night air.

Herr Schiller and his brother crawl to opposite ends of the raft and it settles down. There is just enough room for the rest of us to sit in the middle.

"Now the oars," says Horst. Mother and Brigitta pass them over, whilst I continue to hold the ropes.

"Right," says Herr Schiller, "one at a time. Be

69

quick."

I transfer the ropes to my left hand and, with my right hand, push Brigitta towards the raft. Suddenly a light appears in the distance on the towpath. There's a shout.

"*Wer ist da?*" calls a man's voice, gruff and angry. Who's there?

I turn around in fright and the ropes slip from my hand. Immediately the raft starts to drift away from the bank. Brigitta, who was about to climb aboard, almost topples into the water and Mother grabs her just before she falls. Border guards, still some way off, are running towards us along the towpath.

Herr Schiller and Horst try to paddle back to the shore.

"Jump," calls Herr Schiller, but it is too late. They have already drifted too far and the guards will be on us in seconds.

"Go," I call to him. "Leave us!" I grab hold of Mother and Brigitta and pull them back across the road. We tumble over the fence, back into the allotments. Then we run. We don't stop moving until we are far away from the canal.

The crack of gunshot splinters the night air. We fall to the ground, hugging each other tight. We don't move for ages.

Dieter

Jakobstrasse 51, apartment number five.

It is not far from the *Kneipe* I went to with Bernd. I walk past bullet-scarred tenement blocks, most of them student digs, looking for number fifty-one. A group of young women dressed for a night out walk past, laughing at some joke or other. Rock'n roll music blasts from an open window. From another comes the melancholy sound of a jazz clarinet.

I find number fifty-one wedged between a Turkish bar and a grocer's. The main door is ajar so I enter the unlit entrance hall and search for a light switch. A naked sixty watt bulb flickers into life to reveal a graffiti covered hallway and a staircase with bare wooden treads. I start to climb, looking for apartment number five which I find on the top floor. I knock and wait.

The door is opened by a petite young woman with light brown hair pulled back in a pony-tail. I think I must have the wrong address.

"I'm sorry," I say, "I was looking for someone called Harry." I realise I don't know Harry's surname.

She opens the door wider. "Come in. He's in here."

She turns back inside and I follow her into a narrow corridor, glad I've found the right place but thinking this wasn't what I was expecting.

She stops by a door at the end of the corridor and turns to me. "By the way, I'm Claudia."

"Dieter," I say, holding out my hand to her. She smiles at me and I notice that she has a small dimple in each cheek. Her eyes are hazel brown and framed by long lashes.

She pushes open the door and I follow her into a room furnished with an old sofa, a battered table and half a dozen mismatched chairs. The walls are decorated with posters of American movie stars. At a quick glance I spot Marilyn Monroe, John Wayne and James Dean.

There are two men at the table. One of them is Harry. He is leaning back with his chair balanced on two legs, his hands linked behind his head, a cigarette dangling from his lips. The other man has his chair pulled up close to the table and is hunched over a map of Berlin which is spread out in front of him. He has a pencil in his right hand which he is twirling compulsively between his finger and thumb.

Both men look up as I enter the room. Harry jumps to his feet, takes the cigarette from his mouth and comes over to shake my hand.

"Dieter, you came!" He sounds relieved.

"Of course," I say.

"Dieter, this is Werner," says Harry introducing me to the other man.

Werner tucks the pencil behind his right ear and and stands to shake my hand. He's younger than I first thought, probably in his early twenties, with curly brown hair, cut short, and round, wire-rimmed glasses. "*Guten Abend,*" he says making a slight bow with his head. Good evening. He seems friendly if a little formal. He studies me for a moment before sitting back down to his map.

"Have a beer," says Harry, passing me a bottle from a crate in the corner of the room.

"Thanks."

Claudia and I both pull up chairs and join Harry and Werner at the table. This is all much more informal than I'd been expecting, but everyone seems friendly and I want to hear what they have to say. I wonder how many more people Harry's expecting, but he takes a swig of beer from his bottle and says, "Right, let's get started," and I realise, with some surprise, that it's just going to be the four of us.

"Some people thought Britain and America would put a stop to the Wall," says Harry, "but of course they haven't done a sodding thing."

"What did you expect?" says Claudia rolling her eyes to the ceiling and shaking her head. "You can't rely on politicians to do anything."

Harry ignores her. "Whilst US President Kennedy *cruised* on his yacht and the British Prime Minister, Macmillan, hunted *deer*," – he can't keep the scorn out of his voice – "the East Germans quietly rolled out miles of barbed wire and imprisoned their own population. So…" he takes a breath and looks each of us in the eye, "We need to find a way of getting people out. Simply making a run for it is not realistic. I heard reports this morning that two old guys were shot last night trying to paddle across the *Teltow* Canal on some raft thing or other. The border guards are operating a shoot to kill policy against anyone trying to escape from East Berlin. That is what we're up against."

There's a moment of silence whilst we absorb this chilling fact.

"What about forging identity papers for the people in East Berlin?" I ask. It's the only idea I thought of before coming here and I don't want Harry and the others to think I've got nothing to bring to the party. "If the identity papers say they're from West Germany they'll be allowed to cross at the Checkpoint Charlie."

Harry shakes his head. "You're right that only West Germans and foreigners can cross the checkpoints into and out of East Berlin. For example, I have a West German and an American passport, so I can cross at Checkpoint Charlie whenever I want." He grins to himself, obviously pleased with his special status. "But I don't think false identity papers are the way to go. For a start, they're damn hard to get right and even if we did manage to forge them successfully, we'd only get a handful of people out like that. I want to rescue as many as possible." He stretches his hands into the air to indicate vast crowds. I think he sees himself as Moses leading his people to the Promised Land.

"Now," says Harry, "Werner has a plan that he wants to propose."

I feel a bit put out that my one idea has been so easily quashed, but Claudia gives me an encouraging smile. All attention is now on Werner who takes his glasses off, rubs the bridge of his nose, puts his glasses back on and clears his throat before starting to speak.

Werner, unlike Harry, does not relish being in the limelight. He talks quietly with his head bowed much of the time, but as he gets into his stride his confidence grows and I start to see a spark of genius behind those glasses. He explains he is studying engineering at the Technical University in West Berlin, but he has a girlfriend, Marion, living in East Berlin and that's why he's decided to take a break from his studies to work on this project with Harry; he wants Marion to join him in the West. Then he starts to outline his idea. At first it seems absurd, but as he describes the plan in more detail I can see that he's given this some serious thought and I find myself being persuaded. Escaping *over* the Wall is too risky because of the shoot to kill policy, so he wants the escapees to go *under* it. He wants us to dig a tunnel into East Berlin.

"What do you think?" he asks, twirling his pencil between his fingers. He looks nervous, as if he expects us to laugh at the absurdity of his idea. But no one does.

"I think it's a brilliant idea," I say. "Count me in! I'll dig a tunnel to Moscow if I have to."

"We shouldn't have to go that far," says Werner,

relaxing somewhat and smiling at me.

"You can count me in too," says Claudia taking a swig of beer and looking jubilant.

"Thank you," says Werner to both of us. He turns to Harry. "That all right with you then?"

Harry is frowning and I'm worried he's about to raise an objection. But then he snaps out of it and raises his bottle of beer in a toast. "To the tunnel!"

"To the tunnel!" I reply. *Hold on Sabine, I'm coming for you.*

3 ENEMY OF THE STATE

Sabine

We are still alive, but it is as if part of us has died.

Brigitta is distraught at what happened at the canal and tries to shut it out by reading fairy stories, escaping into a world of make-believe where evil spells are broken by heroic princes. I try to tell her that we don't know if the guards shot Herr Schiller or not. I say, maybe he and Horst jumped off the raft and swam to safety, although I know this is a wild hope. I don't think she believes me.

Mother suffered a panic attack in the allotments after we escaped and it took me nearly an hour to calm her down. We had to hide in Horst's shed. I was terrified the guards would find us. Now she has sunk into a mood of resignation and defeat. She expects she will never see Dieter again.

I am furious that we came so close to escaping and didn't make it. I also think about Herr Schiller and miss him dreadfully. There is an eerie quiet now on the stairs whenever I pass by his apartment. I never thought I'd say this, but I miss the smell of frying cabbage and if I do catch a whiff of it from somewhere then my heart contracts because it reminds me so much of him.

The worst of it is, we can't find out what happened to him because if we were to ask questions of anyone in authority, they would know we were trying to escape with him. That would land us all in prison, for sure. So we keep quiet and miss our friend privately, not knowing if he is dead or alive, but in our hearts fearing the worst.

Whenever I pass Frau Lange on the stairs I sense her watching me. The day after our failed escape, she asked if we had enjoyed the birthday party. I stared at her stupidly, not understanding her question, whilst she watched me through narrowed eyes. After a while I came to my senses and mumbled something incoherent and non-committal. But being the interfering old bat that she is, she couldn't leave the subject alone. "And Herr Schiller, where is he? I have not seen him."

"He is taking a short holiday," I lied.

"Really?" she said, raising her eyebrows in disbelief.

A few days after my encounter with Frau Lange, Hans drops by and suggests we go for a walk. I can see he's got things on his mind. We go to the nearby park with the old nineteenth-century water tower which was used by the Nazis to imprison Communist sympathisers in the 1930s. We sit down on the grass by the tower and Hans starts to talk. Non-stop. He is full of ideas for escaping to West Berlin. He's heard there are students in the West who are forging identity papers and smuggling them into East Berlin but he doesn't know how to get hold of one himself – he intends to look into it. And then there's the sewer system. Apparently anyone can lift the manhole covers with an iron lever. Then it's just – Hans makes it sound so simple – a matter of climbing down the shaft into the sewer system and navigating your way through the network of tunnels until you reach West Berlin where you pop up out of the ground, although he doesn't say how you're meant to get the manhole cover off the exit.

I listen and nod but only take in half of what he is saying. Deep down I am racked with guilt. How can I tell him that we tried to escape but didn't invite him and his mother to join us? Hans would never do a thing like that. And poor Herr Schiller is dead, I'm sure of it, and…

"Sabine, are you listening? Did you hear what I just said?"

I jump at the mention of my name. I realise that Hans must have asked me a question and is waiting for a reply. "I'm sorry, what was it?"

"What do you think I should do first? Investigate false identity papers or the sewer system?"

I don't think Mother will ever have the courage to attempt another escape, but Hans is looking at me expectantly waiting for a reply. "I, er, think maybe…maybe the identity papers. Yes, why don't you look into that?"

"OK, I will." He jumps to his feet as if he intends to look into matters straight away. I get up more slowly and together we walk back to *Stargarder Strasse*.

*

August turns into September. The Wall continues to grow, stone by stone, brick by brick, snaking through the city, around buildings, across roads, over tram-lines. Underground stations on lines leading to West Berlin are closed, their entrances sealed off with metal grilles. From the upper storeys of buildings friends and neighbours wave to each other across the Wall; those on the lower floors whose apartments are by the border can no longer see the opposite side of the street but stare at a concrete barrier when they look out of their windows.

When I go to the shop I overhear snippets of conversation.

"*Die Amerikaner tun nichts.*" The Americans are doing nothing.

"*Die Mauer wird bleiben.*" The Wall is here to stay.

Such things are said in hushed, confidential tones to close friends whilst stocking up on tins of meat and jars of *Sauerkraut*. No one wants to get into trouble with the Stasi for harbouring anti-communist feelings.

Soon it is time to return to school. I normally look forward to the start of a new term, but this time I'm apprehensive. Things are different now. The Wall has created an atmosphere of fear and distrust. Which side are you on? Are you for the Wall or against it?

On the first day of term Mother leaves the apartment at six to go to work so I help Brigitta get ready and then walk with her to the entrance of the *Grundschule*, a grey, bullet damaged building on *Pappelallee*. I hope that a return to school will help her move on from the events at the canal.

"*Tschüs!*" Brigitta waves me good-bye and disappears inside.

"*Tschüs!*" I call after her. Then I continue on to the High School in *Greifenhagener Strasse*. The building dates from the Nineteenth Century, a five-storey brick monolith with rows and rows of identical windows. It looms up at me now as I approach the entrance. This is the final year of school for me - I will take the final exam, the *Abitur*, next summer. I've always wanted to go to university and study languages. I wanted to learn English, but we only learn Russian in East Berlin.

I join the other students entering the building and make my way down the long corridor. Rubber-soled shoes squeak on the linoleum floor. During the holidays the walls have been painted a garish shade of mustard brown. I can't help thinking how I wouldn't be here now if our attempt to escape across the canal had succeeded. That leads me to thinking of Herr Schiller which brings a lump to my throat and I have to push him from my mind so as not to break down and draw attention to myself.

"*Sabine! Warte doch!*" Sabine, wait! The sound of my name being shouted down the corridor brings me back to the present.

I turn round and see my friend Astrid striding towards me, overtaking the other students with her long legs. She looks amazing. The sun has bleached her blond hair golden and her skin is glowing with a healthy tan. Her summer camping trip has obviously done her good.

She catches me up, linking her arm through mine. "Hey, Sabine, good to see you. How are things?"

"Umm, fine." *Under the circumstances*, I think. "How was your holiday?"

"*Ach, wunderbar!*" she laughs. "We camped in the forest for two weeks and we went swimming in the lake every day. And, oh my God Sabine, you should have seen the camp leader." She gives me a look which leaves me in no doubt about the gorgeousness of the camp leader.

I feel better already. It's impossible not to be

cheered up by Astrid's enthusiasm for life.

As we make our way to the classroom, she chatters non-stop, telling me about the camp which was organised by the *Freie Deutsche Jugend*, the Communist youth organisation. She always says she has no interest in the politics, she just likes to go on the organised holidays and have fun. I guess there's no harm in that.

"And we stayed up late every night, drinking beers and telling jokes. You know, Sabine, you should give it a go. Next year…" She falls silent. We've reached the classroom and there's an atmosphere in the room that is at odds with Astrid's frivolous chatter.

There's a group of students in the middle of the room and at the centre of the group are two boys I've known since the first year at the *Grundschule*, Matthias and Joachim. I haven't seen them all summer and I'm struck by how much they've changed. It's not just that Joachim has grown taller, or that Matthias is wearing his hair longer. There's something else different about them. They've never been known for their respect for authority and they're good at making people laugh with their merciless imitations of unpopular school teachers. But today there's a seriousness about them. They are both dressed completely in black – black trousers, black shirts, black sweaters. As Astrid and I enter the room, Matthias is explaining their sartorial choices.

"It's a protest," he says. Joachim, hands thrust deep into his pockets, nods his assent. "We're protesting against the Wall. We're in mourning for the death of freedom in this country." Matthias looks around his audience, inviting them to support him.

And it's clear that they do support him. People start talking about their experiences of being unable to travel to West Berlin because of the Wall; Monika, a pretty girl who is normally shy and quiet, talks heatedly about how she was turned back at the *Bornholmer* Bridge Checkpoint when she tried to visit her cousin in *Wedding*; Gabriele had a similar experience to me at *Friedrichstrasse* station; Jens talks about how he got into a confrontation with an armed guard at *Bernauer Strasse*; everyone, it seems, has watched with horror as the Wall has been built. People have heard rumours of shootings at the Wall. I want to join in and tell my own story about travelling to *Friedrichstrasse* station on the morning the barbed wire was rolled out, but Astrid has walked over to the window and is waiting for me to join her. Her ebullient mood of a moment ago has evaporated.

"*Die Idioten!*" she says under her breath, glancing over at Matthias and Joachim. The idiots.

I'm used to Astrid being quite outspoken but I'm shocked at her abrupt change of mood.

"What do you mean?" I ask, keeping my voice low.

"Wearing black as a sign of protest," she says impatiently. "What are they hoping to achieve?"

"Well they might not achieve anything, but they've got a point," I say. "We've all lost our freedom."

"Yes, I know that. But they don't understand what they're doing. They'll just get themselves into trouble. And anyone who supports them will get into trouble too. They could make life very difficult for the rest of us. Don't you see?"

"I suppose so."

She lets the subject drop as the classroom starts

to fill up. I guess she's right, but even so, I admire Matthias and Joachim for having the courage to take a stand. I do sometimes wonder if the government would have got away with building the Wall if everyone had just stood up against them. But they had plenty of willing supporters in the teams of Factory Fighters and it's difficult to argue with a machine gun. I was going to tell Astrid later about our escape attempt with Herr Schiller, but I decide maybe I'd better not mention it. She would probably think it foolish.

Just then Hans arrives and the guilt I feel about trying to escape without him wells up in me all over again. I realise I must never mention it to Astrid in case she lets something slip and Hans hears about it. He comes over to me.

"*Tag, Sabine, wie geht's?*" Hi, Sabine, how's it going?

I do my best to smile back. "*Gut, danke.*" Good, thanks.

"I've started to make some progress," he says under his breath, "about, you know..."

At that moment Herr Keller, the form teacher, walks in. He's a grumpy man and the summer break has done nothing to improve his mood.

"Tell you later," says Hans.

The chatter dies down and there is a scraping of chairs as everyone finds somewhere to sit.

"*Guten Morgen,*" barks Herr Keller. He drops a pile of papers and books onto the desk. He doesn't bother welcoming us back to school.

The first task of the day is to hand out the timetables. They have been typed on thin, shiny paper by Frau Weber, the school secretary. When I receive mine I scan it quickly - Russian, Physics, Chemistry, Maths, German literature and the compulsory Marxism-Leninism. I count the periods given to the study of Marx and Lenin. There's a lesson at the end of today, Tuesday after break, first thing Wednesday morning and a double session at the end of the day on Friday. My heart sinks. The school has more than doubled the number of lessons in socialist politics. I look around the room. There are mutterings of discontent as people read their timetables and turn to their neighbours.

Hans raises his hand.

"What is it?" snaps Herr Keller.

"There must be a mistake here," says Hans. "There are too many lessons in Marxism-Leninism."

I doubt it's a mistake and Hans is not going to make himself popular with the teachers if he starts questioning the timetable.

Herr Keller glares at Hans. He fidgets with his shirt collar as if he is not entirely comfortable with what he is about to say.

"There is no mistake," says Herr Keller. "The extra lessons are necessary. We cannot hope to build a successful socialist state in this country if its citizens are not properly informed about socialist ideals." He sounds as if he is repeating something he has been taught to say, parrot-fashion.

Hans catches my eye and smirks as if to say, what a load of bullshit. I keep my own face neutral.

"And finally," says Herr Keller, "The headmaster has asked me to tell the boys that they should sign up for military service. There will be an opportunity to do so in the school foyer during the morning break."

The smirk is wiped from Hans' face as surely as if he'd just been slapped. Something else takes its place. Anger. And a steely determination behind those blue eyes of his.

Dieter

Our first job is to find somewhere in the West to dig from. It's Monday morning and I'm back in Claudia's apartment in *Jakobstrasse*, having phoned work to tell them I'm sick. I don't think Herr Pohl believed me.

I stayed late at Claudia's place on Friday night, drinking beers and getting to know my new friends a bit better. Werner loosened up a lot after we agreed to go with his tunnel project. He explained that his girlfriend, Marion, is stuck working in a Trabant factory because the authorities won't let her go to university – something to do with her father making a joke at work about the Communist Party leadership. His colleagues thought it was a very funny joke, but someone must have reported him to the Stasi. He was arrested and sentenced to five months' imprisonment. Now the whole family is under Stasi surveillance. Claudia told us that she has a younger brother and sister who live with their aunt in the East Berlin district of Pankow, but she seemed reluctant to explain how come they're over there and she's over here. I told them about Sabine, Brigitta and Mother. Harry was a bit vague about who he knows in East Berlin but it seems one of his acquaintances is an actor. What I haven't worked out yet is what the relationship is between Harry and Claudia. We're using her apartment as a meeting place, but Harry is clearly the leader of the group, although he leaves all the technical stuff to Werner.

Claudia and I join Werner at the table. The beer bottles from Friday night have been cleared away. Harry doesn't sit down but paces the room like a caged animal.

From his pile of papers Werner pulls out a

detailed map of Berlin and spreads it on the table. The route of the Wall is drawn in red ink, like a river of blood running through the city, along roads, cutting off side-streets, dissecting train and tram lines, crossing the river and the canals.

"I've been thinking about the best place to dig," says Werner. "We can forget about the *Tiergarten* area, it's too open and central. We can't dig all the way under the *Brandenburger Tor* or *Potsdamer Platz*. And *Neukölln* is out because of the *Teltow* Canal. We need somewhere where there are houses close to each other on either side of the Wall. Here in *Kreuzberg* is a possibility, or *Wedding* in the French sector might work."

He points to a street on the map in the *Wedding* district. "Here is *Bernauer Strasse* where the border runs along the edge of the houses."

I nod my head in agreement. It's where I saw the old lady jumping to freedom from her first floor window.

"This would be an ideal area for us to dig," explains Werner. "Many of the houses in the East are now empty or soon will be. People who have escaped in the last week say that compulsory evacuation orders have been issued to those still living there. If we can find a suitable building in the West, we could dig a tunnel from the cellar to a building in the East. What do you think?"

"Sounds good to me," I say. I turn to Claudia. "What do you think?"

Before she has a chance to reply, Harry interrupts.

"Have you made a decision yet?" He's impatient to be off. It's clear that details bore him. Claudia rolls her eyes at me.

"I guess so," says Werner to Harry.

"Right then, let's go."

So the four of us take the *S-bahn* north to *Wedding* and start exploring the streets, looking for suitable properties – empty houses or shops to rent.

Harry takes the lead, striding down *Bernauer Strasse*, his long coat flying open behind him. Metal helmets of the East German border guards are just visible above the Wall that blocks off the side-streets on the eastern side.

On the western side of *Bernauer Strasse*, not far from the junction with *Brunnenstrasse*, we find a shop with its front window boarded up. A hand painted sign above the window reads *Bäckerei*, bakery. There's a cardboard notice propped up in the window with the words, *To Let*, and a phone number to call.

"This could work," says Werner looking up at the deserted property. There's no sign of life in the neighbouring properties either. I suspect living directly opposite the Wall is not popular.

Opposite the bakery are buildings with bricked up windows and, a little further along, the Wall running across the junction with *Brunnenstrasse*. The Wall also runs across an area of ground where there's a gap in the buildings. A bomb must have landed during the war and wiped out a couple of properties. Beyond the Wall, where the bombed houses used to stand, we can see the buildings on *Schönholzer Strasse* which runs parallel to *Bernauer Strasse*.

"We could dig to the basement of one of those houses on *Schönholzer Strasse*," says Werner. "They are about one hundred metres from the border. We don't want the tunnel to emerge too close to the Wall."

As we look in the direction of *Schönholzer Strasse*,

we see a guard marching past the Wall, the top of his helmet the only visible part of him. We'd be digging right under their feet.

Harry takes a notebook from his pocket and jots down the phone number. Then we move on, not wanting to arouse suspicion by hanging around too long.

We don't find any other suitable properties on *Bernauer Strasse* or the streets immediately behind it, so we go into a café where there's a phone and Harry calls the landlord to ask about renting the bakery. The landlord agrees to meet us there in an hour.

When we return, the landlord is waiting for us inside the bakery. He is an old man with a stoop who introduces himself as Herr Becker. He must be a little deaf because we have to repeat our names for him.

Herr Becker regards us with some surprise and not a little suspicion. We clearly don't fit his image of what bakers look like. He shuffles around showing us the shop front and the kitchen out the back with the huge bread ovens. Claudia listens with interest to a speech about how many loaves can be baked in the ovens at any one time, whilst Harry strides around impatiently, opening doors and examining the yard out the back.

Harry comes back in and interrupts Herr Becker. "Could we see the cellar please?"

The landlord mutters something inaudible to himself and, for a moment, I'm worried he's going to throw us out, but then he shuffles over to a row of hooks on the wall and takes down a large metal key. He uses the key to unlock a door at the back of the kitchen. He fumbles for the light switch, flicks it on, and stands aside to let us go down first. The staircase is a steep, wooden one and creaks in protest. At the bottom we find ourselves in a large cellar. There are piles of old furniture stacked in one corner and shelves for storing sacks of bread flour.

Claudia engages Herr Becker in a conversation about the ample storage space in the cellar, whilst the rest of us walk into the middle of the room and kneel down to examine the floor.

"Bare earth," says Werner quietly to Harry and me.

"What's that?" asks Herr Becker shuffling over to us and cupping one hand to his ear.

"Nice big space down here," says Werner.

"Hmmm," nods the old man.

We also check out the living accommodation above the shop. There are three bedrooms, a living room, a small kitchen and an even tinier bathroom. We will need to live on site so there isn't too much coming and going which the border guards would be sure to notice.

It's time to get down to business. We can't afford to pay what the landlord is asking – one hundred Deutschmarks a month. I don't know if we can afford to pay anything, come to think of it.

Harry tries to sweet talk the old man into accepting less. "Look," says Harry in his most genial voice, "the street is half empty. Business is down, understandably, since the Wall went up because half the customers can't get here. How about we agree on fifty Deutschmarks a month and shake hands on it?" He takes his wallet out of his coat pocket.

Herr Becker stands there, unmoving, looking from one of us to the other.

For a minute no one speaks and I can feel the blood pulsing in my temples. Herr Becker suddenly seems to come to a decision.

"I might be old and deaf," he says, "but I'm not stupid. You're not going to open a bakery are you?"

Harry starts to protest, but Herr Becker puts up his hand to stop him. "Save your breath, lad." Herr Becker turns to look out of the window. The helmets of the border guards are visible on the other side of the Wall. When Herr Becker speaks again, his voice starts to crack. "There's only one reason why a group of young people like yourselves would want to rent an old property like this so close to the Wall. You've got some sort of plan up your sleeves for getting people out of East Berlin. Well, I say, good luck to you. You can put your money away. I don't want it."

Herr Becker hands the key over to Harry. "Take it. The place is yours until you've done what you need to do. Just don't let those bastards over there catch you."

Sabine

Matthias and Joachim are attracting lots of attention. People stare and point at them as they walk around the school. Word has spread quickly about their decision to wear black as a political protest. They are receiving a lot of support from their fellow students, but the staff are not amused by it.

The last lesson of the day is Marxism-Leninism with Herr Schmidt, my least favourite teacher.

A short, colourless man with a blotchy, bald head, Herr Schmidt strides towards the desk at the front of the classroom. His weasel-like eyes flit around the room and his nose twitches as if he intends to sniff out dissent at fifty paces. His eyes narrow on Matthias and Joachim sitting at the back of the classroom. I glance at them both. They stare straight back at him, defiant and unrepentant. I expect Herr Schmidt to say something to them, but he doesn't. Instead he looks as if he's making a mental note to exact revenge at a later date.

"Open your exercise books," says Herr Schmidt in his rasping voice. "We will begin by examining some heroes of Socialism and their contribution to our society."

He walks over to the side of the classroom where four portraits of Communist leaders and thinkers are pinned to the wall.

First in this line of socialist demi-gods is Karl Marx sitting on a carved wooden chair, his right hand tucked inside the lapel of his jacket, a gold watch just visible on a chain. His frizzy, unkempt hair and beard make him look like a mad scientist. Alongside Marx is a portrait of his collaborator, Friedrich Engels whose enormous handlebar moustache and beard completely obscure his mouth to the extent that I can't help wondering if he ever managed to eat soup without getting into a terrible mess.

Then there are two twentieth-century practitioners of Marxism: Vladimir Lenin of Russia and our own leader, Walter Ulbricht. They are more restrained than Marx and Engels in their facial hair, both sporting trimmed moustaches and goatee beards. With his arched, black eyebrows and black pointy beard Lenin makes me think of Mephistopheles, the devil from Goethe's Faust. Ulbricht's face is less easy to read. On the surface he looks benign enough with his bald head and silver-rimmed glasses, but I sense that underneath the bland face is a heart of steel. After all, this is the man who said, "No one has any intention of building a Wall."

Marx, Engels, Lenin and Ulbricht observe the lesson from their vantage points like school inspectors come to ensure that Herr Schmidt sticks to the party line.

They needn't have worried. Herr Schmidt recites Marxist and Leninist doctrines like a model pupil. In his monotone voice he drones on about the ideas of Communist ideology and we are obliged to write down everything he says. I find myself scribbling phrases like *dictatorship of the bourgeoisie* (which Herr Schmidt indicates is bad by the scorn in his voice) and *dictatorship of the proletariat* (at which Herr Schmidt purrs like a cat) without understanding what half of it means. If anyone so much as glances out of the window, Herr Schmidt pounces on them with a verbal attack like machine-gun fire.

"Matthias, a socialist society requires the co-operation of *all* its members, and that includes *you*."

"Joachim, since you do not see the need to write down what I am saying I can only assume that you are already familiar with Lenin's programme for the Bolshevik Party as outlined in his *April Theses* of 1917. Maybe you would care to enlighten the class?" Shuffling of paper from the back of the classroom. "*No?* Do I take it that you are not, after all, familiar with Lenin's theories? Then maybe you would do me the courtesy of taking some notes."

"Monika, the concepts of Marxism-Leninism, which I have just explained in great detail, are not to be found on your fingernails, the length of which, I might add, would prevent you from doing any serious manual work, which is the noblest type of work in our society."

Monika, who is sitting across the aisle from me,

blushes scarlet and hides her hands with their elegant, long nails, under the desk.

I keep my head down and long for the bell to ring.

I'm beginning to wonder if the school bell has broken when Herr Schmidt's monologue is interrupted by its strident buzzing. The class exhales a huge sigh of relief. No one can get out fast enough. Astrid drags me through the door and out into the street.

"*Mein Gott,*" she says. "I thought that lesson was never going to end. I still haven't told you everything that happened on the camping trip." She links arms with me as we walk down *Greifenhagener Strasse* and embarks on a story about a midnight hike in the forest when I hear my name being called.

"Sabine!"

I turn around to see Hans running to catch up. Astrid frowns.

"Hi," I say to Hans.

We continue walking, Hans falling into step beside me. Astrid is silent.

"You were telling me about a hiking trip?" I prompt her.

"It doesn't matter. It wasn't anything important."

When we reach the corner of *Stargarder Strasse* Astrid loosens her arm from mine. "Well, I'll leave you two in peace," she says, glancing from me to Hans. She heads off towards *Schönhauser Allee.*

Hans looks bewildered. "Did I interrupt something?"

"No, don't be silly."

"Sabine, you know what Herr Keller said this morning about military service?"

"Yes?"

"Well I'm not going to do it."

I'm not surprised by this. I wait for him to continue.

He leans close and speaks in barely more than a whisper. I can feel his breath tickling the skin on my neck. "I've found a group in West Berlin who can organise false identity papers. They say it might take a while, but still, it's a start."

"That's good," I say smiling at him. We've reached my building.

"I'll let you know," he says, giving me a wink.

I watch him as he walks away down the street, then I go inside and climb the stairs to our apartment.

Brigitta is already there, lying on the top bunk, reading.

"How was school today?" I ask.

"*Nicht gut*," she says. Not good.

"Oh, why?"

She lays her book to one side and explains how the nice Fräulein Peters who was supposed to have been her teacher this year is no longer at the school and instead they have a new teacher called Frau Wolf who's *a real dragon*. Brigitta pulls a face and mimics a wild animal, fingers curled into claws either side of her face.

"Frau Wolf says we all have to join the Young Pioneers," moans Brigitta. This is the Communist youth organisation for young children. Mother never encouraged us to join these groups. She doesn't trust them, saying they remind her too much of the *Bund Deutscher Mädel*, the girl's section of the *Hitler Youth* which she was forced to join as a girl. She used to tell us horror stories of compulsory aerobic exercises, en masse, in the park where the girls were made to wear skimpy white dresses and were ogled by the male instructors.

"I don't want to join the Young Pioneers," says Brigitta, screwing up her face. "I hate their uniforms and the boys are horrible. They march around the playground pretending to be soldiers and shooting at all the girls."

"They can't make you do anything you don't want to do."

Brigitta looks like she doesn't believe me. "I think Frau Wolf is really the evil stepmother from *Snow White*," she says. "She tried to teach us today that the people in West Berlin are evil, but I didn't believe her because Dieter is in West Berlin and I know he isn't evil." She looks like she might cry.

I climb up onto the top bunk and sit beside her. "Let's read a story together," I say. "Which one shall we read?"

"Rapunzel."

How appropriate, I think, as she finds the page. A girl imprisoned in a tower. Everyone in East Berlin is a Rapunzel now.

Dieter

Now that we have a place to dig from, Werner sets to work studying detailed maps of the area, working out distances and the best route for the tunnel to take. Harry has gone to source shovels, spades, pick-axes, buckets and a wheelbarrow. He says he knows somewhere he can get what we need for a fraction of the real cost. I offered to help him, but he waved me away. So Claudia and I take on the job of making the bakery living quarters habitable and tidying the cellar ready for the digging to start.

The bakery has been empty for months and is in a bad way. The shop is filthy and there are mouse droppings in the bakery kitchen.

Claudia pulls open the cast iron door of one of the bread ovens and sticks her head inside.

"We should try and get these working again," she says, her voice echoing in the hollow space.

"What, are you kidding?"

"Not at all," she says turning to face me. She's completely serious. "We're going to need lots of food if we're going to have the strength to dig a tunnel by hand"

"True," I say. Werner has made it clear we won't be able to use machinery for the digging because it would be too noisy and the East German guards would soon hear if there was drilling under their feet.

Upstairs is not much better than downstairs in terms of cleanliness. But at least there's a double bed in one room and bunk beds in the other two. A family with kids must have lived here once. The beds mean that six people will be able to sleep at any one time. Harry has plans for us to work around the clock, in shifts, to try and get the job done quicker. In the kitchen there's a small gas hob, a table and half a dozen chairs. The living room has a sofa with broken springs.

"Comfy," says Claudia bouncing on the sofa and laughing.

But the cellar is where we need to start work. We make our way down the rickety wooden steps.

"These are not safe," says Claudia pointing to a splintered tread. She's right. It's not the only one that's broken. The steps won't last long if dozens of students are stomping up and down day and night.

"I'll fix them," I say, keen to impress her, then immediately wishing I hadn't offered to do that. I've never used a hammer in my life. Still, it can't be that hard.

Claudia opens up an old bag of flour sitting on one of the shelves and peers inside.

"*Scheisse*," she says turning away quickly. "It must be damp down here in the winter. The flour has gone mouldy."

So the first thing we do is carry the heavy sacks of flour up the stairs and dump them in the yard out the back. Then we go back to the cellar and examine the pile of old furniture. There are three-legged chairs, a broken table, and an old chest of drawers.

In the afternoon we get stuck in using wood from the broken furniture to mend the cellar steps and cleaning the apartment. Claudia is full of energy and tackles every job as if she's going into battle. She saws up the drawers from the old chest and I hammer the wood into the stairs. Upstairs in the apartment, she rolls up her sleeves and scrubs the work surfaces, floors and walls until the sweat runs into her eyes and she can't see what she's doing. I do my best to keep up with her, but she seems driven.

By the end of the day we're exhausted. I make us each a mug of coffee and we collapse at the kitchen table. Claudia lifts her mug with two hands, puckers her lips into a rosebud and blows gently over the surface of the hot liquid. She has a smudge of dirt on the tip of her nose. We've been working side by side for hours, but I still hardly know her.

"You said your brother and sister live in East Berlin with your aunt," I say. "How come?"

For ages she stares into her mug of coffee. When she starts to speak it's in a quiet voice.

"My parents were killed in a car crash eighteen months ago."

"I'm sorry."

"Thank you." She gives me a wan smile. "My younger brother and sister, Axel and Bettina, went to live with our aunt in the *Pankow* district of East Berlin. I stayed here to continue my studies in sociology at the university. At first it didn't matter that they were in the Soviet Sector and I was in the West. They were being looked after and I visited them every weekend and took them things like sweets which they couldn't buy easily in the East. And they came to see me in the school holidays. But since the Wall went up, I can't go over there and they can't come here. If I don't get them out of East Berlin, I might never see them again."

She looks at me with her big, hazel eyes which are brimming with tears.

"Don't worry," I say, laying a hand on her arm. "We'll get them out. All of them."

Sabine

The protest started yesterday by Matthias and Joachim is growing. Half the class have come to school today dressed from head to foot in black. One of them is Hans. He walked into the classroom this morning wearing black trousers and a black sweater. Matthias and Joachim have become, in the eyes of many, heroes. Even Monika has eschewed her usual pretty colours for a black blouse and black skirt which make her look much older. Astrid refuses to join in, saying they will all land themselves in serious trouble. I just don't have anything black in my wardrobe.

At registration Herr Keller stands at the front of the classroom eyeing us one by one. I'm sure he's making a mental note of who is wearing what.

When I arrive home from school Frau Mann, from the first floor, is in the hallway, removing some letters from her post box. She starts flicking through them. She's a thin woman in her thirties but looks older, one or two strands of her dark hair already turning grey. Olaf and Michaela, the children, are standing nearby, Olaf sucking his thumb and Michaela twisting a strand of fair hair around her fingers.

"*Guten Tag*, Frau Mann," I say. She is a much nicer neighbour than Frau Lange.

She looks up sharply, stuffing the letters into her coat pocket. "Oh, Sabine," she says with a sigh. "You startled me." Her eyes dart past me, out of the door, as if she's expecting someone else to walk in.

"Is everything all right?" I ask. She's clutching her coat close to her, even though the weather is still very mild.

She glances across at the children, then she leans close to me and speaks in a hushed voice.

"*Nicht gut*," she says shaking her head. Not good. "Helmut can't find a job." Helmut is her husband, a big, jovial man but hardly ever around because he's usually at work.

"Oh?"

"You know, he used to work…" she drops her voice even lower so I have to almost lip read, "*over there*." She means West Berlin. I nod my head to show that I understand her meaning. "But now, he isn't allowed to cross the border to go to work and he can't find a job in East Berlin. He's applied for lots of positions, but no one will take him. I think the Stasi must have something against him."

"That's terrible."

Frau Mann looks as if she's about to say something else but then an upstairs door opens and closes and there is the sound of footsteps on the stairs. Frau Lange appears. She looks from me to Frau Mann and back at me, as if she's drawing some significant conclusion about the fact that we are having a conversation together.

"*Guten Tag*, Frau Lange," I say. I'm determined that she should see we have nothing to hide.

The simple rules of courtesy force her to acknowledge us with a short, sharp *Guten Tag*, but she doesn't stop to chat.

"I must go," says Frau Mann, glancing towards the children. She ushers them out of the building and I'm left standing there, wondering how they're going to manage if Herr Mann can't find a job.

Dieter

I've moved out of the apartment I shared with Bernd, although most of my clothes and things are still there. I've also handed in my notice at the *Hotel Zoo*. I want to dedicate myself totally to the tunnel project and getting Sabine, Brigitta and Mother out of East Berlin. What little money I've saved, I've put into the collective pot for buying equipment and food.

On Thursday evening Harry calls a meeting in the upstairs kitchen to discuss the plans.

Werner arrives carrying a battered old leather briefcase from which he pulls out a sheath of papers and his map of Berlin. He rolls the map out on the table and Harry, Claudia and I listen as he talks us through the details.

Werner has drawn up plans for a tunnel that extends from the bakery on *Bernauer Strasse* to number seventeen *Schönholzer Strasse*. The tunnel will be one hundred and twenty metres long.

"This is a profile of the tunnel," says Werner taking another piece of paper from his briefcase. "We need to dig down vertically four metres before we dig the horizontal tunnel. At the other end we'll dig a slope upwards at an angle of thirty degrees. It's the only way we can reach the surface safely and it also means the escapees will be able to slide down into the tunnel, making their escapes faster."

I'm impressed with Werner's work, but Harry is in an argumentative mood.

"How high will the tunnel be?" he asks.

"Just over one metre," says Werner.

"So people will have to crawl out?"

"It would take too long to dig a taller tunnel."

"And how long is it going to take to dig this one?"

"That depends what the soil is like. If it's mainly sand it will be quick to dig, but if we find clay it will take longer. If we work around the clock I reckon we can get the job done in about four months."

Harry whistles through his teeth. I thought he'd be happier than this.

"Look," I say, "the sooner we get started, the sooner we'll be finished."

Harry ignores my comment and continues interrogating Werner.

"What about noise? Is there any chance the East Germans will be able to hear us?"

"We won't be able to use any noisy machinery," says Werner, "but we already knew that. That's why it's going to take such a long time to dig. And there's another thing, because we're so close to the Wall I think we should have someone on lookout on the roof at all times, so if the East Germans become suspicious we can stop work and lock the cellar immediately."

I'm dismayed that we have to keep a lookout the whole time, but I remind myself that we are planning to invade enemy territory, and if the East Germans caught us digging under their feet we'd most likely be shot.

"Whatever you say," says Harry, although he doesn't sound convinced.

"Good," says Werner in a tone which draws that conversation to a close. Claudia gives me a look to say, glad that's settled.

"Just one last thing," says Harry. "I'll be going in and out of East Berlin because we can't send letters by post – the Stasi steam open and read everything. But I can't visit every escapee personally. We need a contact in the East. Someone who is beyond suspicion. Someone that the Stasi have never had any reason to monitor."

"My girlfriend Marion is plucky enough to do it," says Werner, "but the factory where she works is crawling with Stasi informers. She'd never get away with it. What about your friend, Harry?"

Harry shakes his head. "Manfred is an actor. He's too well known. They watch people like that extra closely."

"My aunt has never had any trouble with the Stasi," says Claudia. "But she's busy all day working at the hospital and looking after my brother and sister in the evenings."

"Don't worry," I say excitedly. "I know just the person." Everyone turns to look at me. "My sister Sabine could be our contact in the East. The Stasi have never had a reason to suspect her of anything. She'd be perfect for the job."

"What's she like, this sister of yours?" asks Harry.

"Well she's seventeen and still at school, but don't let that put you off. She's very mature and sensible. She's never been in any sort of trouble with the Stasi, or anything like that."

"Hmmm," says Harry. "Well, if she's the best we've got, she'll have to do."

I'm disappointed by Harry's reaction, but I try not to let it show.

"I'm sure she'll be great," says Claudia confidently.

I think so too. And so will Harry once he's met her.

Sabine

The atmosphere at school is deteriorating. Hans and the other boys are coming under increasing pressure from the Headmaster to sign up for military service. So far they've all refused. Most of them are wearing black in support of the protest started by Matthias and Joachim. And there are men I don't recognise in the corridors. Dressed in suits of grey, they must be Party officials, probably Stasi. And they are watching us.

When the final bell rings on Thursday, Astrid grabs me by the arm.

"Come on, let's get out of here. It feels like we're under surveillance."

"We are."

"Well I've had enough of it." She hurries me outside. "Want to come back to my place for a bit?"

"Sure."

We head off towards *Schönhauser Allee* where Astrid lives in a modern apartment with her parents and younger brother, Frank. As we walk, Astrid does a merciless impression of the politics teacher Herr Schmidt, knitting her eyebrows together and preparing to launch into a lecture of Marxist political theory. It feels good to laugh.

When we reach her building we climb the stairs to the first floor. The stairwell is bright with electric lights that don't run on a timer and looks, and smells, as if it has been newly painted. She opens the door to the apartment and I follow her into the lounge as she embarks on another impersonation of Herr Schmidt.

Frank is lying on a red rug watching *Meister Nadeloehr*, the only children's programme on television. Like most young boys his age he is dressed in the uniform of the Young Pioneers, blue shorts, white shirt and a blue neckerchief.

"*Shhh!*" he says, frowning at us. Astrid ceases her chatter for a moment and we stand there watching the flickering screen. A man with a bouffant hair-do and dressed in a frilly white shirt and dinner jacket is singing a song about fairy tales whilst pretending to play a guitar that looks like a plank of wood. Then he starts to pack a rucksack so he and his teddy bear companion can go hiking in the forest and watch animals through a pair of binoculars. I think, *is this really the best East German television can do for kids?*

"Papa will want to watch the news when he gets in," says Astrid. Frank sticks his tongue out at her.

I once asked Astrid what her father does for a living but she just said he had a boring job working in an office.

"Astrid, is that you?" calls her mother from the kitchen. The smell of *Bratwurst* and *Apfelstrudel* wafts into the room. "Tea will be ready in half an hour. Oh, hello Sabine, will you stay for something to eat?"

It's tempting, but I'll have to go home and prepare food for Brigitta, so I thank Astrid's mother for her kind offer, but say I can't stay long.

Astrid is lucky the apartment is large enough that she doesn't have to share a bedroom with her brother but has her own modern furnished room overlooking *Schönhauser Allee*. She takes me there now and we sit on her bed which is much softer than the bunk bed I share with Brigitta.

I ask Astrid what she makes of all the Party officials roaming around the school.

She shrugs her shoulders. "It's like I said on the first day back. Matthias and Joachim are causing trouble for everyone."

"What do you think will happen?"

"How do I know? Anyway, who cares? Want to hear my new record?"

She jumps up off the bed and goes over to a record player in the corner of the room where she has a collection of discs. We spend the next half hour listening to music. But I can't get the sight of those Party officials out of my mind, stalking the corridors of the school like predators on the hunt for prey.

I'm still thinking of predators on the way home when I turn into *Stargarder Strasse* and notice a man walking along the pavement towards me. My first instinct is to keep my head down. But there's something about him that makes me want to look. He's not like one of the locals in their drab factory clothes. And he's not like one of the grey-suited officials roaming the school corridors. He's tall with blond hair swept back off his face and he's wearing a long overcoat which flaps behind him in the breeze. As we approach one another he reaches a hand into the pocket of his coat and pulls out a map which he starts to unfold. I'm almost level with him now and am just about to walk past when he turns to me.

"*Entschuldigen Sie, bitte.*" Excuse me. His German is tinged with a foreign accent that I can't quite place. Possibly American. He holds up his map. "I'm looking for the Jewish Cemetery in *Prenzlauer Berg* and I have become a little lost. I wonder if you could point me in the right direction please."

This is odd, I think, *a foreigner wandering around East Berlin, looking for the Jewish Cemetery*. It was all but destroyed by the Nazis. And how come he is in East Berlin anyway? Then I remember, westerners, like Americans and Britons, are still allowed through the checkpoints. He fumbles with the zig-zag folds of the map and opens it on a page nowhere near where we actually are. He holds the map open in front of me and I see a small envelope in the folds of the paper. What is going on here? The envelope has my name on it. I recognise the handwriting and feel a little dizzy.

"Take it," he whispers. Then in a louder voice, pointing at the map, "Am I anywhere near here?"

I don't know what to make of this strange man with the foreign accent. I reach for the envelope and slip it into my pocket whilst saying, "No, you've gone completely astray. If you're looking for the Jewish Cemetery you need to go back down this road," I point at the map with a trembling finger, "and keep going until you reach this crossroads. Then it's two blocks away."

"*Vielen Dank.*" Many thanks. He folds the map and tucks it back inside his coat. "You have been very helpful."

He gives me the faintest of winks with his right eye. Then he strides away in completely the wrong direction for the Jewish Cemetery. He doesn't look to me like a man who is lost. He obviously knew exactly who I was.

I hurry home and run up the stairs two at a time. I shut myself in the bedroom and rip open the envelope. Inside is a short message from Dieter. He explains that the man I've just met is called Harry. He's half American, half German. And, this is the bit I re-read a dozen times before it starts to make sense…Dieter, Harry and some others are going to dig a tunnel into East Berlin so that we can escape.

A tear splashes on the paper and I realise that I'm crying. Dieter is coming for us. He is going to rescue us.

Dieter

It's late when Harry returns from East Berlin. He saunters into the kitchen, takes his coat off and throws it over the back of a chair.

"How did it go?" I ask him. I'm desperate to hear if he managed to make contact with Sabine. I want to know how she is.

"Oh, easy as always," says Harry running his fingers through his hair. "Those guys at Checkpoint Charlie make a big show of examining my passport and acting like they're not going to let me through, but they have to and they know it." He laughs.

He's always like this when he's been to East Berlin. He relishes the thrill of walking into enemy territory; of plotting against the East Germans. In war time he would have made a good spy. But I don't want to hear about the antics at Checkpoint Charlie.

"What about Sabine?" I say. "Did you see her?

How was she?"

"Hey, she's not bad looking your sister, is she?" He gives me a wink. Claudia cuts herself as the knife she's using to chop vegetables slips in her hand. She swears under her breath.

Harry's words annoy me, but I let them go. "So you saw her then?"

He nods. "All sorted. I've given her your message. And you were right."

"About what?"

"She'll make a great contact. She won't get on the wrong side of the Stasi."

Sabine

At last it is Friday and the final lesson of the day. Unfortunately, it is Marxism-Leninism with Herr Schmidt.

I've been delayed, talking to Frau Nijinsky, the Russian teacher, about which Russian novels I should be reading so I rush into Herr Schmidt's classroom at the last minute. The only seat left is at the front, in the middle. No one wants to sit right under Herr Schmidt's nose. I'm hot from rushing so I take off my cardigan and fling it over the back of the chair. Then I retrieve my exercise book and pencil case from my bag. Just in time.

Moments later Herr Schmidt enters the room, strides up to his desk and slams down a copy of *Das Kapital*. There are red blotches on his bald head. The class falls quiet. He's standing so close I can smell stale tobacco and sweat on him. I keep my head down, pretending to be interested in re-reading the notes I took in Wednesday's lesson.

Herr Schmidt makes a sound in his throat as if

he's swallowed *Sauerkraut* laced with barbed wire. This is the signal that the lesson is about to begin. With a sigh I turn to a fresh page in my notebook and write down today's date. Herr Schmidt starts to talk.

"Today we will be examining Marx's theories of the class struggle – the conflict between an ownership class and a working class. Karl Marx," - Herr Schmidt walks over to the portraits of the Communist leaders and thinkers on the classroom wall – "was a great man who understood the problems faced by the workers in an unjust, bourgeois society."

As Herr Schmidt drones on I switch my brain off and just scribble down everything he says, like an automaton. I fill two pages of my notebook and am about to turn over to a third page (Herr Schmidt has just started describing in minute detail Marx's collaboration with Friedrich Engels) when the great orator splutters mid-sentence and comes to a stop.

This is so unexpected that I look up to see what is happening. Herr Schmidt is standing at the front of the classroom, mouth hanging open and eyes bulging in indignation. I follow his gaze to the back of the room to see who or what he is looking at. Hans is sitting in the corner seat by the window. He has put his hand up to ask a question.

"What is it?" snaps Herr Schmidt. No one ever interrupts Herr Schmidt.

Hans' lips curl at the corners in a faint smirk. I know he's going to try and say something clever to rile Herr Schmidt. My heart sinks.

When Hans speaks there's a pretend naivety in his voice as if he were a child asking an innocent question of a loving parent. "We call ourselves the German Democratic Republic, but how can we be a democratic country when there is only one political party?"

He might as well have launched a hand grenade at Herr Schmidt. That is the sort of question that can land you behind bars in a country like ours. I have to resist the urge to dive under the desk in anticipation of the fallout which such a question is likely to trigger. I'm sure no one is breathing.

Herr Schmidt looks as if he might explode at any moment. The red blotches on his head have turned a nasty shade of purple. He makes more of the *Sauerkraut*-mixed-with-barbed-wire rasping noises in his throat.

"The working class only needs one party to represent their interests and that party is the Communist Party. Therefore there is no need for free elections because the working class has no need of choice."

Hans pretends to consider this absurd argument for a moment. Matthias and Joachim are grinning in delight, enjoying every moment of this charade. I try to signal to Hans to stop before he lands himself in real trouble, but I'm too far away and he doesn't see me grimacing at him.

"But surely," says Hans in a genial voice as if he and Herr Schmidt were enjoying a light-hearted discussion over a couple of beers, "a party needs to win an election where there is a choice in order to demonstrate that it has the support of the people."

Is Hans out of his mind? He could get expelled for this.

Matthias and Joachim look in Hans' direction and nod their heads in agreement. Astrid looks at me and rolls her eyes to the ceiling. I wish the bell would ring and we could all go home.

All eyes are turned on Herr Schmidt now,

waiting to see how he will respond to Hans' argument.

Herr Schmidt walks up to Hans, places both his hands down on the desk and leans forward. Hans flinches at the nearness of Herr Schmidt.

"An ignorant and impudent young man like you," says Herr Schmidt, spraying Hans with spittle, "cannot yet appreciate the values of our socialist society. But a stint of compulsory service in the National People's Army will soon put that right."

The smirk slips from Hans' face.

Brrrrng! At the sound of the bell everyone jumps to their feet, not waiting to be dismissed.

Astrid appears at my side. "*Komm*," she says. "Let's get out of here."

I hurriedly pack my things away, sling my bag over my shoulder and follow her out into the crush of students. She's walking fast and it's difficult to keep up with her.

"*Mein Gott*," says Astrid to me over her shoulder. "Can't you knock some sense into that boyfriend of yours?"

"He's not my boyfriend."

"Well, whatever he is, tell him not to be so stupid. Does he think he's going to single-handedly change the political system of the whole country?"

"I don't think he's trying to do that." But Astrid isn't listening to me, and anyway, this is not the place to get into a discussion about political opposition, not with Stasi spies lurking around every corner. We're almost at the end of the corridor when I suddenly remember that I've left my cardigan in the classroom.

"Sorry," I say to Astrid. "I have to go back. Won't be a minute."

"I'll wait here for you." She leans against the

wall. "Be quick."

I head back to the classroom, weaving my way through the tide of bodies flowing in the opposite direction. I open the classroom door and see my cardigan on the back of the chair where I left it. Herr Schmidt's copy of *Das Kapital*, I notice, is also still on his desk. As I enter the room I become aware of a noise to my left. I turn and see Matthias and Joachim standing by the portraits of Marx, Engels, Lenin and Ulbricht. At the sight of me entering the room they practically jump out of their skins and run for the door without so much as an *Auf Wiedersehen*. In their rush to leave, one of them drops something on the floor. It lands with a clatter and rolls to its resting place by the leg of a nearby desk. *How odd,* I think, as I look towards the door which they have left swinging.

I pick up my cardigan then I walk over to where they were standing to see what they dropped. There's a black pen on the floor. I bend down to pick it up.

Just then Herr Schmidt walks in. He goes to his desk and picks up *Das Kapital*. He looks up and sees me standing there, holding the black pen. Then his eyes dart to the pictures of the Communist leaders on the wall, then back to me. His face turns purple. He looks as if he would like to shoot me.

I turn to the portraits on the wall to see what he was looking at and feel the blood draining from my face. The portraits have been defaced. Marx has donned a pair of black rimmed glasses; Engels has insects crawling around in his bushy beard; Lenin has sprouted horns which make him look even more like Mephistopheles and Ulbricht's straggly, grey moustache has turned into a short, black, toothbrush moustache in the style of Adolf Hitler.

I look at the pen in my hand and my legs start to shake. I'm in for it now. I can see Herr Schmidt weighing up the evidence. I might as well be holding a bloodied dagger beside a mutilated corpse. Guilt must be written all over my face even though I'm innocent.

Herr Schmidt starts to walk towards me. I can imagine what is going through his mind. The glasses on Karl Marx and the insects in Engels' beard are bad enough although they could possibly, just possibly, be excused as foolish teenage pranks. But, in this society which forbids political protest, the devil's horns on Lenin and the Hitler moustache on Ulbricht are crimes of treason; the first as good as blasphemous, the second suggesting an uncomfortable parallel between the dictatorships of Communism and Fascism.

"Give me the pen," says Herr Schmidt. His voice is cold. I pass it to him. He holds it gingerly between his forefinger and thumb as if it is itself contaminated with treacherous ideology.

"What is the meaning of this…this excrescence?" he hisses, leaning towards me. I recoil at the sourness of his breath.

"It wasn't me," I say, shaking my head.

"Who was it then?" he asks, fixing me with his weasel-like eyes.

"I didn't see, they had already gone by the time I came back," I lie. "I only came back to get my cardigan."

"*They?*" he asks, his lips curling at the edges. "So there was more than one?"

"I…I don't know." I blush to the roots of my hair. He knows I'm lying, I'm sure of it. I don't want to snitch on my classmates but if I refuse to give their names then I'm as good as condoning their actions and therefore, in his eyes, just as guilty.

He touches Ulbricht's Hitler-style moustache with a nicotine-stained finger. The tip of his finger comes away black.

"The ink isn't yet dry," he says, with a note of triumph in his voice. "The culprits, if it really wasn't you as you claim," his voice is full of scepticism, "can't have been gone long. Are you sure you didn't see them?"

"Not properly," I say. "I was over there," I point to the front of the classroom, "collecting my cardigan, and someone rushed out. I don't know who it was."

This is a ridiculous thing to say. It's inconceivable that I wouldn't recognise my own classmates who I've been at school with for years, even if I only saw them briefly from behind. But I'm determined not to back down now. For all I know he saw them leaving the room and knows exactly who they are. I can believe that he's playing with me like this for the pure pleasure of tormenting me.

"This," he jabs a finger at the portraits, "is a very serious matter. You may go now but do not think you have heard the last of this."

I pick up my bag and walk out of the room. In the few minutes that I spent in there, everything has changed. I am not the same person I was five minutes ago. I am a marked person. I have become an Enemy of the State.

Astrid is leaning against the wall at the end of the corridor. She looks at her watch as I approach.

"What took you so long?"

"Not here," I say looking behind me.

When we are outside and clear of the building I tell her about the portraits and how I stupidly picked up the pen and Herr Schmidt found me. I don't tell her it was Matthias and Joachim who did it. Even though she's my friend, I don't want to be responsible for spreading gossip that could get the boys into trouble.

"Don't worry," says Astrid putting her arm around me. "It won't come to anything."

But I know she's just saying that to make me feel better. The fact is, I'm scared. Very scared.

4 STASI

Sabine

I was right to be scared yesterday.

It's Brigitta who notices the car at half past seven in the morning. Mother is at work. I told them last night what had happened at the end of Herr Schimdt's lesson and warned them that the Stasi might want to question me about it. Still, it's a nasty shock to realise they've come so soon.

Brigitta is standing by the edge of the sitting room window, half hidden behind the curtain. She calls me over, her voice quivering with fear.

"Look," she whispers. There's a pale green Wartburg parked outside our building. The large car, with its long sleek bonnet and gently curving roof is conspicuous. Hardly anyone around here owns a car and those that do all have box-like Trabis. There are two men sitting in the front of the car, looking up at the building. Stasi officers.

The man in the passenger seat looks at his watch, then nods to the driver. They open the car doors and climb out. The man who gets out of the passenger side is tall, with square shoulders and steel grey, bristly hair. The driver is shorter and stockier. From this height I can see that he has a bald patch on the top of his head. Both men are wearing brown, anonymous raincoats. Civilian clothes.

They slam the car doors and walk towards the building. I lose sight of them as they enter through the door. It will only be a matter of seconds now before they arrive at the apartment. For a moment I feel paralysed, unable even to think. I shake my head and pull myself together.

"Quick," I say to Brigitta. "Dieter's letter is in my notebook in the chest of drawers. Burn it now." I have no idea if the men will search the apartment, looking for more evidence that I am a traitor to the state, but Dieter's note explaining his plans to dig a tunnel into East Berlin could put me behind bars for the rest of my life.

Brigitta runs to the bedroom, retrieves the letter, runs back to the living room, and tosses it into the *Kachelofen* just as there's a sharp rap on the door.

I walk down the hall, my legs shaking with each step. I take a deep breath and open the door to the apartment. The two men are standing there. The tall, grey-haired one has a face etched with deep lines like cracks in a dry riverbed. He is standing in front of the driver who has stationed himself off to one side with his feet apart and arms crossed as if he expects me to make a run for it and is getting ready to tackle me. The tall one introduces himself matter-of-factly.

"Herr Stein from the *Staatssicherheitsdienst*." The State Secret Police. The Stasi.

"Fräulein Neumann, we need to ask you a few questions about a matter of state security. You are required to come with us." I note that he doesn't ask if I am Fräulein Neumann. He already knows that.

There's no point pretending I don't know what he's talking about, so I nod my head deciding that it's probably best to appear co-operative.

"But first I must say goodbye to my sister." Without waiting for them to object, I walk back to the sitting room, where Brigitta is curled up in her favourite reading chair, clutching her book of fairy tales to her chest. There's a look of terror on her face.

"Don't worry," I say giving her a hug. "Stay inside and don't open the door to anyone." She nods. "When Mother gets back from work, tell her what's happened but tell her not to worry. I'll be back soon." I kiss her forehead. Then I return to the hallway where the two men are waiting for me.

I follow Herr Stein down the stairs, the driver bringing up the rear. Just as I think things can't get any worse, we encounter Frau Lange on her way back from the shop. She doesn't say anything and I refuse to look in her direction, but I can imagine the smirk on her face.

We step outside and I have a sudden urge to sprint as fast as I can down the street, but Herr Stein seems to anticipate my thoughts and before I know what is happening he opens the rear passenger door and pushes me into the car. The men get in the front. The inside of the car smells of cigarettes and men's hair oil.

The driver starts the engine and we pull away from the curb. I slump back, defeated. The familiar streets of *Prenzlauer Berg* slide past the window, but none of them seem real.

To focus my mind and stop myself from panicking, I try to concentrate on where we are going. We seem to be heading in a south east direction towards the suburb of *Lichtenberg*. We take the *Dimitroffstrasse*, then the *Frankfurter Allee*, a rigidly straight Prussian road. Twenty minutes or so after we set off, the car turns into *Normannenstrasse* and then pulls into a vast, soulless square surrounded on all sides by enormous, inter-connected multi-storey blocks. We stop in front of a brown concrete building. I know, without needing to be told, that this is Stasi Headquarters and the surrounding buildings are where the Stasi machine operates from.

The men jump out of the car and the driver opens my door. I climb out feeling small and helpless next to the megalithic architecture. Herr Stein steers me into the brown concrete building and into an ascending Paternoster lift. I stand well back from the edge for fear of falling out. On the second floor, he takes me by the arm and we jump out of the moving lift. He escorts me down the corridor to a small, square room.

"In here," he says.

I walk into the room which is barely furnished with a gun-metal filing cabinet and a desk with two chairs, one on either side. The desk is empty save for a dun-coloured telephone with rows of extra buttons next to the handset and a large metal box with two reels of tape. I've never seen such a machine before, but I think it must be a tape recorder. This will be the start of the file that the Stasi keeps on me, if they haven't got one already.

Herr Stein indicates the nearest chair, the one with its back to the door.

"*Setzen Sie sich!*" Sit down!

There's a cloth on the seat of the chair. I don't know why it's there. I think maybe one of the cleaners left it. I pick it up, intending to drop it on the floor, but Herr Stein shouts at me.

"Leave it!"

I look at him, startled.

"You must sit on that," he says.

I don't know why I need to sit on the cloth, but I don't want to aggravate him any further so I smooth it flat and sit down, bolt upright with my hands clasped in my lap. This is all so unnerving, I can feel myself trembling. I look from the telephone to the tape recorder, then back to the telephone. They're only inanimate objects, but they're making me nervous.

I thought Herr Stein was going to question me, but he seems to be waiting for someone else. I know he's still there, behind me, because I can hear his breathing. I sit and wait.

Dieter

"So what made you want to do this?" I'm on my way to the Technische Universität with Harry to help him recruit students to work on the digging. I know what is motivating Claudia and Werner, but I've never known what made Harry want to pursue this dangerous project.

"Do what?" he asks with his usual casualness.

"You know, organise an escape route for people in the East. You don't have family over there do you? You're not even from Berlin." He's already told us that his father was American and his mother was from Hamburg. He grew up in Boston and has dual American and West German nationality. He uses his American passport to get himself through Checkpoint Charlie, although the West German one would do the job just as well. He reckons letting an

American through pisses the East German guards off more than letting a West German through. I'm still waiting for him to answer my question.

"You're right," he says. "I don't have family over there behind the Wall. But the thing is... my dad was killed in the war when his plane was shot down over Dresden. I was seven at the time. I spent the rest of my childhood desperate to come to Europe and see where he died. I came here in 1954 at the age of eighteen." He pauses and stares straight ahead. When he speaks his voice is so low I have to lean in close to hear what he's saying. "My dad died trying to free Europe from the tyranny of Hitler. Now I'm doing what I can to free people from the tyranny of Communism. Happy now?"

I've never heard him speak so seriously before. I feel humbled. I'm doing what I'm doing because I want to get Sabine, Brigitta and Mother out of East Berlin. Would I be selfless enough to do this if I didn't have family over there?

Sabine

There are quick footsteps in the corridor. They stop outside the room. Then a woman's voice addresses Herr Stein.

"*Danke. Sie können gehen.*" Thank you. You can go.

For some reason I had been expecting a man so this comes as a bit of a surprise. I'm curious, but I daren't turn round to see.

The woman closes the door, walks to the front of the desk and sits down opposite me. Her appearance does nothing to calm my nerves.

She is tall, middle-aged and with close cropped

black hair which looks dyed. Her eyebrows have been plucked to nothing and redrawn with black kohl arches that give her a questioning look which, I suppose, befits her job. Her lips, plastered in a dark red lipstick, compete for attention with her eyebrows. She looks artificial, like something produced in a laboratory. She doesn't smile but introduces herself as Frau Biedermeier. There is no need for me to introduce myself because she already knows who I am, where I go to school, where I live and no doubt many other facts about my life.

As she shuffles her papers and prepares to begin the interrogation, I give myself courage by thinking of Dieter and the tunnelers in West Berlin. As far as I'm aware even the Stasi haven't yet mastered the art of mind-reading. What wouldn't she do for that information? Sell her own grandmother, I imagine, if she hasn't already.

She reaches out a finger and presses a button on the tape recording machine. Her nails are painted the same shade of red as her lips. The reels start to turn, making a whirring noise which I find very distracting. She brings the tips of her fingers together and assesses me with cold, grey eyes.

"So," she says, "you were discovered by Herr Schmidt, your politics teacher, standing by some portraits of great socialist leaders, holding a black pen with which you had shamefully and crudely defaced the portraits, thereby showing your contempt for our socialist system. What do you have to say?" She raises her kohl eyebrows and waits for me to speak.

"It wasn't me. I didn't draw on the portraits." My voice doesn't sound like my own. It's too thin and quiet. The tape recorder whirrs.

"Nonsense. You defaced those portraits and the

sooner you admit it the sooner this interview will be over."

"I didn't do it." My voice is louder this time. She's not going to get me to admit to something I didn't do.

"Then how do you account for the fact that you were holding the black pen?"

"I went back into the classroom to collect my cardigan which I had left on my chair." Just stick to the facts, I tell myself. "As I entered the room I startled some students who left in a hurry. One of them dropped the pen. I went to pick it up and that's when Herr Schmidt reappeared."

"So you picked up the black pen. This must have been the same pen that was used to deface the portraits, yes?"

"I suppose so."

"And you've already said that someone in the room dropped the pen."

I nod my head miserably, wishing I hadn't said that much.

"Could you speak up please."

"Yes," I mumble.

"So you agree that one of the students in the room was holding the black pen. Therefore it seems logical that the student holding the pen is the person who defaced the portraits?"

"Possibly."

"Did you see this person defacing the portraits?"

"No."

"But you noticed that he or she had dropped the black pen?"

"Er, yes."

Frau Biedermeier leans across the desk, her eyes glistening with the thrill of the hunt. "Who was it?"

I bite my tongue. I'm not going to give her the

answer. "I don't know."

The kohl eyebrows go up even further. "Surely you don't expect me to believe that. You've been at that school for years. You must have recognised the person concerned. *Who* was it?"

I shake my head. "I told you, I don't know." My voice wobbles. I'm sure she knows I'm lying. I'm perspiring and my throat is dry. I can feel the beginnings of a headache.

She glances across at the tape recorder. Only about a quarter of the tape has spooled from one reel to the other. There's plenty more recording time left. Frau Biedermeier sits back in her chair, leans her head to one side and prepares to launch her next question.

"How many students were in the room when you went back in?"

She's using a different tack, trying to catch me out. "Er, I don't know. Maybe two or three. I couldn't say for sure."

"But you must have seen them when you entered the room."

"I went in to pick up my cardigan, so I wasn't looking in their direction."

"But you must have realised there was someone else in the classroom as soon as you walked into it. Didn't you look to see who it was?"

"Well, not really, I was in a hurry to fetch my cardigan. My friend was waiting for me in the corridor."

"Yes, you've mentioned your cardigan numerous times now, but I repeat my point, you must have seen who was in the classroom when you went back in."

I'm starting to feel dizzy. When I speak I can hear there's a note of desperation in my voice. "No,

I didn't see who was there. I wasn't looking in that direction. I'd been sitting at the front of the classroom and the boys were at the back."

"So it was some boys who did this?" She pounces on my words like a cat springing on a mouse. The silence that follows is filled with the whirring of the tape recorder.

Scheisse! I realise I've made my first big slip and I try to back-peddle.

"I'm not saying it was boys who did it, just that they were sitting at the back of the classroom during the lesson." It sounds pathetic. "There may have been some girls involved." I stop myself. What am I saying? In my efforts to protect Matthias and Joachim I'm doing a pretty good job of incriminating other innocent people.

"But you indicated a moment ago that they were most probably boys."

"Maybe."

Frau Biedermeier is like a Rottweiler that refuses to let go of a bone. She is relentless in her questioning and is starting to wear me out. I have to stay focused and stick to my story.

"So," says Frau Biedermeier, "since you can't or won't say who did it, I have to come to the conclusion that *you* defaced the portraits."

"I didn't do it." We're back to where we started and I just know we're going to go over all the same ground as before. There's still plenty of tape left.

After another half hour or so of being grilled, I haven't given her any new information. She fixes me with a stare, then appears to come to a decision.

"Maybe you need a little time to jog your memory of who was in the classroom," she says.

I don't know what she means by this. She stops the tape recorder and presses one of the buttons on her phone. There are footsteps in the corridor, the door opens and Herr Stein appears. Frau Biedermeier addresses him.

"Fräulein Neumann needs some time to think," she says.

"Certainly," says Herr Stein.

He takes me by the arm and leads me out into the corridor. I have no idea where he's taking me, but I'm under no illusion that I'm being allowed to go home.

We return to the Paternoster lift and this time jump into the one going down. When we reach the ground floor, Herr Stein once again takes me by the arm, his thumb and fingers pressing into my flesh, and leads me outside. We walk across the courtyard to one of the other buildings and go inside. This building has an eerie quiet to it which I don't like. The door clangs shut behind us.

A uniformed guard steps forward to meet us and that's when I really start to feel frightened.

We follow the guard up some stairs and along a corridor. The guard stops in front of a steel door and unlocks it with a key on a chain tied to his waist. He stands aside as Herr Stein escorts me inside.

"You can stay here," says Herr Stein, "until you remember a few more details. Use your time wisely."

Then he walks out and the guard closes the door, locking it with his key.

I can't believe they have locked me up. And all because I refused to tell Frau Biedermeier what she wanted to hear. Suddenly fury wells up inside me and I run to the door, banging on it with my fists.

"*Nein!*" I scream. "Let me out!"

No one comes.

I let my forehead fall against the door and close my eyes. I must calm down and try not to lose control. I take a deep breath, open my eyes and walk away from the door.

It's a small room with a window of frosted glass, high up. There is a narrow camp bed; a toilet and a sink; a table and chair. Nothing else. I notice a spy hole in the door. Herr Stein or the guard could be watching me right this minute. I am determined not to break down and cry. I won't give them that satisfaction.

I sit down on the edge of the bed and try to think rationally about my situation. Frau Biedermeier is obsessed with finding out who defaced the portraits. I'm glad I didn't give her any useful information. And the knowledge that I have a far greater secret, namely the tunnel, gives me strength. I will continue to deny all knowledge of who drew on the portraits. What Matthias and Joachim did might have been ill-judged, but I don't want to become the sort of person who betrays her friends, like an informer.

Dieter

"*Siebzehn Studenten.*" Seventeen students. Harry rocks back on his chair, looking pleased with himself.

"That's fantastic," says Claudia smiling at him. "Where did you find them all?"

"At the *Technische Universität*," I say, hoping that she'll acknowledge my part in helping to recruit so many extra pairs of hands, but she keeps her eyes on Harry.

"The uni is swarming with people keen to help in a project like this," says Harry airily. He pulls a sheet of paper out of his coat pocket. "We signed up twelve guys and five girls, so with you three that makes twenty people to do the digging."

I think, *shouldn't that be twenty-one with Harry?* But Werner doesn't say anything so I keep quiet. I guess Harry sees his role as a supervisory one.

"How do you know they're all to be trusted?" asks Werner, looking up from a map of the underground sewer system which he's been poring over all evening.

"We questioned them intensively," I say. "About their motives." Actually Harry charmed most of them into joining with his charismatic personality.

Harry tosses the piece of paper over to me. "Can you draw up a twenty-four hour rota Dieter? We need four shifts of six hours around the clock. If we have five people on each shift that will mean two to dig, two to remove the buckets of rubble and one on lookout duty on the roof."

"Sure," I say, looking down the list of names. I'm as keen as anyone to get started and will make sure I'm on the first shift. Tomorrow we start digging.

Sabine

I wait for someone to take me back to the interrogation room, but no one comes. The guard brings me bread and thin, watery soup. I don't have much of an appetite, but I force myself to eat. I will need to keep my strength up if I'm to face another round of questioning.

The light at the window starts to fade and eventually turns dark. I had hoped to be home by now, not still stuck here, helpless and alone. I imagine Brigitta telling Mother about the two men who came to take me away. This could push Mother right over the edge.

I stay awake long after it has turned dark outside. The light is still on in my room. I start to feel tired. It must be well past midnight, so I lie down on the bed and close my eyes. As soon as I do, the cell door opens and the guard stomps in.

"Get up!" he shouts.

I sit up, feeling scared. Then he grabs me by the arm and marches me back to the interrogation room for another round of questioning.

Frau Biedermeier must have reapplied her lipstick because her lips are redder and angrier than ever. I take a deep breath as she rests her elbows on the desk, fingertips together, eyebrows arched. What has she got in store for me this time? The adrenalin pumping through my veins is keeping me awake.

"I hope you've used your time to reconsider your answers to my questions."

I say nothing.

We go over all the same questions as before - *Didn't you see who was in the room when you went back in? Didn't you even bother to look? How many of them were there? Were they boys or girls or both? Why did you pick up the pen? It was you who defaced the portraits wasn't it?* – and some new questions designed to test my socialist credentials - *Do you consider yourself to be a good socialist? Do you listen to RIAS radio? Do you believe in the German Democratic Republic?*

I stick doggedly to my story about what happened in the classroom, that I didn't see who it was, and I do my best to sound like a true and faithful member of the socialist state, even trying to remember some of the phrases about the class struggle that Herr Schmidt regularly spouts.

By the time Frau Biedermeier draws this

interview to a close the adrenalin rush I experienced at the start has drained away, leaving me feeling weak and exhausted. It must be about four or five in the morning.

The guard takes me back to my cell where I collapse on the bed. The light is turned off and I am permitted to sleep. But it's not enough. Before I know what is happening the light is switched back on and the guard shouts at me through the spy-hole to wake up.

I open my eyes with a groan. Outside it's already light. I think I've had about two hours' sleep, no more. I continue to lie there, my whole body aching from the lack of sleep and the hard mattress. The cell door opens and the guard marches over to the bed, grabs hold of my wrists and pulls me to my feet.

"Didn't you hear what I said?" he shouts. "You have to wake up. That means get up. No lying down, no sitting. Stand there."

He pushes me into the centre of the room, then walks out, slamming the door behind him.

I'm so shocked at this behaviour, I just stand there, staring at the door. My body is screaming at me to lie down, but I tell myself to be strong and stay awake. *Don't let them beat you, Sabine.*

A few times my eyes close and I sway on my feet, almost falling over. But I always wake up just before I lose my balance. When I think I can't stand there a second longer, the door opens and I am taken back to the interrogation room.

Frau Biedermeier repeats the whole performance as before and I give her the same answers as previously. There's a new reel in the tape recorder.

I'm so tired I can hardly concentrate on Frau Biedermeier's questions. I wonder what she hopes to achieve. Then I realise this is part of her plan. To disorientate me, so that I let slip the names of the perpetrators. Or just give in so they'll let me go to sleep. I tell her nothing.

I'm taken back to the cell and given some bread and water. It's going to be another long day.

Dieter

I'm up early, keen to make a start on the tunnel. A couple of the new recruits arrive just before nine o'clock and I let them into the bakery, locking the door behind them. We can't risk anyone wandering in and discovering our plans. Werner was saying only last night that a half-built tunnel in another part of Berlin had to be abandoned when the team digging it was infiltrated by Stasi spies from the East.

The pair who've come to help dig today are students that Harry and I recruited from the university. Andreas is an engineering student who looks as if he could single-handedly dig his way out of Colditz. I wish we had more like him. Thomas is studying maths and, if I'm honest, doesn't look as if he's built for hard, physical labour. Still, we need all the hands we can get, and I'm not exactly Hercules either. Neither of them have friends or family in East Berlin, but they volunteered their services out of hatred of the totalitarian regime in East Germany.

"Right," says Andreas, rubbing his hands together. "Show us where to dig."

I take them both down to the cellar to meet Claudia and Werner. Werner is kneeling at a couple of upturned crates he's using as a makeshift desk. He's still studying the plans. He must have gone over them a hundred times, measuring distances on the map and working out angles. Last night he even asked me to check them. I never dreamt, when I was at school, that one day I'd be using Pythagoras' Theorem for something useful. Claudia is busy examining the tools, weighing the pick-axes and shovels in her hands.

"This is Andreas and Thomas," I say. "They're here to help with the digging, so let's get started."

Werner looks up, removes his glasses, rubs the bridge of his nose and puts his glasses back on. Then he claps his hands together and another, more decisive Werner suddenly seems to appear. "Right, first we need to decide who's doing what." He turns to Claudia. "I thought you could do the first lookout duty." He picks up a pair of binoculars and a radio transmitter and holds them out to her.

Claudia has a pick-axe in her right hand and is tapping the handle against her left palm. For a moment she looks at Werner as if she'd like to attack him with it. Then she rolls her eyes to the ceiling, and drops the pick-axe on the floor.

"Sure, I'll do lookout duty," she says taking the proffered binoculars and radio transmitter. "Just give me a shout when you guys get tired digging." She stomps up the stairs. I make a mental note to check she's all right later.

"OK," says Werner, "the first task is to dig a vertical shaft. I've marked out where we're going to dig on the floor over here." He walks over to the middle of the cellar and shows us a chalk circle, one and a half metres in diameter. "We won't know how difficult it is to dig until we get started so I suggest we just get on with it."

"Great," says Andreas. Thomas looks a little less confident.

132

We each choose a pick-axe and shovel and position ourselves around the chalk circle.

Werner lifts his pick-axe over his shoulder and swings it into the ground. "East Berlin, here we come!"

Sabine

I spend the whole of the afternoon in my room, watching the light outside the window changing from the bright light of mid-afternoon to dusk. I am permitted to sit on the edge of the bed. My one attempt to lie down results in the guard marching into the cell and forcing me to stand up for the next hour. After that I stay sitting in an upright position. I have a headache from dehydration and lack of sleep. Mother and Brigitta will be beside themselves with worry that I didn't come home yesterday. I have to use the toilet in the room and hate the thought that the guard outside could be watching me through the spy hole. The evening deepens and eventually it's dark outside. I know what's going to happen now. I am taken back to the interrogation room. This time there's no adrenalin keeping me awake. I'm a spent force. I hate what Frau Biedermeier is doing to me, but it makes me even less inclined to co-operate with her.

We go over all the same ground as before until I'm falling asleep where I sit. When Frau Biedermeier feels she's had enough she calls the guard and tells him to take me back to the room. She mutters under her breath, "She's a hard one to crack."

I lie down on the mattress, determined to make the most of the two hours I've got before the light comes back on. I dream of nothing.

Dieter

I stagger into the kitchen on Monday morning feeling as if I've been run over by a Soviet tank. I did ten hours of digging yesterday and now the muscles in my arms, shoulders and back feel as if they've been pulverized. I can't stand up straight, my lower back is so stiff. *Scheisse*, I think, *I'm not used to hard physical labour.* And we only managed to dig down about three metres yesterday. There's still a hell of a long way to go.

Harry is standing in the kitchen, dressed in his overcoat and swigging back a black coffee.

"You look crap," he says, laughing.

"Thanks. Any coffee left?"

"A bit." He pours me half a cup. It's lukewarm.

"Going out?" I ask.

"Sure am," he says. "I'm going to see that gorgeous sister of yours again. I want to give her some instructions about contacting the other escapees."

"Well you better hurry," I say. "She'll be off to school early."

"Righto!" says Harry giving me a mock salute. To my relief he leaves and I collapse onto a chair at the table. Someone has left some bread and cheese out so I eat a hurried breakfast then, feeling a bit better, I make my way down to the cellar.

Andreas is hacking at the earth with his pick-axe and shoveling mounds of rubble into the buckets which Werner and Thomas are carrying out to the back yard.

"Hi guys," I say, reaching for a spade. I can see

they've already shifted bucket loads of earth this morning.

Werner takes one look at me. "Why don't you do lookout duty today?"

I never thought I'd be so happy to hear him say those words. "Sure," I say, dropping the spade. "I'll go swap with Claudia." After all, I tell myself, someone's got to do it.

Sabine

The light comes on and I sit up like a robot. I'm dog-tired, but I don't want the guard coming in, bullying me. I eat my bread and drink the water. I'm left alone for an hour or so, then I'm taken to the interrogation room. I assume it's going to be more of the same but this morning Frau Biedermeier is in a different frame of mind. She informs me they have received new information from the school about the "enemies of the state" who defaced the portraits. She watches me closely, keen to see how I react. I'm surprised by this news but I try not to let it show. Has someone snitched on Matthias and Joachim or is Frau Biedermeier just trying to trick me into revealing what I know?

But she doesn't pursue the matter. Instead, she says she has a proposition she wants to put to me. She attempts a smile but it doesn't work because it's only her red-painted mouth that curls at the corners. Her eyes play no part in this charade of friendship.

"You could be of great service to us," she says. "I hear you hope to go to university and study languages. In return for a little co-operation from you, I'm sure we could arrange to make your future studies at university...how shall I put it...more

135

congenial."

She slides a piece of paper across the table to me and hands me a pen.

I glance at the paper and two words leap out at me: *Inoffizielle Mitarbeiter*. Unofficial collaborator. She wants me to sign up as an informer, to spy on my family and friends, to pass information to the Stasi which could be used against other people. The thought disgusts me. How could I do such a thing? I wouldn't be able to respect myself if I was spying on my friends. What sort of a person would that make me?

"Lots of people help us," she says, "including young people like yourself."

I don't believe her. None of my friends would ever stoop so low. I shake my head.

"You will not sign?" All the mock friendliness has vanished from her voice.

"No, I will not."

She takes the paper back, looking sterner than ever. I have disappointed her and I'm glad.

She walks to the door and calls the guard. I assume I will be taken back to the cell, so I can hardly believe it when the guard escorts me to the main door of the building and lets me leave.

I walk out of the Stasi Headquarters into the bright morning light and take a deep breath of air. The pale green Wartburg that brought me here is parked outside, but Herr Stein and the driver are not around. I wasn't expecting them to drive me home and I'd rather be on my own. I walk as quickly as I can away from the complex of buildings.

They have let me go, but I know that life will be very different from now on. The Stasi have a file on me. I have been marked as a suspicious person; someone not to be trusted; a traitor to the cause of socialism. They will be watching me from now on. I must be careful who I'm seen with and who I talk to, otherwise they too will come under suspicion.

I take the *S-bahn* from *Frankfurter Allee* to *Prenzlauer Allee*, then walk the rest of the way home. I can't shake the feeling, though, that I am being followed. I keep glancing over my shoulder. Why is that woman in the red coat looking in my direction? Why did that man with the newspaper under his arm just cross over to my side of the street? Why is there a white Trabant parked on the corner? Normally I wouldn't have given any of these people a second thought, but forty-eight hours in Stasi custody has made me paranoid.

I turn into *Stargarder Strasse* and see someone I recognise walking towards me. It's Harry.

This is the worst possible timing. If I am being followed then I mustn't speak to him. It could spell the end of the tunnel project.

When I see him looking my way, I give an infinitesimal shake of my head and then cross the road very deliberately. I hope he gets the message. The white Trabant that was parked on the corner is crawling down the road behind me. I think Harry must have understood because he turns and walks into a bar. I wonder what he wanted to see me about.

By the time I reach my building I'm shaking from the strain of being followed. I feel like a hunted animal. I wish I could have spoken to Harry, but it was out of the question.

It has never been more effort to climb the stairs to our apartment. By the time I reach the top I'm almost in a state of collapse. I open the door and walk in.

Mother and Brigitta rush to meet me.

"*Komm, Sabine,*" says Mother leading me to a chair in the living room. "You don't have to say anything now." I'm too distraught to speak and sit in a state of shock, not quite able to believe that I'm home.

Brigitta runs into our bedroom and comes back waving a piece of paper.

"This was in the post box," she says giving it to me. I unfold it and glance down the page. I can't take it all in now, but I can see it's a letter from Harry. It contains instructions on what he wants me to do.

I feel an overwhelming sense of relief. There was no need to speak to Harry after all. Everything I need to know is here in this letter.

It's only then that the tears start to fall down my face.

Dieter

I push open the skylight, climb out onto the roof and look for Claudia. She's about three metres away, crouched behind a low stone parapet, peering through the binoculars. There's a narrow walkway between the parapet and the main roof space. I crawl along it now.

"Hi," I say, tapping her on the shoulder.

She puts the binoculars down and turns to face me. "God, you look awful."

"You're not the first person to point that out today."

"Sorry." She gives me a warm smile.

It's the first time I've been up here and I'm amazed at what a good view we have into East Berlin. I can clearly see the border guards on the other side of the Wall with their metal helmets and rifles. I can also see the house on *Schönholzer Strasse* that we are aiming for.

"What's happening over there?" I ask.

"Not a lot. The guards just patrol the Wall. Every few hours a truck turns up and new guards take over."

"Well I can take over here if you like," I say. "You can go and dig. Show Werner that you're up to the job."

"Great," she says grinning at me. She hands me the binoculars.

There's not much space on the roof and as we exchange places we find ourselves squashed up against one another. She looks so delicate, I'm suddenly overcome with an urge to take her in my arms. She shouldn't be risking her life in this dangerous project.

"Sorry," she says, squeezing past.

"Don't apologise."

She looks at me with her big hazel eyes, and then she's gone, through the skylight.

I sit down by the edge of the parapet and prepare to spend the next few hours watching the guards on the other side of the Wall.

Sabine

I spend the rest of Monday morning and half the afternoon in bed, catching up on my sleep. When I wake up, Brigitta, who has refused to go to school today, brings me a hot drink and something to eat. But on Tuesday I return to school. Life must go on and I think it would do me good to see my friends.

A white Trabant is parked outside our building.

As Brigitta and I walk along *Stargarder Strasse* the Trabant's engine coughs into life and the car pulls away from the curb. I can hear it trailing us in a low gear. I tell Brigitta not to look but she turns and stares anyway. She informs me there are two men in the car. I sigh. Have these people nothing better to do? Before I enter the school building I can't resist turning to look. The Trabant is parked about twenty metres away. Are they planning to stay there all day?

I make my way to the classroom, looking forward to chatting with people, but there's hardly anyone there. Astrid hasn't arrived yet. Matthias and Joachim are not in. Neither is Hans. Or Monika. Where is everyone? The few people who are at school are talking quietly in small groups. Conversations fall silent as I walk past. I sit down at my desk and wonder what on earth is going on.

Just then Astrid breezes into the room. She sees me sitting at my desk and comes straight over.

"Am I glad to see you," she says, giving me a big smile. "You weren't here yesterday and so obviously we all thought…" her voice trails away.

"What did you think?"

She looks over her shoulder then turns back to me. "That you'd been *arrested*." She speaks the last word sotto voce.

"I *was*," I say. "I was questioned by the Stasi. They locked me up overnight."

Astrid looks horrified. "No way! Was it to do with the portraits?"

I nod.

"What did you tell them? Did you say it was *Matthias* and *Joachim*?" She mouths their names.

"No, of course I didn't." I wonder how she knows that. I didn't tell her. Maybe she saw them leaving the classroom.

She pulls up a chair and sits down next to me. "But what was it like?" she asks. "It must have been horrendous for you."

I can see she's desperate to hear the gory details, so I tell her about the men turning up at the apartment, the cell at Stasi HQ, the interrogation room, Frau Biedermeier. All the time Astrid looks at me with wide eyes and nods her head in sympathy. Then I mention the cloth on the chair and the way Herr Stein shouted at me when I tried to remove it.

"You know what that was for?" she asks.

"No, what?"

"It was to collect your smell, your personal scent. They'll put the cloth into a sealed jar with your name on it and if they ever need to track you down they'll give the cloth to a sniffer dog."

I think of how I sat on that cloth, sweating with nerves and the strain of not giving anything away, and I feel physically sick.

"Anyway, don't worry about it," says Astrid. "You told them you didn't do it and it looks like they believed you because they let you go. They've got the culprits now."

"How do you know?" I ask. "And what's happened here?" I indicate the classroom with a wave of my hand. "Where is everyone? Where are Matthias and Joachim? And Hans? Why is everyone so quiet?"

Astrid rolls her eyes. "Of course, you don't know."

"Know what?"

She leans closer and whispers. "They've all been expelled."

Her words hit me like a thunderbolt. For a few seconds I just stare at her in disbelief. "Expelled! But why?"

"For wearing black. For protesting against the Wall. As the ringleaders, Matthias and Joachim have been arrested. They'll be charged with defacing the portraits."

At that moment Herr Keller enters the room and Astrid moves away to sit at her own desk. I realise that I'm trembling like a leaf.

Dieter

There's a noise in the street directly below me. I look down and see a woman with a small boy of about eight and an older boy, a teenager. The older boy is carrying a wooden step ladder under his arm. It has five steps and is the sort of thing you would use to decorate a room or reach a high shelf. They stop a short distance from the bakery and the older boy sets the step ladder up next to a lamppost bearing the sign *Bernauer Strasse*.

The younger boy can hardly contain his excitement. When the ladder is ready, he climbs up the five steps, the woman standing behind him, holding onto his legs to make sure he doesn't fall. The little boy is now higher than the street sign. With one hand he leans on the sign and with the other he stretches up as far as he can and waves towards one of the buildings in *Brunnenstrasse*.

I pick up my binoculars and look in the same direction as the little boy, trying to see who he's waving at. At first I don't see anything, but then I notice a movement at a window. I focus the binoculars and an old woman comes into view. She is standing by an open top floor window in one of the five-storey houses. She is waving a white handkerchief.

"*Da ist sie!*" shouts the little boy. "*Da ist Oma.*" There's Grandma. It must seem like a game to him, waving at his grandmother who is on the other side of the Wall.

"*Shhh*," says the woman. "Remember we have to be quiet."

The child's shout has attracted the attention of the guards who turn to look at the old woman at the window behind them. She disappears in a flash, slamming the window closed. Then a helmeted head appears above the Wall. The guard looks in disbelief at the family with the step ladder. Then he seems to focus his attention on the bakery. We have a sign in the window that reads *Closed for renovation.*

"She's gone!" wails the little boy, pointing towards his grandmother's house.

"But we saw her, didn't we," says the woman, injecting her voice with forced cheerfulness. She turns to the older boy. "Bring the ladder please Axel. We have to go home now."

"But *mummy*," wails the little boy. "Just one more…"

"*No*," says his mother, her voice cracking. "We'll see Oma again one day."

I doubt it.

Sabine

I can't concentrate on anything all day and I sit at my desk like a zombie. Almost half the class has been expelled. Those who remain are understandably subdued. I understand now why people were surprised to see me this morning – they must have thought I'd been expelled as well when I didn't come in yesterday. I hope they don't think

I've turned informer and been allowed back to school for "good behaviour." Astrid stands by me as if nothing has happened and I'm grateful for her unflinching support.

But I keep thinking about Hans. He's never been in any sort of trouble with the authorities before despite his tendency to rash behaviour. But this expulsion means the end of his school career and his university prospects. He'll want to get out of East Berlin more than ever. I must go and see him as soon as I can and tell him about the tunnel project.

As for Matthias and Joachim, I shudder to think what the Stasi is doing to them. Were they arrested just for being the ringleaders of the "black protest" or was it because of the portraits? No matter how many times Frau Biedermeier asked me who had defaced the portraits, I never told her, so how would the Stasi know it was Matthias and Joachim? Astrid seems certain of the facts, but is that just through idle gossip? Did Herr Schmidt know the truth all along and did he inform the Stasi? But if he knew the truth, why was I arrested? These questions chase each other around my brain until my head starts to hurt. I start looking at my classmates with suspicion and realise that I'm becoming like the Stasi – paranoid.

After morning break we have Marxism-Leninism with Herr Schmidt. I don't want to go back into that classroom, I'd rather be anywhere else, but I force myself to arrive early so I can sit next to the window and not right under his nose. The offending portraits have all been removed and the wall is now blank, the only clue to their former existence being the brighter patches of paintwork where they used to hang.

I just want this lesson to be over.

Herr Schmidt enters and looks around the room, noting who is still here and who isn't. I can hardly bear to look at him. His lips curl in a smile of satisfaction at the sight of the empty chairs. I strongly suspect him of informing on Matthias and Joachim and I despise him more than ever.

When school finishes my only thought is to go and see Hans. I make an excuse to Astrid about needing to get home quickly for Brigitta and then I rush off.

Frau Fischer answers the door to me. She looks older than the last time I saw her, greyer and more tired. But she smiles and invites me inside.

"Sabine, it's good to see you." She takes my hand in both of hers. She looks unbearably sad.

"I heard what happened to Hans," I say as we walk into the living room.

She shakes her head at me. "The Stasi questioned us both, you know."

"Whatever for?"

"They wanted me to admit that I have failed to bring him up as a true socialist. Apparently I have failed in my son's political education." Her voice is serious but there's a twinkle of defiance in her eyes as if she thinks this assessment of her maternal qualities is a load of *Scheisse*.

"What utter nonsense," I say.

She shrugs. "That is the way they see things. Hans is in his room. Go and talk to him. He is spending far too much time in there."

I knock on his door.

"Who is it?"

"It's me, Sabine."

He opens the door and lets me in. He looks terrible. His hair is a mess and there are dark rings under his eyes as if he hasn't slept properly. He sits down on the bed without saying a word. I sit down next to him.

"I'm sorry you got expelled," I say. "Astrid told me this morning."

He laughs bitterly. "She'll enjoy having something to gossip about."

I think this is a bit unfair on Astrid, but Hans is clearly upset about his own situation so I let it go.

He turns to look at me properly for the first time since I arrived. "You weren't at school yesterday. What happened to you?"

I tell him about my arrest and interrogation and he listens with a growing look of anger.

"*Die Arschlöcher!*" he says when I've finished telling him about my ordeal. He looks as if he'd like to punch someone. I lay a hand on his arm to calm him down.

"It's all over now," I say. "Forget about it. Anyway listen, I didn't come here to tell you about my arrest. I came to tell you that I've heard from Dieter."

"Oh?" There's a look of genuine surprise on his face.

"He's joined a group of people in West Berlin who are digging a tunnel into the East so they can rescue their friends and family."

I feel very proud of Dieter and I wait for Hans to say something positive. But his face falls and he looks away from me.

"Didn't you hear what I just said?" I ask, frustrated by his lack of response.

He stands up and walks to the window, pressing his forehead against the glass. "Sure. Dieter's digging a tunnel. That's great, but how long will it take?"

I shrug. "A few months I suppose."

He turns to face me. "That's way too long.

They'll be discovered before they've finished it. Then they'll all be arrested. And meanwhile we're stuck here wasting our lives."

"You don't know they'll be discovered! I'm sure they're being careful." I'm cross with him for pouring cold water on Dieter's plan before they've even given it a chance. "At least Dieter's doing something productive instead of just wearing black which hasn't achieved anything except get you into trouble with the Stasi."

He flinches at my words and I regret them as soon as they're out of my mouth.

"Is that what you think of my actions?" he asks.

"I'm sorry," I say. "I didn't mean to offend you, but Dieter's doing what he can and you shouldn't write him off. I thought you'd be pleased to hear about the tunnel."

He hangs his head, looking defeated. After a few moments he looks up at me. "Look, I'm pleased Dieter is doing something, of course I am, but the problem with this tunnel idea is that it's just going to take too long. I can't wait months."

"Well, what about your plan to get false identities?" I ask.

He nods his head. "That still might work. I have my contacts. But I can't wait forever. Don't you see? I've been expelled from school which means I'll never get my *Abitur* and never be able to go to university. As soon as I step outside the Stasi will be watching me. If I can't get the false identities sorted out soon, then I have other ideas."

"To do what?"

He drops his voice to a whisper. "I could go to Czechoslovakia and from there try and cross the border into Austria."

I think this idea is absurd. "Are you crazy?

You'll be shot trying a stunt like that. At least Dieter and his friends will be hidden from view underground. Trying to cross the border in Czechoslovakia is way too obvious. Astrid thinks…"

He turns on me and cuts me off. "I don't give a fig what Astrid thinks."

I'm stunned. "Why not?"

He shrugs his shoulders and looks away.

"Why not?" I insist. "What have you got against her?"

"I don't trust her."

"Why ever not?"

He sighs. "Oh, I don't know. She's probably harmless. She just gets on my nerves with her endless gossiping. Be careful what you tell her."

I'm furious at this insult to the only person at school who has shown me any kindness today. "You're telling *me* to be careful, when you're planning on running across national borders?"

He looks like I've just slapped him in the face.

I stand up to leave, wishing I'd never come. "If you're still here when the tunnel is ready, then you're welcome to come with us."

He doesn't answer.

I walk home in a foul temper. Astrid was right. Wearing black as a protest hasn't achieved anything except get the participants into trouble. And if Hans isn't prepared to wait for the tunnel to be built, well he can go and take his chances at the Czechoslovak border and see if I care!

I'm walking with my arms folded and head down so I don't notice the group of young people walking towards me until I almost collide with them.

"Vorsicht!" snaps a voice in my ear. Watch out!

I look up to see a group of three teenagers, two

boys and a girl. They are all wearing the unmistakable bright blue shirts, with the yellow rising sun motif on the sleeve, of the *Freie Deutsche Jugend*. It was the girl who spoke. She frowns at me and flicks her head, tossing two long braids of blond hair over her shoulders. For some reason she is clutching a compass in her right hand. I suppose I almost made her drop it when I nearly walked into her. The boys are each carrying clipboards and pencils.

"Entschuldigung!" I mutter. Sorry! I'm not in the mood for a confrontation with these young enthusiasts of the socialist system. I just want to go home.

They let me pass and I continue on my way. But at the entrance to my building I turn round to look at them. They are standing where I left them, the girl holding the compass in her outstretched palm, the boys looking up at the roofs of the buildings and then writing something on their clipboards. What on earth are they doing?

Just then Frau Lange appears in the doorway. She is on her way out.

She greets me with her usual formality and lack of friendliness. *"Guten Tag,* Fräulein Neumann."

"Guten Tag, Frau Lange."

She notices the group a little way off and gives a nod of approval. Then she turns back to me. "I see you are not out with your comrades."

"Er, no," I say. I don't add that I'm not actually a member of the *Freie Deutsche Jugend*.

"A fine job they are doing," she says looking in the direction of the two boys and girl who have now moved down the street and are repeating their performance with the compass and clipboards.

"And what are they doing?" I ask.

She looks incredulous at my stupidity. "They are checking the television aerials of course."

"What about them?" There aren't that many television aerials in this street but I can see now they are standing by a building which does happen to possess a couple of these rare but prized pieces of technology.

Frau Lange makes a tutting noise with her tongue and then answers my question as if I was five years old. "They're checking to see whose aerial is pointing to the West. That's why they're using a compass. People shouldn't be watching western television. It's corrupting and immoral." Then she turns on her heel and marches down the street.

Despite the terrible day I've had, I laugh out loud. She can probably hear me but I don't care. We don't have a television but I've seen a bit of Western television when I've visited Dieter and I thought it looked much more interesting than the dreary rubbish we get over here. I think of Astrid's brother, Frank, watching that ridiculous *Meister Nadeloehr* and how he'd really enjoy a decent cartoon.

I climb the stairs to our apartment feeling unbearably sad about life here in the East. If we wear black as a sign of protest we get expelled from school. If we say what we think we are liable to be arrested. If we watch western television we are traitors to the state.

Two days later the *Freie Deutsche Jugend* are back but this time they are on the roofs of houses and apartment blocks, repointing western facing television aerials back towards the East. It is the end of American movies and western news coverage for East Berliners. From now on there will be nothing but the State news channel and *Meister Nadeloehr*.

5 MOTHER COURAGE

Sabine

October arrives and brings with it a blustery wind that shakes the leaves from the trees. I haven't seen Hans for a couple of weeks now. I've been hoping that he would call round and tell me he's changed his mind about the tunnel; that he's happy to wait for it to be finished. But there's been no sign of him. And deep down I've still been cross with him for being so mean about Astrid. So I've gone to school each day and tried to carry on as normal. For a while the white Trabant followed me everywhere, but I haven't noticed it in the last few days. Maybe the Stasi think I've learned my lesson.

By the end of the week I realise that I'm missing seeing Hans at school and decide to pay him a visit. I want to try and patch things up between us. I call round after school on Friday. Frau Fischer answers the door to me.

"I'm sorry, Sabine," she says, drying her hands on a tea towel, "but he went out a couple of hours ago. I don't know when he'll be back."

She's going about her daily chores and doesn't sound at all worried, but a knot tightens in my stomach. I was so sure of finding him at home that I can't help thinking the worst when I find he's not here. What if he has decided to flee to Czechoslovakia without telling her? He could be on a train right this moment. I don't know if she knows anything about his plans. Presumably not, otherwise she wouldn't be so relaxed at the idea of him going out.

"Can I give him a message?" she asks, smiling at me. She really isn't at all worried so I try to relax a little.

I shake my head. "No. No message. Just tell him I called, please."

"Of course, dear."

I return home and try to put Hans out of my mind by fetching Harry's last letter from its hiding place inside the pages of my notebook. It's the letter Brigitta gave me the day I was released from Stasi Headquarters. I haven't acted on it yet because I was worried about being followed by the Stasi. I take it into the kitchen and re-read it carefully.

It contains a set of instructions, a list of three names and a couple of photographs. Harry wants me to contact the people on this list and they in turn will contact other people who want to escape from East Berlin and who can be trusted to keep the tunnel project secret. That way we'll be able to spread the word about the tunnel without the need for Harry to get in touch with everyone individually. If he tried to do that he could put himself under suspicion and the whole project would be in jeopardy.

Re-reading the letter now, I notice with some

alarm that Harry has appointed me the primary contact in the East. If I don't pass this information on, then no one will know what the plans are. I suspect Dieter volunteered me for this role, thinking that I've never been in any sort of trouble with the Stasi. If only that were still the case. Just because I haven't seen the white Trabant for a few days doesn't mean I can afford to relax my guard. I have a Stasi file which means they'll watch me from a distance and will be on the lookout for any unusual behaviour.

I study the names, addresses and photographs of the people I'm supposed to contact. The two pictures are holiday snaps taken in happier times, before the Wall went up, and must have been supplied by the tunnelers in the West. I try to commit the names, faces and addresses to memory in case I need to destroy this letter at a later date.

The first person on the list is a woman called Marion Weber. She's the girlfriend of Werner, the tunnel engineer. The photograph shows a blond haired woman on the arm of a young man with wire-rimmed glasses. They are standing outside the Palace of *Charlottenburg* in West Berlin looking happy and relaxed. But her real address is very far from this leafy district. She actually lives southeast of *Prenzlauer Berg* in the East Berlin district of *Biesdorf*. As well as her home address I have the name of the Trabant factory where she works on the production line. Visiting her will mean a long journey on the *U-bahn*. I put her picture to one side and pick up the next photograph.

It is a holiday snap of Ingrid Huber who, the letter explains, is Claudia's aunt. The photograph shows a picnic on the beach. It must be somewhere on the North Sea. She is sitting beside a checked cloth next to two young children who must be Claudia's brother and sister. They live in *Pankow* which is immediately north of *Prenzlauer Berg*. Ingrid works at the local hospital, but I have her home address.

The final names on the list are those of Manfred Heilmann, his wife Gisela, their young son Peter and baby daughter Karin. There is no photograph of them but the letter tells me that Manfred is a friend of Harry's and an actor with the *Berliner Ensemble* theatre group. He's about to appear in a production of Brecht's play, *Mother Courage and Her Children*, which is opening at the *Theater am Schiffbauerdamm* in a week's time. Hitler banned Brecht's work in the 1930s but the Communists are enthusiastic in reviving the plays because of their socialist themes. It occurs to me that it might help my own reputation with the Stasi if I go to a performance of Brecht so I call Brigitta over from the living room where she is reading a book.

"How would you like to go to the theatre?"

Her eyes light up at once. "What are we going to see?"

If she's hoping for a production of *Schneewittchen* or *Hänsel und Gretel* she's going to be disappointed but I can't help that.

"*Mutter Courage und ihre Kinder*," I inform her.

"*Ja, gut*," she says brightly.

"Right then," I say. "Let's go and buy the tickets."

Dieter

Progress in the past week has been good. By having teams working round the clock we've managed to dig a deep, vertical shaft. I climb down to the bottom using the hand and footholds which Claudia and I made from the remains of the old furniture that was lying around in the cellar.

"Here it comes," says Werner leaning over the edge of the hole. He lowers a rope knotted at one metre intervals and weighted at the end with a hammer. I grab hold of the hammer and pull the rope tight. The hammer just reaches the floor of the shaft.

"We've done it," I call back up. There's a shout of joy from Claudia and the other students.

After weeks of back-breaking work the vertical shaft is now four metres deep. We've installed a pulley system to lift the buckets of earth up to the surface. Werner pulls the rope up and I scramble back to the surface. Claudia runs over and hugs me then runs to Werner and hugs him. He takes off his glasses and rubs his eyes. Despite the sense of achievement, we know this is only the beginning. We now have the gargantuan task of digging a horizontal tunnel one hundred and twenty metres long. The first section will run under *Bernauer Strasse* and then we will cross the border into the German Democratic Republic. We will be invading an enemy land.

Harry steps forward from the shadows. I didn't even know he was in the cellar. "Well done guys. Good work. Any chance of speeding things up a bit now? We've still got a hell of a long way to go."

I think, *how dare he!* We've been slogging away at that vertical shaft and it's not as if Harry has so much as lifted a finger to help.

"Look," I say, but Werner steps forward, cutting me off.

"We're making good progress and we're on track

with the plan. Things are speeding up now we're developing some muscle," he glances at me, "but digging the horizontal tunnel is going to take longer than the vertical shaft because we'll need to shore up the sides and roof with wood as we go."

Harry sighs. "How long will that take?"

"Not as long as it will take if the tunnel collapses," says Werner looking Harry straight in the eye. There's an uncomfortable silence for a few seconds as Harry and Werner continue to stare each other out.

Claudia intervenes. "Werner's right. We can't afford to take that risk."

"And," says Werner, "we will need to be extra quiet. The guards are patrolling all the time and they have dogs that might sense something going on under their noses."

"Okay, okay," says Harry throwing his hands in the air. "You're the technical expert, so we have to do what you say."

"Come on," I say. "Let's get back to work. We're wasting time here." I'm keen to get going again. Werner's right about us all getting stronger. I've noticed that my arms don't hurt as much after digging and I can keep going for longer.

"Yes," says Claudia. *"Vorwärts!"* Onwards!

Sabine

After another strained week at school where everyone is on the lookout for suspicious behaviour and people have lost the confidence to say what they really think of the Wall, it's finally the opening night of *Mother Courage and Her Children.* But as always when there's something you've been waiting for, time slows to a crawl and the day drags even more than usual. The final straw is in Marxism-Leninism where Herr Schmidt is particularly vehement in his defence of Marxist theory, arguing that class struggle is a necessary prerequisite of progress in a society. Apparently the Wall dividing East and West Berlin is an essential element in the progress of our country. The only progress I'm interested in is the progress Dieter and his friends are making with the tunnel.

When Herr Schmidt's lesson is finally over, I'm the first out of the door.

"Warte mal!" calls Astrid who's busy gathering her things together. Hang on!

"Sorry," I say, waiting for her by the door. "Didn't mean to leave you behind. Just got things to do this evening."

As we walk, Astrid chatters non-stop about an upcoming camping trip with the *Freie Deutsche Jugend.* I half-listen, nodding my head and saying *gut* or *wunderbar* at appropriate points. By the time we reach the corner of *Stargarder Strasse* I haven't had a chance to mention this evening's trip to the theatre and, to be honest, I'm glad. It's not that I want to hide things from Astrid, but if I told her we were going to see a Brecht play she'd want to hear all about it, down to the very last detail of what the actors were like and whether the direction was any good. The fact is, I don't know how much of the play we'll actually see because the main task is to try and find a way of contacting Manfred Heilmann. I tell myself it's better for her sake if she doesn't know about the tunnel project. Then if it all goes wrong, she can't be accused of consorting with traitors.

When I arrive home, Brigitta is already there. She

is very excited at the prospect of going to the theatre and even more excited at the thought of our secret mission. I'm just nervous in case we fail to contact Manfred and the whole thing is a waste of time and money or, worse still, we're observed by the Stasi.

I have written a note for Manfred and put it into a small white envelope. I will need to try and pass it to him, although how I am supposed to achieve this feat of conjuring I have no idea.

I hide my letter to Manfred Heilmann inside my coat pocket, then I check I've got the tickets and we set off.

We take the *S-bahn* to *Friedrichstrasse* and I am reminded of the journey we made back in August when we were looking forward to a day at the lake with Dieter and instead we discovered that the border had been closed and we were trapped in the East.

Brigitta slips her hand into mine as we leave the station and walk the short distance to the theatre. Oma used to have a picture postcard of the theatre taken before the war. The main entrance was an ornate tower decorated with carvings, scrolls and turrets. After it was destroyed in the war the entrance was rebuilt in a plainer style, the elaborate stone carvings replaced with straight lines and the fancy gothic tower on the top replaced with a circular metal sign announcing the building as the home of the *Berliner Ensemble*, the theatre group that Brecht founded.

Before we go inside I glance up and down the street. It's become a habit with me now, checking to see if there is a white Trabant parked nearby, or a man standing on a street corner perusing a newspaper, or a woman peering into a shop window. I trust no one who seems to be just hanging around. There are lots of people making their way to the theatre, but none of them looks suspicious. But then, I suppose, the best spies are the ones who blend in so you don't notice them.

There's a crush of people inside queuing to leave their coats in the garderobe. I decide it's better if we keep our coats on. I don't want to be seen carrying Manfred's letter in my hand.

We climb the stairs to the balcony and find our seats, which are in the second row from the back, in the middle. They were the only ones we could afford.

With its red velvet upholstery and grand chandelier hanging from the centre of the roof, this is the most opulent place either of us has ever been.

"I want to see the rest of the theatre," says Brigitta, so we walk down the side of the balcony, lean over the edge and peer down into the auditorium below. There are three layers of seating, the stalls at the bottom, the circle in the middle and the balcony at the top. The seats in the circle are the best seats in the house, raised up above the flat stalls, but not so far away, like those in the balcony, as to make the actors appear like little dolls.

Pillars in the guise of semi-clad Greek maidens bear the weight of the balcony on their shoulders. I'm pointing out this architectural flight of fancy to Brigitta when a movement below us in the front row of the circle makes me stop.

The people in the outer seats are standing to make way for some new arrivals who are making their way to the middle of the row. From this angle I can only see the tops of their heads but there's something familiar about them. There's a tall man with a bald patch, a woman with her hair in a neat bun, a young boy and an older girl...I don't believe it. It can't be. They shuffle around until they are happy with who's sitting where and then they sit down. Then the girl turns round and I see that I'm not mistaken. It *is* Astrid and her family.

She hasn't seen me. I draw back from the edge of the balcony. I'm surprised to see her and feel somewhat put out. Why didn't she tell me she was coming to the theatre? She usually talks non-stop about her plans for the weekend. I accept, not without a hint of shame, that I kept my own theatre plans a secret, *but*, I remind myself, I had good reasons for that. Astrid is presumably here just for a night out, to enjoy herself. So why didn't she mention it?

For a while I watch her, unobserved. She is sitting between her brother Frank and her father. Her father is talking to two grey-suited men sitting on his left. Her mother is busy wiping Frank's nose with a handkerchief. With no one to talk to, Astrid is flicking through the programme.

"*Komm*," I say to Brigitta, pulling her away from the edge of the balcony. "We should go back to our seats. The play will be starting soon."

The balcony is rapidly filling up. Some people, judging from their clothes, look as if they've come straight from work. Others look like students.

Whilst we wait Brigitta asks me to tell her what the play is about. I explain that it's set in the Seventeenth Century and it's about a woman in the Thirty Years' War in Sweden known as *Canteen Anna* or *Mother Courage*. She hopes to make a lot of money in the war and starts trading with the armies of both sides, but all three of her children die as a result of the war. "It's an anti-war play," I add, somewhat unnecessarily.

Brigitta nods her understanding. No one in East

Germany is in any doubt that war is a bad thing. It's just that over here, behind the Wall, peace isn't much fun either.

From Harry's letter I know that Manfred Heilmann is playing the role of the Swedish Commander. The poster outside the theatre announced that Mother Courage will be played by the actress Elisabeth Borgmann.

The lights dim and there is a hush from the audience. A couple of latecomers shuffle apologetically along our row. The audience settles down and prepares to be entertained, although that's probably not the right word for this rather grim type of drama.

It's warm in the theatre, but I keep my coat on because I don't want to risk losing the letter which must be crumpled by now. Somehow, in the interval, or straight after the performance, I'm going to have to find a way of passing it to Manfred Heilmann. The curtain rises and I try to sit back and enjoy the play but I'm nervous and can't concentrate on the dialogue.

As Mother Courage drags her unwieldy wooden cart around the stage, doing deals with the army generals, and switching allegiance from Protestant to Catholic as the situation demands, I sit and worry about the task ahead of me. After an hour or so of onstage wheeling and dealing, her youngest son (who goes by the unlikely name of Swiss Cheese) is shot dead and the curtain falls for the interval. By now I have a knot in my stomach. I wish Astrid wasn't here. If I bump into her it'll be really awkward.

Brigitta and I stand up and follow the crowds heading for the foyer. It's hard to move in the crush of people and impossible to tell if there are Stasi agents amongst the audience, although I'm sure there must be because they infiltrate all public gatherings, like flies that invade houses in the summer even when you keep the windows closed.

In the foyer the doors have been opened to let in some air. People are spilling out into the street, drinking, smoking and discussing the first act of the play. I keep an eye open for Astrid but don't see her anywhere so I try and focus on the task in hand which is to find a way backstage, but the audience and actors inhabit two distinct worlds and I can't see how to cross from one to the other. We've now only got about ten minutes before the curtain rises again.

Brigitta tugs on my arm. "This way."

She starts to weave her way through the crowds of people and I struggle to keep sight of her. She heads outside and I arrive just in time to see her dart around the side of the theatre into *Marienstrasse*. I run to catch her up.

"Look," she says with a big smile on her face. She is pointing at a small black door in the side of the building. "It's the stage entrance." Brigitta is already reaching out for the door handle. I glance up and down the street, but there is no one loitering on the corner and there are no parked cars with men sitting inside them.

"Quick," I say. She pushes the door open and we disappear inside, into the dark.

Dieter

The dark. I'm on my knees, hunched over in the confined space of the tunnel. I have mud and dirt in my hair, on my face, stuck down my fingernails and over my clothes. I want to stand up and stretch my

162

legs, ease out my back, but the space I'm in is way too small. I've been down here for four hours, hacking at the tunnel face with the pick-axe and shovelling the earth into buckets. I now know what it must feel like to be a mole, living and digging underground and never seeing the light of day.

Werner is down here too, rigging up an electric cable so we can have some light and don't need to rely on torches.

"I could do with a bit more space," says Werner rolling out an electric extension lead. "Why don't you go and take a break."

"OK," I say.

I crawl back to the vertical shaft and stand up straight for the first time in hours, pushing my hands into my lower back and leaning backwards.

I limp up the stairs to the kitchen and collapse onto one of the chairs. My jeans are ripped and my knees are grazed and bleeding. My whole body aches. The kitchen door opens and Claudia walks in, also covered in mud and filth. She's been emptying the buckets of earth into the yard. She's given up trying to keep the living quarters clean. It's not possible when we spend hours every day digging in the dirt.

She takes one look at me and shakes her head. "Coffee?"

"Yes please." I'm glad someone's got the strength to put the kettle on because I haven't.

Digging the horizontal tunnel is much harder than digging the vertical shaft. I spend hours crouched or kneeling on the rough ground chipping away at the wall of earth in front of me. My legs cramp up and my back is hunched. I think I'm going to turn into Quasimodo.

Progress is painfully slow. There's only room for

one person to dig at the tunnel face at any one time so the other members of the team are put to work passing buckets of rubble along the tunnel and shoring up the tunnel walls and roof with planks of wood.

Claudia places two mugs of coffee on the table, then kneels down and examines my bleeding knees.

"You should wrap bandages round your legs before you start digging," she says.

"Yeah, I know," I sigh. "Thanks for the advice."

Sabine

After a few moments our eyes adjust to the dark and we find ourselves in a narrow corridor. At the end of the corridor is a short flight of steps leading downwards.

Backstage there is none of the luxury that adorns the public areas of the theatre; no carpet, or red velvet or carved pillars. The floor is laid in a cheap, brown linoleum like the one we have in our apartment. Exposed pipes, covered in a layer of dust, run along the wall at ankle level. A flickering strip-light does a half-hearted job of illuminating its dingy surrounds. I'm just relieved that we seem to have got in unnoticed. We head off down the stairs in search of the dressing rooms.

The sound of voices reaches us from round the corner. I grab hold of Brigitta and pull her behind a rail of peasants' costumes which someone has left in the corridor. Two men appear carrying a bulky piece of scenery. They are concentrating on not letting it topple over, so they don't notice Brigitta and me hiding behind the tunics and capes.

When they've gone I peer out to check the coast

is clear. We need to hurry before anyone else appears.

We continue round the corner, where the men carrying the scenery had come from. There are doors on either side. I think these must be the dressing rooms but I don't know how we're going to find the right one.

Half way down the corridor a door opens and six actors dressed as Swedish soldiers emerge. There is nowhere for us to hide now, but they head off in the opposite direction and don't notice us. The interval must be over and Act II about to begin.

We hurry down the corridor, looking at each of the doors in turn. To my relief I see that the names of the principle actors are on the doors. We reach the door of Elisabeth Borgmann, the actress playing Mutter Courage, when suddenly there's a shout.

"*Was tun Sie da?*" What are you doing there?

We freeze. A red-faced man is striding towards us. He looks hassled, as if he hasn't got time to be dealing with uninvited strangers wandering around backstage.

"I asked, what are you doing?" His voice is stern and he fixes us with a hard stare.

Whilst I stand there tongue-tied, Brigitta gives him her sweetest smile and says, "It's my fault we're here. I'm such a big fan of Elisabeth Borgmann and I just wanted to get her autograph. She's a real heroine of mine."

The man looks taken aback. He clearly wasn't expecting such a straightforward and innocent answer.

Brigitta doesn't flinch or blush like I would do telling such an outright lie. She keeps her poise and I think, *she should be an actress one day*.

The man grunts and looks at his watch. "This is

all very irregular, but I suppose if you're very quick she might just have time to give you an autograph. She's on stage in five minutes."

He knocks on the door. We wait. I wish he'd go away but he stands there as if he's about to present us to the Queen of Sheba. The door opens and *Mutter Courage* appears, aka Elisabeth Borgmann. She is in full costume - a coarse grey woollen dress, a grubby apron and a length of brown cloth wrapped turban-style around her hair. She stands with her arms akimbo, looking at the man with raised eyebrows. She doesn't smile.

"A young fan of yours," says the man, pointing at Brigitta.

Elisabeth looks down at Brigitta who is still radiating innocence. The actress looks as if she doesn't believe a word of it but nods her head at Brigitta and me. "You'd better come in."

She ushers us into her dressing room and closes the door on the man. Then she turns on us.

"I don't know who you are," she says, "but you shouldn't be snooping around backstage like a couple of thieves. Don't you know you can get arrested in this country for acting suspiciously?" I'm all too aware of that and don't need reminding. But now we're here, I need to decide if we can trust her.

She turns back to her dressing table, picks up a kohl pencil and starts to accentuate her eyebrows with it. For one dreadful moment I'm reminded of Frau Biedermeier, my interrogator at Stasi HQ.

"You heard the man," she says. "I haven't got long before I'm back on stage. What do you want?" She lays the kohl pencil down and picks up a powder compact. Amongst the clutter of make-up, hair brushes and cigarette packets on her dressing table there's a photograph of a boy in a silver frame.

He looks to be about fifteen. She catches my eye in the mirror.

"That is my son," she says picking up the photograph. "He lives in West Berlin with his grandmother." This admission is all I need to know I can trust her.

"We're looking for Manfred Heilmann," I say. "I have a letter for him."

"Come with me," she says getting up from her dressing table. We follow her down the corridor and wait whilst she taps on a door. She doesn't wait for an answer but opens the door and pushes us inside.

"You have some visitors," she says. Manfred Heilmann is standing there in full Swedish regalia. Elisabeth closes the door on us and disappears, presumably not wanting to be caught aiding and abetting traitors.

Manfred Heilmann looks alarmed and his right hand flics to the hilt of his sword. He's much taller than he appeared on stage.

"I have a letter for you," I say, getting straight to the point and handing him the envelope.

He removes his hand from his sword and takes the letter, all the time watching me closely.

He rips open the envelope, takes out the letter and peruses its contents quickly. It's just a short note explaining about Harry and the tunnel. As he reads, the expression on his face softens.

"*Danke*," he says, smiling at me.

At that moment there is a call for Manfred to be on stage. He tucks the letter inside his tunic and hurries off ready for his cue.

We sneak back out the way we came in. It's too late to return to our seats in the balcony so we will have to miss the second half of the play. But we are principle actors in our own real-life drama.

Dieter

I'm back at the tunnel face and making better progress than yesterday. I took Claudia's advice and wrapped my knees in strips of cloth torn from an old shirt. I got some sarcastic comments from Andreas about suffering from housemaid's knee, but I just ignored him.

I thrust the spade into the wall of earth in front of me and remove a clod of thick, brown soil. Andreas is some way behind me, knocking planks of wood into the walls and roof of the tunnel, following Werner's instructions to shore up the sides as we go. Claudia arrives to remove the buckets I've already filled.

"Hey, you're doing great there," she says. I give her a grateful smile.

She takes away the full buckets, leaving me with empty ones. I'll have them filled in no time at this rate.

Andreas appears behind me. "We need more wood," he says. "I'll be back in half an hour or so."

"OK," I say without pausing to turn around. I'm determined to dig as far as I can whilst he's gone. Werner said we shouldn't dig too far ahead of the shored up section, but if I don't make real progress Andreas will no doubt give me some stick when he gets back. He clearly doesn't think I'm up to the job, but I'll show him.

I keep hacking at the earth. Werner's light makes being down here a lot less depressing and the clay is becoming sandier so it's easier to dig. I soon fill the buckets Claudia brought me. She takes those away and then returns with a fresh pair.

"Want to swap over for a bit?" she asks.

"All right," I say. I move back to let her through.

She squeezes past me. I inhale the sweet smell of her soap. She always smells nice, even in the mud and filth of the tunnel.

She pushes the spade into the soil. Werner was wrong to think she couldn't do as good a job as the rest of us. "Go on then," she says turning to look at me with a grin on her face. "Take the buckets away."

"Yes, boss. Sorry." I pick up the buckets of rubble and make my way back up the tunnel, hunched over like an old man. When I reach the vertical shaft I fix the first bucket onto the hook on the end of the pulley system and give the rope a yank.

"Bucket coming up," I call.

Werner hauls it to the surface. I do the same with the second bucket, then start to climb up the shaft myself. I'm right at the top when I hear a thud and a muffled scream from inside the tunnel.

Werner looks at me. "What the hell was that?"

I don't answer. I'm already scrambling back down the shaft, my feet and hands slipping on the footholds in my desperation to reach the tunnel face. I jump the last couple of metres, then run, as best I can bent double, back down the tunnel.

Where, a few moments before, I'd left Claudia digging, now there is only a pile of earth. Her right foot is sticking out of the rubble. The rest of her is completely buried.

I go into overdrive, tearing at the earth with my bare hands.

"Claudia! Claudia! Can you hear me?" I shout at her, oblivious of the East German guards above our heads. *Please God*, I think, *let her be all right. Let her still be alive.*

My fingers scrabble through the soil until they

touch something warm and soft. Flesh. I can feel her arm. I grab hold of it and start to pull but I can't get her out. The weight of the earth on top of her is too heavy.

There's a noise behind me in the tunnel. It's Werner. Together, we shovel armfuls of earth off her body until suddenly Claudia's face emerges, then her neck and shoulders. We grab hold of her and pull her free.

She sits up coughing and spitting out mouthfuls of brown, slimy earth. I try to rub the dirt from her face and hair. She doesn't say anything.

"Help me carry her upstairs," I say to Werner.

"I'm OK," croaks Claudia.

"No you're not," I say. "You could have died under there."

I feel sick to the pit of my stomach. If I hadn't tried to dig so far ahead of the shored up section this would never have happened. Neither Werner nor Claudia says anything, but I know this accident was all my fault.

Sabine

At school on Monday Astrid doesn't say anything about being at the theatre on Friday night. When I ask her how her weekend was she just shrugs her shoulders and says nothing much happened. I'm puzzled by this but can't ask her about it without giving away the fact that I was at the theatre too, so I let it drop. Knowing Astrid, she probably found the play so boring she doesn't think it's worth mentioning.

Anyway, I've got other things on my mind. Encouraged by the success with Manfred Heilmann,

I plan to contact Marion Weber, Werner's girlfriend, this afternoon as soon as school has finished. When the bell rings, I make an excuse to Astrid about needing to take Brigitta to buy some new shoes (I hate all this lying and subterfuge) and head off towards the *U-bahn* at *Schönhauser Allee*. I'm going to *Biesdorf-Süd* to look for Marion Weber at the factory where she works.

I find the Trabant factory easily enough from the plumes of grey smoke pouring out of the tall, brick chimneys. The main gates to the factory are closed but I peer through them and realise from the sight of the sprawling buildings that this place must employ hundreds, if not thousands, of people. I wonder if I've made a mistake in hoping to find Marion amongst all the workers who will be coming out at half past five.

I've still got twenty minutes before clocking off time and I can't stand outside the factory that long without drawing attention to myself so I go to a café which I passed on the way here, order a coffee and sit down at a table by the window.

I return to the factory gates a minute before half past five. On the dot of five thirty the doors to the factory open and dozens of factory workers in identical blue overalls spill out onto the forecourt and make their way towards the gates. How am I going to find Marion in this crowd? I sneak a quick look at her photograph which I have in my pocket then I look back at the faces of the workers. I see tired, grim-faced men and women who are bored by the monotony of their lives and who do not smile. At first glance everyone looks the same.

Then I see her. She's hard to miss. She stands out from the crowd because she has a spring to her step, even after a long, hard day at the factory. She manages to wear her overalls as if they were an item of fashion clothing instead of functional work wear. She looks to be about two or three years older than me. As she walks towards the gates she unties her hair and shakes out the bottle blond curls that fall over her shoulders.

I start to move towards her, wanting to catch her before she disappears from view. She sees me walking in her direction, pauses for a fraction of a second and then keeps moving. I follow her. She looks back, appears to assess me, then gives me the tiniest nod of encouragement. I run to catch her up. To my surprise, she slips her arm through mine.

"Just act normal and pretend we're best friends," she whispers.

I try to do as she suggests and we continue down the street in the direction of the *U-bahn* station.

"I have a message from Werner," I say.

"I hoped that was what it was," she says.

I quickly tell her about the tunnel and pass her a note which she slips inside her overalls without reading it.

"Listen," she says, gripping my arm tighter and leaning in close, "you must be very careful around here. You know that don't you?"

"Because of informers?" I ask.

She nods. "There are spies and collaborators swarming all over the factory. Tomorrow, if anyone asks me who you are I'll say you're an old friend from school and you just dropped by to say hello."

"Of course." I like the idea of being an "old friend" of Marion's.

At the *U-bahn* we go our separate ways. She is travelling east towards *Cottbusser Platz* and I must return to *Prenzlauer Allee*. Although I've only just met her, I hope we really can be friends once we make it to West Berlin. I have to believe that we will make it. It's the only thing that keeps me going.

Dieter

Claudia is resting on the sofa, bathed and patched up. Werner ordered her to take a day off after her ordeal even though she insisted she was fine. She doesn't look fine to me. She's covered in cuts and bruises and she's still coughing like a nineteenth-century consumptive and complaining of a headache. I've taken ten minutes off from the digging to make her a mug of coffee and check how she is.

"Thanks Dieter," she says taking the steaming mug from my hands. "You really don't need to fuss over me, you know."

I still feel really guilty about what happened to her yesterday and I want her to know how sorry I am. I kneel down on the floor beside her.

"Listen, Claudia, I..."

The door bursts open and Harry charges into the room. I've never seen him look so angry. Come to think of it, I haven't seen him for a couple of days.

He takes one look at Claudia lying on the sofa then turns on me. "What the hell was going on yesterday?"

"What do you mean?" I ask, getting to my feet. He might at least have asked Claudia how she is.

"*This!*" Harry says, indicating the prone Claudia who immediately tries to sit up but falls back with her hand on her head. I'm worried she's suffering from concussion and should see a doctor but Werner doesn't want to risk anyone finding out what we're doing.

Harry ignores Claudia's plight and addresses his comments to me. "Werner tells me the fucking tunnel collapsed because it wasn't shored up properly."

"It was being shored up," I say, trying to keep my temper. "Andreas had gone to fetch more wood."

"But you carried on digging. You should have stopped work and waited for him to come back."

I think this is a bit rich coming from someone who is always so impatient to see progress and yet hasn't shifted so much as a thimbleful of soil himself.

"What are you saying?" I round on him. "That this is all my fault?"

"Yes, I am as a matter of fact."

I'm furious. Even though I do blame myself for being too keen to make progress, the last thing I need right now is Harry giving me his opinion. If I hadn't handed over to Claudia it would have been me under that rubble. It *should* have been me. But I'm still not prepared to take this kind of crap from someone who doesn't actually do any digging himself.

"Instead of criticising other people," I shout at him, "how about you get your lazy arse down there and do some of the hard work for a change?"

The anger flares in his eyes. "You know what I do. I risk my freedom every time I go to East Berlin."

"Yeah right," I snort, "like you don't enjoy swanning around like some secret agent in a war film. This is all a game to you isn't it?"

Claudia tries to sit up. "Dieter, please..."

But I'm not in a mood to listen to reason. I take a step towards Harry and jab my finger at his chest.

"Why don't *you* get yourself down that tunnel and see what it feels like to spend hour after hour hacking away at the earth, living like a rat in a sewer? Or *what?* Too afraid of getting dirty are you?"

For a moment I think he's going to punch me. He lifts his fist to shoulder height and his eyes are blazing.

Claudia screams at us to stop.

Harry's fist hovers in the air. I stand my ground and look him straight in the eye. He lets his hand fall to his side. Then he turns and storms out of the room, slamming the door behind him.

Sabine

I have one more person I need to contact - Ingrid Huber, Claudia's aunt in *Pankow*. So on Saturday I take the *S-bahn* to *Pankow-Heinersdorf*, leaving Mother and Brigitta at home baking a cake for Michaela Mann who is going to be seven tomorrow.

I find Ingrid's house in a quiet street of white-washed bungalows with square patches of lawn and neatly trimmed hedges out the front. I recognise Ingrid from the photograph of the picnic on the beach. She is in the garden pruning rose bushes with a pair of secateurs. She is a small woman with her brown hair tied tightly in a ponytail. She is wearing thick leather gloves to protect her hands from the thorns. I can hear children running around in the back garden.

"*Guten Tag,*" I call to her over the low wall which separates the property from the road.

She looks up from her pruning, startled. I can see the suspicion in her eyes, thinking, *who is this stranger?*

"Sind Sie Frau Huber?" Even though I already know who she is, it only seems polite to ask.

"Ja." She is holding herself very rigid as if she expects me to denounce her as a traitor. For all she knows, I could be from the Stasi. "And you are?" she asks in a tentative voice.

"Sabine Neumann. I have news from Claudia."

At the mention of Claudia's name Ingrid breathes out a sigh of relief, puts the secateurs into her pocket and takes off her gardening gloves.

"Oh, thank goodness. I thought for a moment…" she doesn't finish what she was going to say but instead opens the garden gate. "Please, come in."

As I enter the garden two children run round the corner of the bungalow, chasing each other. A girl and a boy. The girl looks to be about eight, the same age as Brigitta. The boy is maybe a couple of years younger. At the sight of me they stop dead in their tracks and stare. They have obviously been taught to be wary of strangers.

"It's all right children," says Ingrid. "This lady is a friend. Go and play until I call you for tea." With those words of reassurance the children disappear round the side of the bungalow. Ingrid leads me inside.

Whilst she makes us both some tea, I tell her how Claudia and my brother are working as part of a team to build a tunnel so we can escape from East Berlin.

"I knew Claudia would do something," she says, setting two mugs of steaming tea down on the table. "She's a brave girl."

"Yes," I say. "We owe them a great deal."

I stay half an hour chatting to her about Claudia

and the two younger children whose names, I learn, are Stefanie and Jens. During the week Stefanie goes to school and Jens attends the *Kindergarten*. Ingrid is a nurse at the local hospital.

"For my own sake," she tells me, leaning across the table and speaking confidentially, "I would probably just stay here and make the best of things. The hospital lost so many doctors and qualified nurses to the West before the Wall went up. But Stefanie and Jens deserve a better life than they'll get in East Berlin."

I thank her for the tea and promise to be back in touch as soon as I have more news of when the tunnel will be ready. Then I head for home.

I'm keen to tell Brigitta and Mother that I have made contact with all the people on Harry's list and, as far as I'm aware, I haven't been followed. I exit the *S-bahn* at *Schönhauser Allee* and walk quickly up *Stargarder Strasse*. As I'm nearing our building a brown Skoda drives away from the other side of the street.

Inside, I peer through the grilles of the letter box but it's empty. No messages today. I press the light switch and start up the stairs. The Mann apartment is quiet. On the second floor Frau Lange's door is ajar. It closes just as I turn the corner of the stairs. I have developed the habit of hurrying past Herr Schiller's door on the third floor because the memories are so painful. I run up the last flight of stairs, trying to reach the apartment before the light times out. The top landing is eerily quiet and an unfamiliar smell catches my nose. I turn my key in the lock and go inside calling, "Brigitta! Mother!"

No answer.

The apartment is in darkness. I fumble for the light switch by the door. Somebody has been here. I can smell it. It's the same smell I noticed on the landing, only more intense. Aftershave and cigarette smoke.

"Brigitta! Mother!"

I go to the kitchen and find the cake ingredients spread out on the table – flour, sugar, butter, eggs – but no sign of my mother or sister.

Then I remember the brown Skoda, and I know what has happened. My legs start to shake and I have to grab a chair and sit down. Whilst I was visiting Ingrid Huber in *Pankow*, the Stasi came calling. They have taken my mother and sister away. For questioning.

I can picture it in my mind's eye. The knock at the door. The strange men standing there, demanding that Mother and Brigitta accompany them to Stasi HQ. But then what? Have the Stasi locked them in a cell? Together? Apart? And why?

I rush to the bedroom where I keep Harry's letters tucked inside my notebook in the chest of drawers. The first letter ended up in the *Kachelofen* the day the Stasi came for me, but the second one, the one with the names, addresses and photos of the people I'm supposed to contact was still inside the notebook when I left home this morning.

I wrench open the drawer. The notebook has gone.

I throw myself down on the bed and weep.

6 ORANGES FOR CHRISTMAS

Sabine

I don't leave the apartment all day. I want to be here in case Mother and Brigitta return, but realistically I don't expect to see them again today. I blame myself for their arrests. If I hadn't stayed chatting with Ingrid Huber I would have been home when the Stasi came. They could have taken me instead. I would have done anything to prevent them taking Mother and Brigitta.

I'm incensed that the Stasi would want to interrogate an eight year old child, but, if I'm honest, I'm more worried about Mother than my little sister. Brigitta can be resilient and resourceful as she proved at the theatre, but I dread to think what Mother might say if she's put under pressure.

And as for the notebook and the letter inside it - how could I have been so stupid not to have destroyed that letter as soon as I'd read it? I memorised the names and addresses from the start, so I should never have kept it. I may have jeopardised the whole tunnel project. And what will the Stasi do with the notebook? It contains names and addresses of family and friends. They could track down Dieter.

Night falls and I know I should try to get some rest. I don't undress but lie down on the lower bunk in my clothes. I lie there for ages, picturing the interrogation room at Stasi HQ. Frau Biedermeier comes unbidden into my mind's eye, her eyebrows blacker and her lips redder than ever.

I must have fallen asleep in the early hours because I wake up shivering. I forgot to close the curtains last night and outside it's a grey, cold morning with drizzle running down the window.

I sit up and rub my arms to warm myself up. We will need to start fetching coal from the cellar soon. I make my way to the kitchen, conscious of how empty and quiet the apartment is without Brigitta to brighten it up.

The ingredients of yesterday's baking session are still laid out on the table. Mother and Brigitta had got as far as weighing the flour and butter and putting them together in a mixing bowl. Fortunately they hadn't cracked any of the eggs. It had been a rare treat to find butter, sugar and eggs in the shop and Brigitta had insisted on baking a cake for Michaela's birthday. I cover the flour and butter mixture with a cloth and make myself some tea. I don't feel like eating. Then I take the tea to Brigitta's favourite reading chair in the living room and sit and wait.

Dieter

There's no progress for a day whilst we clear the

collapsed earth out of the tunnel and make doubly certain the walls and roof are properly shored up. Claudia insists on coming back down the tunnel to help out. Even Harry has rolled up his sleeves and is operating the pulley mechanism, lifting the buckets of rubble up to the surface. We haven't spoken since our row.

Claudia and I are taking our empty buckets back down the tunnel when she stops and puts a hand on my arm.

"Dieter, I don't think I've thanked you properly for saving my life the other day."

Her words make me feel terrible and I stare at my feet. "But it's my fault you were nearly killed," I say. "I shouldn't have let you dig there. I should have waited for Andreas to bring more wood. I'm really sorry."

"Nonsense," says Claudia. "Don't listen to Harry. No one else is blaming you. It wasn't your fault, it really wasn't. It was my decision to dig." Then she continues in a quieter voice. "You know I wasn't sure if I'd be able to stand it down here anymore. I was worried I might freak out, coming back into this cramped space. But it's like what they say when you fall off a horse - you have to get straight back on otherwise you lose your nerve."

"I hope you haven't lost your nerve," I say, looking into her big, hazel eyes.

"No," she laughs. "I can keep going for a while longer." Then she leans forward and gives me a peck on the cheek. I remain where I am, in stunned silence, as she disappears back down the tunnel.

Sabine

Brigitta and Mother don't return until Sunday evening. At the sound of Mother's key in the lock I leap up from where I've been sitting all day and rush to meet them. Brigitta runs into the apartment and hugs me tight. Mother walks in more slowly and lays a hand on my shoulder.

"Come into the kitchen and sit down," I tell them. I realise that I haven't eaten anything all day and I'm hungry. I'm sure they must be too.

Whilst I cut slices of *Schwarzbrot* and boil the kettle, they tell me that the Stasi came for them at ten o'clock on Saturday morning, so they've been gone for over thirty hours. Brigitta looks a bit tired but otherwise fine. Mother looks tense and drawn. There are dark rings under her eyes.

I set the bread and tea on the table and sit down myself.

"Tell me what happened," I say.

Mother stares at her plate, so I turn to Brigitta.

"Did they come for you in a brown Skoda?" I ask.

She nods. "Yes. Two men." She takes a large bite out of her bread, chews it, swallows then carries on with her story. "I saw the car pull up outside the building and two men got out. I thought they looked suspicious. When I saw them heading this way I went into the bedroom and took Harry's letter from your notebook. I burned it in the *Kachelofen* like the last one. I hope that was the right thing to do?"

A mountain of worry falls from my shoulders and crumbles to dust.

"Yes," I say, squeezing her hand. "It was exactly the right thing to do. Thank you. Where did you put the notebook?"

Brigitta looks confused. "I left it in the drawer of course."

"Ah, OK." This is not good news. If Brigitta left it in the drawer then the Stasi must have taken it. Maybe someone searched the apartment after Mother and Brigitta were driven away. I don't want to worry them any more at this point, so I ask, "Where did they take you?"

"To their headquarters I think."

"And did they keep you together or were you separated?"

"They separated us," says Brigitta. "We were each interviewed by Frau Biedermeier." She does such a good impersonation of Frau Biedermeier with her arched eyebrows and stern mouth that, despite everything, I smile.

"So what did Frau Biedermeier want to know?"

At last Mother looks up. "She wanted us to tell her why you have been meeting people that you don't normally see."

"And what did you tell her?" I try to keep my voice steady, but my hands are trembling and I drop them onto my lap so that Brigitta and Mother can't see.

"I didn't tell them anything," announces Brigitta confidently. "I just said you had a few friends that you didn't see very often. I didn't tell them why you'd been to visit these people."

"Good," I say. I turn to Mother. "And what did you tell Frau Biedermeier?"

For a moment she doesn't say anything. The silence stretches between us until I think I can't stand it anymore. Then she shakes her head at me. "No, Sabine. I didn't tell them anything. But they know something is going on. I'm sure of it. If this tunnel isn't ready soon, then it might be too late for all of us."

Dieter

"Any chance of a coffee?" I ask, staggering into the kitchen. I've just been digging for four hours non-stop and am in desperate need of caffeine and sugar.

"Sure," says Claudia, reaching for the kettle. Werner is sitting at the table studying the work rota. Harry is staring out of the window, smoking a cigarette. I ignore him and sit down opposite Werner. Despite Harry's efforts on the pulley system the other day, things are still tense between us.

"How are we doing against the plan?" I ask Werner. It seems to me we've been making excellent progress for about a week now. The only good thing to come out of the tunnel collapse (except Claudia giving me a peck on the cheek) is that the team is really pulling together. Harry still hasn't lifted a finger as far as the digging is concerned, but the rest of us are working harder than ever.

Werner puts the rota to one side and picks up his map of the tunnel. "We're not doing too badly," he says. "By my calculation, we're about here." He draws a cross on the map. "That's about five metres short of the border."

"Great." I, for one, can't wait to start digging under the feet of the enemy.

"But," says Werner, "there's still a long way to go before we reach the houses on *Schönholzer Strasse*, and we've got a problem."

"Oh, what's that?" I ask. Claudia places a mug of steaming black coffee in front of me and I start spooning in the sugars.

"Andreas needs to take some time off to look after his younger brother and sister," explains Werner. "His mother's sick. That leaves us a man short."

This is bad news. "We'll be more than one man short," I say, sipping at the hot coffee. "Andreas does the work of at least two people." I've given up trying to compete with Andreas – he's built like a tank whereas I'm more of a clapped out Trabi.

"Is there any chance of recruiting someone else?" asks Claudia. "What do you think Harry?"

Harry turns round from the window. "What I think," he says, "is that if you hadn't spent two days dealing with the tunnel collapse we'd be under the feet of those East German bastards by now."

"For fuck's sake," I say standing up to face him. "Can't you let it go? We, all right *I*, made a mistake. But we've been making really good progress since then, no thanks to you."

"What's that supposed to mean?"

"It means that you never lift a bloody finger to help us." Harry looks as if he's about to protest but I cut him off. "Since we're going to be missing Andreas for a while, how about you get yourself down that tunnel and do some real work for a change?"

"But…"

"What?"

"I…"

"Too afraid of the mud?"

"No."

"Well then, I'll see you in the cellar tomorrow morning. Don't be late." I walk out, slamming the door behind me.

Sabine

Today Herr Schmidt has organised a visit to the cinema to watch a government film about East German agricultural and industrial productivity. I expect it will be nothing but lies and propaganda, but at least we won't have to sit and listen to Herr Schmidt expounding Marx's theories on the dictatorship of the proletariat.

Our class gathers in the entrance hall, those of us still at school that is. There are rumours that Matthias and Joachim have been sent to prison for instigating crimes against the state. Those who were expelled for wearing black have not been allowed to return. I suspect Hans wouldn't want to come back to this place even if he was given the opportunity.

I haven't seen Hans for weeks. Not since I told him about the tunnel and we argued. I've been too busy contacting the people on Harry's list and then keeping a low profile after what happened to Mother and Brigitta.

"Cheer up," says Astrid. "We're off to see a movie."

"Oh yeah? Is John Wayne in it?"

Astrid gives me a puzzled look then shrugs her shoulders. "Anyway, it's better than being in school."

Herr Schmidt arrives wearing a brown overcoat, looking like a comedy Stasi spy. He marches to the head of the group and commands us to follow him. We walk the short distance to the state-owned cinema and take our places in the drab auditorium with its worn velvet seats.

The film shows scene after scene of industrious farm and factory workers who, judging from the smiles on their faces, find their backbreaking and monotonous labour nothing but a source of joy and personal satisfaction.

It occurs to me that with no prospect of finishing his education in this country, this is exactly the sort of work Hans will end up doing if he doesn't make it to West Berlin.

At the end of the film I can't get out of the cinema quickly enough. Having sat through an hour and a half of watching happy workers and being told that production in East German factories has increased by an astounding forty percent this year alone, I need the company of someone who always says exactly what's on his mind. I set off to see Hans.

I meet Frau Fischer on the landing. She is on her way out.

"Go straight in, Sabine," she says. "You know where to find him." She looks towards his bedroom door and the look on her face clearly says, Teenage boys!

I tap on Hans' door.

"Komm 'rein," he calls. Come in.

I go in and find him sprawled on his bed with a map of Berlin spread out in front of him.

"Oh, Sabine, it's you." He starts up, surprised, and tries to fold the map away, but not before I've seen that he's drawn the route of the Wall on it in red ink. He stashes the crumpled map under his bed.

"What was that?" I ask, trying to keep my voice casual sounding.

"Nothing," he says, flustered. "I was just…it's nothing."

I know he's trying to hide something from me, but I pretend not to notice.

"So, how are things?" I ask. I'd rather not refer to our previous encounter, hoping that we can just forget about it and move on.

"Actually, I have some good news," he says.

"Oh?"

He reaches under his bed and pulls out a shoebox. "You remember I said I was looking into false identity papers?"

"Yes. And?"

He doesn't reply but takes the lid off the box and pulls out a wig with dark, shoulder length curls.

I laugh. "You're not going to wear that are you?"

"No! Of course not. It's not for me." He looks towards the door and drops his voice. "It's for her." He takes a piece of paper out of the box and passes it to me. It's an identity paper.

I unfold it and see a picture of a middle-aged woman with dark, curly hair and a round, smiling face. Her name is Frau Roth and she comes from Hamburg in West Germany. I look at the wig which Hans is holding up and look back at the picture of Frau Roth. She's not dissimilar, facially, to Frau Fischer.

"Where did you get this?" I ask.

"Some students from West Germany are providing them. Frau Roth kindly loaned them her papers so that someone similar in appearance could escape to the West. With the wig on, Mother will look just like Frau Roth and as a West German citizen she'll be able to walk through Checkpoint Charlie without any problems."

"Cool," I say, handing back the identity papers. It's a huge risk, crossing the border in disguise, but I don't want to put a damper on things. "What about you? Do you have a false identity too?"

Hans puts the papers and wig back in the box and hides them under his bed. "No, not yet."

"And what does your mother think of this plan?"

Hans grimaces. "I haven't told her about it yet. But she'll be fine with it, I'm sure. Anyway, how's the great tunnel project coming along?"

"To be honest," I say, "I haven't heard anything about the tunnel for ages. I've no idea how far they've got."

Hans doesn't say anything but there's a flicker of I told you so on his face. When he speaks he's sympathetic sounding though.

"It will take them months," he says. "Even assuming they don't get found out."

"I know."

"Do you want me to try and get false identity papers for you?"

It's tempting, but I shake my head. "Thanks for the offer, but Mother would never have the nerve to present false documents to a border guard. And we'd need papers for me and Brigitta too. No, the only way my family will get out of East Berlin is in secret, underground."

Dieter

"Right, let's get started," I say.

I'm in the cellar with Harry who has turned up wearing an old pair of khaki trousers and a scruffy shirt. He looks quite different out of his usual stylish clothes. Claudia is doing lookout duty and Werner and Thomas will be along in a minute to work on shoring up the walls and roof. I want to get Harry started on the digging, show him the best way to work in the tight space. I lower myself into the vertical shaft, searching for the familiar footholds with my feet. I've been up and down so often now that I've developed some speed and agility.

I reach the bottom of the shaft whilst Harry is still lowering himself over the edge.

"Don't worry," I call up to him. "You get used to it." I want to try and make things up between us but I start to get impatient as he makes his slow and faltering way down the shaft.

Eventually he joins me at the bottom. He's out of breath already so I don't rate his chances after an hour of digging. Still, it's only fair he should do his bit.

"This way," I say. I bend over and start to make my way towards the tunnel face. Harry follows close behind. His breathing is noisy, like an old air-conditioning system.

The lighting system that Werner installed is rigged up on an extension cable and hung from the roof rafters, but it stops five metres or so short of the tunnel face. One of Werner's jobs this week is to find another extension cable to attach to the first.

"Bit dark down here, isn't it?" says Harry.

"Don't worry, your eyes will adjust after a while."

We reach the tunnel face and I show Harry the best way of hacking at the earth with a pick-axe. Whilst I'm talking, he stays focused on the wall of earth in front of us, not looking at me once.

"Here, you have a go," I say, passing him the pick-axe.

He makes a couple of feeble stabs at the earth, flinching as the soil starts to crumble.

"You're doing great," I lie. I shovel the loosened earth into buckets. "I'll go and empty these." Harry keeps hacking at the earth and doesn't answer. I hope he improves with a bit of practice.

Werner and Thomas have still not arrived, so I hook the first bucket onto the pulley system, climb up the shaft and hoist it to the surface. Then I repeat the whole exercise with the second bucket. There's no more space in the backyard for all the earth we've dug out, so we've started dumping it in the corner of the cellar where the broken furniture used to be.

I'm on my way back down the tunnel with the empty buckets when I sense something is wrong.

From the direction of the tunnel face, I can hear the sound of panting. I start to run, which is not easy seeing as I can't stand upright. I find Harry sitting on the tunnel floor, clutching his throat with his hands. The pick-axe is lying abandoned on the ground. With every breath he takes, his chest rises and falls like a piston. His eyes are tight shut and sweat is pouring off his face.

I grab him by the arms and shout, "Harry! Harry! What's the matter?"

He's trembling and he doesn't seem to hear me. I have to try and bring him to his senses.

"Harry!"

He starts to babble nonsensical words. I don't know what to do. I can't seem to make him hear me. In exasperation I slap him on the face. The babbling stops and he opens his eyes, staring at me in terror.

"Harry, for God's sake, what's the matter with you?"

"I can't...I can't...." His breath catches in his throat.

"Can't what?" I find I'm having trouble breathing too. I think Harry's behaviour is having an effect on me.

"I...have...to...get...out."

And then I understand. He's claustrophobic. That's why he's never helped with the digging.

"Okay," I say. "Let's get you out of here. Can you move?"

He shakes his head.

"Well, there's only one way out, and that's the way we came in. You have to follow me." I speak with as much command as I can muster and he nods his head slowly.

I start making my way back down the tunnel. Harry crawls on all fours behind me. It takes an age for him to reach the vertical shaft. I let him go ahead of me and he climbs up to the top in a fraction of the time it took him to come down. I follow him up to make sure he's all right. He's lying on his back on the cellar floor, gulping in lungfuls of air. I sit down next to him and wait for him to calm down.

After a few minutes he sits up. "Sorry about that," he says, running his fingers through his hair.

"No, I'm sorry," I say. "I shouldn't have made such a big deal of getting you to dig. But why didn't you just say you were claustrophobic?"

He shrugs. "No one likes to admit their weaknesses, do they?"

I can understand that. "Go back to playing the spy," I say, slapping him on the back. "It's what you do best."

Sabine

November has arrived and with it comes the first really cold weather of winter. Now when I wake up in the morning I can see my breath misting and when I climb out of bed the linoleum floor feels damp as well as cold. In the bathroom I hop from one foot to the other whilst I wait for hot water to come out of the tap. The pipes bang and clank like a tuneless percussion section of an orchestra.

We need to fetch coal from the cellar for the *Kachelofen*. Herr Schiller used to carry coal up from the cellar for all the neighbours, dismissing our thanks with a wave of his big, paw-like hand and saying that the exercise kept him fit. But now we must do that job for ourselves. Brigitta offers to help me. We take a metal bucket down the stairs to the ground floor and open the cellar door. The light is on. Someone must be down here already. We descend the flight of wooden steps and find our own section of the cellar, separated from those of our neighbours by wooden partitions.

I raise the lid on the bunker and peer into the blackness. This is a dirty job which will leave us with coal smudges on our hands and clothes if we are not careful. We start to shovel coal into the bucket, the coal dust making us both cough. We have almost filled our bucket when, from another part of the cellar, a coal bunker lid slams shut. A moment later there is a cry of pain, like a wounded animal.

We drop our shovels and run around the wooden partitions in the direction of the sound which has turned into a high-pitched moaning. Frau Lange is standing with a large bucket of coal by her feet, hands to her back, her eyes screwed tight shut.

"Are you all right Frau Lange?" I ask.

"Of course I'm not all right." She opens her eyes and glares at us. "I've injured my back trying to lift this bucket of coal." She rubs her lower spine with one hand and points at a full bucket of coal with the other.

"Would you like Brigitta and me to help you carry it upstairs?" I can't believe I'm saying this, but it seems like the only thing to do in the circumstances.

She looks at us in surprise. "Yes. Thank you. That would be very helpful."

Brigitta frowns at me, but I tell her to help me lift the bucket. We carry it between us, up the cellar stairs and up to Frau Lange's apartment on the second floor. I'm not surprised she injured her back, it weighs a tonne. Frau Lange hobbles behind us.

We stand aside whilst she unlocks her door. "Bring that inside, will you?" she asks. We follow her into her apartment.

Brigitta and I have never been inside Frau Lange's apartment before. As we follow her down the entrance hall and into the living room, I'm struck by how different it is to our rather shabby apartment. The modern, rectangular sofa and square chairs have been arranged with geometric precision around a beige rug. There's a tall bookcase with hardbacks and paperbacks arranged according to height and all the spines perfectly flush with the edge of the shelves. There are no pictures on the walls but there is a black and white photograph on top of an otherwise empty sideboard. It's a picture of a good looking, young man with thoughtful eyes and a playful smile on his lips. It's no one I recognise.

We take the bucket over to the *Kachelofen* in the corner of the room and put it down on a black iron grate. There's a moment of awkwardness when no one knows what to say. Frau Lange leans against the sideboard, rubbing her back with one hand. Her other hand is near the picture of the good looking young man.

"He looks nice," says Brigitta. I put a hand on her shoulder to silence her, worried that Frau Lange will think her impertinent.

"My husband," says Frau Lange. "His name was Bruno."

This is more information about herself than Frau Lange has ever volunteered in the past.

"Was your husband killed in the war?" It seems only polite to ask and is the most obvious explanation for his non-existence. If they were divorced she wouldn't have a picture of him prominently displayed in her living room.

Frau Lange shakes her head. "No, he wasn't killed in the war. He was killed before the war even started." Frau Lange isn't looking at us but is directing her gaze towards the photograph. "Bruno was a good man," she says nodding her head. "He was a committed Communist. Like all Communists in the 1930s, he opposed Hitler. He thought the Nazis were evil, and he was right."

"Yes, of course," I say. If this is a test to see if my family supported the Nazis, then I want her to know that my conscience is clear on that front.

"You've heard of the fire in February 1933 that destroyed the *Reichstag* Parliament building?" she asks.

"Yes." Although it was years before I was born, the *Reichstag* fire is one of the most infamous events of the early years of Hitler's dictatorship. Father often talked about it. I wait to see what Frau Lange has to say on the subject. When she speaks there is real bitterness in her voice.

"We thought at the time, and I still think to this day, that the Nazis started it themselves and then blamed it on the Communists." She looks past us, at a place deep inside her memory that only she can see. "Of course the fire was a ploy to give the Nazis an excuse to arrest hundreds of Communists, trade unionists and intellectuals from the university – the sort of people that the Nazis detested. That particular time Bruno and I managed to escape. We were lucky. But things got worse. In May the Nazis started burning books in the *Opernplatz*. They burnt anything they considered subversive to their political ideas. They didn't believe in free speech." I glance at her bookcase and notice volumes of Brecht and other authors banned by the Nazis. "Then in June 1933 the Nazis stepped up their campaign." Her voice rises in pitch. "They carried out raids and abducted over five hundred Communists from their homes. I was out at a meeting the night they came to our apartment. I returned home to find that the door had been broken down and Bruno was gone. I knew he'd been taken." Her eyes well with tears. "There was nothing I could do. I hid with friends for two weeks. Then I escaped to Poland and eventually to Russia. It was only safe for me to return to Berlin after the Soviets had liberated the city."

I never expected her to tell us so much about herself. I suppose it's her way of thanking us for helping her with the coal.

"Would you like me to put some coal in the *Kachelofen* for you?" I ask.

She looks startled as if she'd forgotten we were still there. "No thank you. I can manage now." Her old, closed look has returned.

"We'll be off then," I say. She nods curtly in our direction.

We leave her standing there, looking at the portrait of her dead husband, and go back to the cellar to fetch our own bucket of coal.

Dieter

We've dug as far as the border with East Berlin, but Werner isn't happy.

"We have a serious problem," he says when Claudia and I report for duty in the morning. "There isn't enough oxygen in the tunnel. When Harry had his panic attack the other day, it was exacerbated by the fact that not enough oxygen's getting through."

"How do we fix that?" asks Claudia.

"We need to install a ventilation system," says Werner. "I've sent Harry off to see if he can source some pipes and an electric ventilator which we'll fix up in the cellar. It should take us about a day to get it sorted."

Great, I think. *More delay to the project.* But without oxygen we'll be going nowhere fast. Still, we've made it to the border and are now digging right under the feet of the border guards patrolling the Wall.

Harry turns up later that morning with metres of piping which he managed to pick up cheap from a factory that had closed and a second-hand ventilator that a contact let him have *for a song*. I have to hand it to him – he might be useless at digging but he's resourceful when he needs to be.

Under Werner's technical guidance Claudia and I install the piping in the tunnel whilst Werner gets the ventilator cleaned up and running. By the end of the day we've got a functional air conditioning system and we're ready to start digging again. I can hardly wait.

Sabine

I pull the scarf up around my face to keep out the biting wind and make my way, head bowed, to the shop. We need bread, if there is some that isn't stale, and milk, if there is any that isn't sour, and vegetables although I don't expect to find anything other than the usual bruised and limp specimens.

As I approach the shop I'm surprised to hear the chatter of voices. I look up and see a queue of women outside the shop, all talking excitedly. I recognise Frau Klein from the hairdresser's on *Pappelallee*. I join the back of the queue, curious to see what has brought so many people to the shop.

"I haven't seen anything so bright and beautiful for months," says Frau Klein to the woman next to her. The queue shuffles forward and I crane my neck to see what she's talking about. In the corner of the window is a crate of oranges. Piled high in a bright golden pyramid, they look like a gift from the gods.

"Where have they come from?" asks a woman in a chequered headscarf.

"They've been imported for Christmas," says Frau Klein knowingly. "To cheer us all up." There are wry smiles at this, no one quite sure if she is being sarcastic. The queue moves forward a few more paces.

After about ten minutes of waiting outside, I finally make it into the shop. Frau Maier, the shop keeper, is rationing out the oranges to ensure as many people as possible are able to buy them. When it's my turn I pick three large oranges, one each for Brigitta, Mother and myself, laying them carefully in my basket. The skin is firm and unblemished. They are perfect. Then as an afterthought I ask Frau

Maier if I can have two more for the Mann children. Michaela never did get the cake we had planned to make.

"Of course," says Frau Maier, passing me two more plump fruits.

I do the rest of my shopping, not really caring about the poor quality of the vegetables on display or worrying about the age of the milk. I pay at the till and hurry home.

On the way upstairs I stop at the Mann's door on the first floor. I haven't seen Frau Mann for ages and wonder if her husband has been able to find work. Herr Schmidt always tell us that this country has zero unemployment thanks to the Communist system, but what he fails to mention is that no one will employ you if the Stasi tell them not to. I hope that Frau Mann will not be too proud to accept a couple of oranges for the children. I knock on the door and wait. There is no answer, so I try again.

"There's no point waiting," says a voice behind me.

I turn and see Frau Lange coming down the stairs.

"Why is that?" I ask, dreading what she might say.

"They've gone." She inclines her head towards the Mann's door.

"Gone?"

"Yes. And good riddance too. They didn't believe in the socialist society."

I feel like saying that the *socialist society* didn't believe in them because no one would give Herr Mann a job, but Frau Lange doesn't wait to hear my reply. I stare at her back as she disappears through the door, thinking how can she be so heartless?

I turn away from the Mann's door and climb the

rest of the stairs, the five oranges suddenly feeling heavy in my shopping bag. Brigitta meets me in the kitchen to help unload the shopping.

"Oranges!" she says delving into the bag and pulling out two golden spheres. She holds them up, one in each hand.

I feel bad about the Manns and can only hope that if they have tried to escape then they have done so successfully, but seeing Brigitta's face light up at the sight of the oranges makes me smile.

I hunt in the cupboard for a bowl that isn't chipped, and we arrange the oranges inside. Then I place it in the centre of the kitchen table. They are the most colourful objects in the room and they are giving off a tangy, citrus scent.

Brigitta puts her nose up to the fruit and sniffs them. She hasn't tasted fruit like this in months.

"We'll save them for Christmas," I say.

Dieter

It's my turn to do lookout duty. Andreas is back so it makes sense for him to dig. We've passed the border now and are crossing *Brunnenstrasse* in a diagonal line, right under the boots of the border guards.

I climb up to the roof and sit huddled behind the parapet, blowing on my hands to keep them warm. The weather has turned bitterly cold and dark clouds are gathering in the sky. At least the tunnel stays a constant six degrees above zero and you soon get warm digging. Up here, there's no protection from the wind or rain. I expect we'll soon have snow.

I pick up the binoculars and look to see what's

happening on the other side of the Wall. As usual two guards are patrolling at *Brunnenstrasse*. I expect they're as bored as I am. I lay the binoculars to one side and wrap my arms around myself in an effort to keep out the wind. I'm so tired I shut my eyes for a moment. Nothing ever happens on lookout duty.

There's a rumbling in the distance, like thunder.

Scheisse, I think, *not a storm!*

That's just my luck to be stuck up here in the middle of a downpour. I look up at the sky. It looks like it's going to chuck it down any minute. I pull my collar up around my neck. I wish I'd thought to bring a hat. The rumbling stops for a moment. Then it starts again, only this time it's louder and it doesn't sound like thunder any more.

I grab the binoculars and look down *Brunnenstrasse*. Because of the angle I don't have a clear view straight down the road, but I can see for about fifty metres. I shift my position to try and get a better view. The rumbling noise increases. Then two army trucks appear in my line of vision and behind them, a tank. It's the caterpillar tracks of the tank on the road that are making the thunderous noise. It's loud even from this distance. I can feel the tiles on the roof vibrating.

I watch, transfixed, as the vehicles trundle down the road and come to a stop about ten metres from the border. A dozen or so soldiers jump down from the trucks. Two of them have guard dogs, large vicious-looking brutes, straining at their leads. The dog handlers walk up and down, right above the tunnel, and the dogs go berserk, barking and pawing at the ground.

Stupid animals, I think.

Then I come to my senses, throw the binoculars to one side and grab the radio. I jab at the buttons, trying to make contact with Werner and the rest of the team down below.

"Can you hear me? Can you hear me? There's a tank. Stop work immediately. Repeat, stop work immediately."

I've no idea if I'm getting through. Although we tested the radio equipment at the start, we've never actually needed to use it for real. After an agonising few seconds, there's a crackle and Claudia's voice comes over the airwaves. "Message received."

I reach for the binoculars once more. The soldiers have moved away from the location of the tunnel and are gathering at one spot. One of the dogs is barking and pulling at its lead. It knows there's something going on a few metres away, under the earth. But the soldier holding its lead isn't interested in that patch of ground and gives the animal a sharp kick with the toe of his boot. The dog howls then shuts up. It knows it's beaten.

Two of the soldiers have long metal bars. They bend down and wrench open a manhole cover, then four of them descend into the sewer. The others stand guard around the hole, rifles at the ready.

Everyone waits.

After a few moments the guards around the manhole jump to attention. There are screams and shouts. I watch in horror as, one by one, a group of East Berlin escapees are hauled out of the manhole and dragged off to the waiting trucks. They were trying to escape through the sewers and didn't quite make it, poor sods.

Then I almost cry out as I recognise the last four people to emerge from the tunnel. It's the family who live in the same building as Sabine, Brigitta and Mother. I think their name is Mann. The children, a boy and a girl, are lifted out of the hole, followed by their mother and father. The children look confused and frightened. Frau Mann is in tears. Her husband tries to comfort her, but he is dragged away by one of the guards and shoved into the back of one of the trucks. Frau Mann and the children are taken to the other truck.

The soldiers replace the manhole cover and return to their vehicles. Then they drive away, taking their prisoners goodness knows where, probably to some godforsaken work camp to live out the rest of their days in captivity and drudgery.

Sabine

Christmas Day dawns cold and miserable. Normally we would stay inside warming ourselves around the *Kachelofen* but this year Mother, Brigitta and I join the crowds at the Church of Reconciliation in *Bernauer Strasse*.

We wrap up against the freezing cold and gather with dozens of other East Berliners outside the church which lies in East Berlin, no more than a few metres from the Wall. With half its congregation in West Berlin and unable to access the building, the church is now closed. The government of East Germany has no interest in the spiritual welfare of its citizens.

There are crowds of people on both sides of the Wall, waving white handkerchiefs to each other. I have no idea if Dieter will show up, but I wanted to come here just in case.

The Wall, here, is about one and a half metres high and built of concrete blocks, crudely cemented together. Not everyone can see over the top. Children in the East are standing on wooden crates, those in the West are sharing small step ladders. The border guards on this side of the Wall are patrolling, looking tense and nervous. They wouldn't normally allow people so close to the Wall, but they seem to be making an exception for Christmas.

We squeeze our way to the front. A kind man offers us the use of his crate and we huddle together, looking over the Wall into a sea of faces in West Berlin.

"Fröhliche Weihnachten!" Merry Christmas! People on both sides shout to each other, whether they know the people they are talking to or not.

I scan the faces in the West, looking for Dieter. Brigitta and Mother are doing the same.

Then Brigitta jumps up excitedly. *"Da ist er!"* There he is!

She points straight ahead into the crowd on the other side and calls his name. "Dieter!"

He hears her voice and weaves his way to the Wall. He reaches up and takes hold of our hands. Tomorrow this will again become impossible.

Mother clings to him, not wanting to let go. *"Mein Sohn,"* she cries. My son. The tears start to fall down her cheeks. It's all too much for her. She hasn't seen Dieter for months and now all she can do is touch his hand over the Wall.

"It's so good to see you all," says Dieter. His voice is choked and there are tears in his eyes.

I want to ask Dieter about the progress of the tunnel but it's too dangerous with so many people nearby. There are bound to be Stasi informers mingling amongst the crowd. I give him a questioning look with my eyes, confident that he'll understand me. He gives the faintest nod and I have to be satisfied with that.

Eventually we let go of each other's hands so

that more people can come to the Wall in search of their loved ones and make our way back to Stargarder Strasse. When we arrive home the oranges are still in the bowl on the kitchen table, giving off their tangy fragrance.

To cheer everyone up I fetch three plates from the kitchen cupboard and a sharp knife. Then I pick one of the oranges and cut into it, slicing it around the equator. Juice squirts out and splashes into my eye, making me blink. Brigitta laughs and passes me a handkerchief. I dab my eye, but I'm laughing too.

"Soon," she says, "we won't just have oranges for Christmas. Once we've escaped to West Berlin, we'll be able to have them every day."

I do hope so.

7 *NEUES JAHR* - NEW YEAR

Sabine

It's late on New Year's Eve when I decide to call on Hans and his mother. We still have two oranges left. They are starting to lose their plumpness and I want to give them to someone before they become inedible.

I place the two remaining oranges in my shopping bag and head out into the cold night. Flakes of snow swirl in front of my face. I walk quickly along the pavement, keeping my head down.

The door to the building is ajar so I let myself in without pressing the buzzer and climb the stairs to Hans' apartment. I knock on the door.

There's no answer. It makes me feel uneasy, reminding me of the last time I knocked on the Mann's door.

I try again, more loudly.

The door on the opposite side of the landing clicks open. I turn to see who's there. A head appears, poking round the door. It's Hans' elderly neighbour, Frau Winkler. She's a tiny woman with white hair tied back in a bun and quick, darting eyes. When she sees it's me she opens the door more fully. I've visited her once or twice with Hans. She is leaning on a walking stick with one hand. With the other hand she crooks a gnarled finger and beckons me over.

"*Guten Abend,* Frau Winkler," I say. Good evening.

"Come inside," she says in a hushed voice.

Confused, I follow her into her apartment and on into the living room. The *Kachelofen* in the corner is radiating a fierce heat and the room smells of *Bratwurst* and cabbage.

Frau Winkler fixes me with her eyes. I can tell something's wrong. I start to sweat, whether from the heat of the *Kachelofen* or nerves, I don't know.

"They are not at home," she says, tilting her head in the direction of Hans' apartment.

"You mean they've gone out for the evening?" I know this is unlikely, but I don't want to jump to conclusions. The worst explanation for their absence would be that the Stasi have taken them in for questioning.

Frau Winkler gives me a significant look and shakes her head. Her eyes are twinkling and there's a smile playing about her lips.

"Do you mean…they've gone *west*?" I whisper the last word.

Frau Winkler gives an infinitesimal nod of her head.

I don't know whether to feel glad for them, or sad that I didn't get to say good-bye. And does this mean that Hans managed to obtain false identity papers for himself after all? I wonder how much Frau Winkler knows or how much she's prepared to tell me.

"Did they go together?" I ask.

She shakes her head and invites me to sit down on a chair by the table. It is covered in a cream, embroidered table cloth. She sits down next to me, leaning forward with both hands on her walking stick.

"Frau Fischer went a week ago."

"I see. And Hans?"

"Just this evening."

I can't believe I've only just missed him. "And how did he look? I mean, was he like himself?"

"Oh, yes," says Frau Winkler surprised at my question. "I'd recognise that boy anywhere. I've known him since he was a tot."

This worries me. If Hans looked like himself then maybe he didn't manage to obtain false identity papers. I hope he's not planning something reckless. I realise I need to go into Hans' apartment and try and find out what's happening.

"Frau Winkler," I say, leaning towards her, "do you possibly have a key for Frau Fischer's apartment? You see, it's just that I left something there the last time I visited them. A book. And I was really hoping to be able to pick it up tonight."

She looks at me with those bright eyes of hers. I try to smile sweetly. I don't know if she believes me, but she nods her head and, leaning on her stick, rises to her feet. She hobbles over to an antique writing bureau, lifts the lid and takes something from one of the compartments.

"Here you are," she says, passing me a key on a blue, velvet ribbon.

"Thank you so much," I say, getting to my feet and taking it from her. "I won't be a minute. I'll bring the key straight back."

"Take as long as you like, dear. And you can keep the key. I won't be needing it."

"*Auf Wiedersehen*, Frau Winkler," I say, moving towards the door.

She waves her hand at me and sits back down. She suddenly looks very tired.

I leave the warmth of her apartment and tiptoe across the cold landing. I slide the key into the lock, feeling like a criminal. I tell myself that Frau Fischer and Hans wouldn't mind.

Inside, the apartment is cold. Frau Winkler said Hans only left this evening, but already there's an emptiness here. I hover for a while in the hallway, not sure what to do. I decide to start in Hans' bedroom.

The room is a mess with dirty clothes flung on the floor and unwashed mugs on the bedside table. The wardrobe doors are hanging open, as if Hans dressed himself in a hurry and didn't have time to close them again.

The shoebox that contained the identity papers of Frau Roth, the West German woman from Hamburg, and the dark, curly wig, is lying empty on the floor. But there's something else on the floor that catches my attention. It's the map of Berlin that Hans tried to hide from me the last time I was here. The map with the Wall marked in red ink.

I pick up the map and spread it out on the bed. I gaze at the line of the Wall as it zig-zags around the central district of *Mitte*, south along the *Teltow* Canal and north along the *S-bahn* line. I stare at the map, trying to work out what Hans' plan might be, willing it to give me a clue.

The central section of the map is smudged and dirty, as if it has been the subject of more intense scrutiny.

I follow the red line with my finger, past the *Brandenburger Tor* and round *Potsdamer Platz*. There's a big red cross at the Checkpoint Charlie border crossing on *Friedrichstrasse* which draws my attention. From there I run my finger east along *Zimmerstrasse*. One of the houses on *Zimmerstrasse* is marked with a tiny red dot. It's not much to go on, but it's all I have. I leave the map on the bed, then I head out into the night.

Dieter

"Tonight is a golden opportunity to press ahead," says Werner. "Whilst the East German guards are distracted by fireworks going off in the West, they are less likely to notice the digging that is going on right under their feet."

I agree. I would normally spend New Year's Eve out in *Kreuzberg*, celebrating with Bernd. We'd go round the bars, drinking beer, and watching the fireworks being let off over the city, at least in West Berlin. But this year no one on the team wants to go out partying. We just want to keep digging. The horizontal tunnel is now sixty metres long and the sandy soil is easy to dig.

"But we still need to be careful," says Claudia, pulling on a woolly hat and wrapping a scarf around her neck in readiness for lookout duty. "They do regular patrols of the empty houses on *Bernauer Strasse*. They're more likely to hear us from one of the houses than from the street."

"Good point," says Werner.

I grab a pick-axe and spade and start to climb down the tunnel shaft. It's started snowing and I'm glad to be in the relative warmth of the tunnel. I'll take over from Claudia on the roof later in the evening.

Sabine

I don't return home but head straight for the *S-bahn*. There are no New Year's Eve celebrations on this side of the Wall and it's so cold the streets are quiet.

I take the train to *Friedrichstrasse* station and then walk south down *Friedrichstrasse* itself. Ahead of me, at the junction with *Zimmerstrasse*, is Checkpoint Charlie, the border crossing for foreigners. That will be how Harry gets into and out of East Berlin. Even from this distance I can see the guards standing outside the squat, pre-fabricated building, stamping their feet to keep warm. I don't want to get too close to them so I turn left into *Leipziger Strasse* and head down the back streets towards *Zimmerstrasse*.

Zimmerstrasse is a ghost street. On the north side the houses lie dark and abandoned, a result of the recent enforced evacuations. On the south side is the Wall, a metre and a half high and topped with three rows of barbed wire supported on metal struts. On the other side of the Wall is the trendy West Berlin district of *Kreuzberg*. People in *Kreuzberg* really know how to party. I can hear the beat of rock'n roll from a café or nightclub. The West Berliners are out to celebrate the New Year and will no doubt want to show the East German border guards that the Wall isn't going to stop them having a good time.

I walk slowly along *Zimmerstrasse* keeping close to the houses. There is no sign of any life and I wonder if I've come to the wrong place. Snow is settling on the ground like a fine blanket.

I'm about one hundred metres from Checkpoint Charlie now. I don't want to get any closer. If Hans is here, I'm sure he wouldn't position himself so close to the checkpoint. I can see the guards standing in front of the barriers, clearly visible in the strong floodlights that illuminate the area.

A car appears from *Friedrichstrasse*. It's a western model, sleek and sporty, not a patched up old Trabi. The guards flag it down and the driver has to get out whilst they open the bonnet and boot, hunting for an East Berliner being smuggled out of the country. But their search reveals nothing and reluctantly they are forced to lift the barrier and let the driver through. The guards look frustrated. Finding an illegal escapee would have made their day. One of them has a dog on a lead. He starts to walk in my direction. I draw back into the shadow of a doorway, willing myself to become invisible.

The guard's boots crunch in the frozen snow. The dog's breath comes in short, sharp pants. I can hear them getting closer. Then they come into view. The guard is a thick-set man who walks with his legs wide apart. The dog is a fierce-looking Alsatian, ears pricked at the ready, sniffing the air with its nose and pulling on its lead. I pray it doesn't pick up my scent.

They walk past me and continue down the street for about fifty metres. Then they turn around and head back again. I hold my breath once more. The dog turns its head in my direction. But the guard tugs on the lead and threatens to kick the animal. It obeys its master immediately.

"Come on, there's nothing there." The dog doesn't look convinced, but it has no choice but to accompany the guard back to the checkpoint.

I slip out of my hiding place and head back down *Zimmerstrasse*. There's no point staying here any longer. I'm about to turn into one of the side streets when a figure emerges from one of the buildings about twenty metres ahead of me. A firework explodes in West Berlin and in the shower of red and green light I recognise Hans.

Dieter

A shower of red and green light bursts into the sky.

I've been on the roof for the last half hour, keeping an eye on the border guards in *Brunnenstrasse*, but also watching the fireworks that are illuminating the sky above West Berlin. Sparkling silvers, greens, blues and reds. East Berlin, on the other hand, remains shrouded in darkness.

There's a noise behind me and I turn to see Claudia crawling through the hatch in the roof, two bottles of beer in her hand. She nestles down beside me and passes me one of the bottles.

We sit in companionable silence, sipping the beer and watching rockets exploding in the sky.

Claudia looks at her watch. "Two minutes to go."

"You should make a wish."

"There's only one thing I want," she says.

There's an explosion of red in the sky towards the south.

"Happy New Year," she says leaning forwards and giving me a kiss.

I take hold of her hand. "Claudia," I say, "when this is all over…"

"Yes," she says, putting a finger to my lips.

"When this is all over. But not now. I have to go back and help with the digging."

I watch as she disappears down the hatch.

Snowflakes fall on my face, but I don't feel the cold.

Sabine

"*Hans!*" I whisper his name but the sound carries in the deserted street. He turns to look in my direction, sees me, then shrinks back inside the doorway of the building. I run to him. He kicks open the door and pulls me inside the entrance hall. It smells stale and dusty.

"What the hell are you doing here?" He stares at me in astonishment.

"I called on you earlier. Your neighbour, Frau Winkler, told me you'd gone. She gave me the key to your apartment. I'm sorry, I know I shouldn't have gone snooping, but I was worried about you."

He runs a hand through his hair. "Sabine, I don't know what to say…I…"

"What happened to your mother?" I ask. "Did she get to West Berlin?"

He nods. "A week ago. She just walked straight through Checkpoint Charlie wearing that curly wig. It was so easy."

"That's good," I say. "But what about you? Couldn't you get false identity papers too?"

He looks down at the floor and shakes his head. "I tried, but the border guards got suspicious of the students coming over from West Germany. Maybe a Stasi spy pretended to be an escapee and infiltrated their ranks or something, I don't know, anyway they were found out and arrested. On the very day they

214

were supposed to be bringing me a false identity! I would have been caught myself if I hadn't turned back from the meeting place. There was a Trabi parked nearby with two men in it and I just *knew* the game was up. I'm sure they spotted me though. I'm on their books already and they'll tighten the noose even more, particularly when they find out Mother has gone." He looks me straight in the eye. "That's why I can't stay here a moment longer. I'm going over that Wall tonight."

"Are you crazy? There are armed guards out there. I saw one of them walking up and down with a dog."

"I know. I'm not stupid. Look, I've been watching them for the last hour. One of them walks up and down every ten minutes. The last one went a couple of minutes ago so there won't be another for at least six or seven minutes. I can get over the Wall in that time. Plus, they're distracted by the fireworks. Why do you think I chose tonight?"

"Hans, this is madness, I don't want you to…"

"Shut up," he says, pulling me towards him. He wraps his arms around me and kisses me hard on the lips. It's as if a firework explodes inside me and suddenly I'm kissing him back, tasting him, inhaling the familiar smell of him and forgetting where we are and the fact that there are armed guards outside. I want this moment to last forever, but Hans pulls away from me and holds me at arm's length. "I'll go and find Dieter and help him build this damn tunnel if you like. Then you'll be able to get out quicker."

I just stare at him, like a dumb animal.

He checks his watch. "I have to go. Before the guard returns. And Sabine…"

"*Ja?*"

"*Ich liebe dich!*" I love you!

215

I nod, speechless. I never knew how he felt about me until now. I don't think I knew how I felt about him either.

He opens the door and peers into the street.

He looks back one more time. "*Auf Wiedersehen*, Sabine!" Then he runs.

There's nothing I can do to stop him. I stand by the doorway, watching, urging him on.

He's across the street in no time, then he launches himself into the air and grabs the top of the Wall with both hands. His feet scrabble at the concrete blocks as he tries to haul himself over the top. His shoes make a scraping noise against the rough surface. I pray the guard dog won't hear. He's going to have to squeeze himself between the lines of barbed wire on top of the Wall.

Go on! I shout silently, mouthing the words at him. *Go on! You can do it!*

He manages to get his elbows onto the top of the Wall and then he swings his right foot up so that he's almost horizontal. If he can just flatten the lowest strip of barbed wire with his foot then he might be able to squeeze through. *Do it!* I yell at him, but of course no sound comes from my mouth.

Suddenly there's frenzied barking. Then a shout. The wretched dog I saw earlier runs down the street, barking like a mad thing, all sharp teeth and drooling saliva. Running behind the dog, struggling to keep up with it, is its handler. More guards are leaving their post at the checkpoint to follow.

"Stop!" The guard's voice rasps through the night air. He is still about fifty metres away, but he has a clear view of what Hans is doing.

"Stop or I shoot!" The guard raises his right arm and fires a warning shot into the sky. But at the same time a series of fireworks explodes on the other side of the Wall and the gunshot is lost amongst the bangs and explosions.

"Stop!" The guard shouts the command a third time.

Hans pays no attention. His right leg is pressing down on the barbed wire. He's trying to squeeze his upper body through the gap. His left leg is still dangling on this side of the Wall. The dog jumps up, trying to bite Hans on the ankle. Hans kicks the animal away.

The guard has walked forwards and is now standing directly between me and Hans. He positions his feet squarely on the ground, raises his right arm, supports his right wrist with his left hand and aims the gun at Hans. The dog returns to the guard and stands motionless at his side, ears pricked, its breath misting in the cold night air. The guard takes a deep breath and pulls the trigger.

It's as if time slows down. The steel bullet slices through the swirling snowflakes, splitting the air molecules. It hits its target and in the flash of a brilliant white rocket, a shower of red sprays out against the snow.

Hans balances for a moment on top of the Wall, face frozen in astonishment. His body jerks, then he tumbles to the ground. He's still in the East.

I feel as if someone has launched a hand grenade into my chest. I turn from the door and throw up over the floor of the deserted building. My head is spinning, my ears are ringing and I keep retching until my throat burns and I can't breathe. I stagger to the wall, thinking I'm going to faint.

After a moment, when I realise I'm still conscious, I creep back to the door, open it a crack and peer outside.

Five guards are now standing in the middle of the street looking at Hans who is lying on the ground, curled on his side. No one approaches him. No one touches him. No one goes to see if he is dead or alive.

I want to run to him, help him, but if I do the guards will shoot me without a second thought. They'll think I was planning to escape with him.

Then something unexpected happens. Faces appear on the other side of the Wall. People in West Berlin must have heard the shots. They must be standing on something, maybe chairs from the nearby café, in order to see over the Wall. Their faces reveal shock, horror, disgust. And anger.

Then I hear a sound like an animal caught in a trap, a moaning and choking noise. It's Hans! He's still alive. He's lying on his side, curled on the ground and he's making a dreadful high-pitched wailing noise. He's calling for help.

The West Berliners shout at the guards.

"He's alive!"

"Fetch help!"

"Take him to hospital, you fucking idiots!"

One of the Westerners, a man who looks like he's had a fair bit to drink, tries to climb over the Wall into the East.

Two of the guards point their guns at him. "Get back! You are breaching the national border of the German Democratic Republic."

He points a finger at the guards. "Commie bastards!"

The guards prepare to fire. Someone else on the Western side pulls the drunken man back and he disappears from view.

The other onlookers continue shouting at the guards, telling them to fetch help. But none of the guards does anything. Instead they stand around, looking at Hans and shrugging their shoulders. A couple of them walk back to Checkpoint Charlie.

Someone drops something over the Wall, some sort of package. I think it's a first aid kit, but Hans is in no position to use it and the guards refuse to help him.

Instead of dealing with Hans, the guards turn their attention to the crowds leaning over the Wall.

The crowd is becoming even more abusive, shouting insults at the guards.

"Commie arseholes!"

"Stasi pigs!"

"Murderers!"

The guards threaten to shoot if the crowd doesn't go away.

Hans lies forgotten.

As the argument between the guards and the Westerners intensifies, I watch Hans, listening out for his cries, looking out for any sign of movement. The snow is falling on him, settling on him like a veil and I realise that his cries are becoming fainter and fainter. I strain my ears to hear his voice but it is no longer there. He is silent.

I cannot feel my hands or my feet because of the cold. But more than that, I can no longer feel my heart. Something has died inside me.

A senior looking border guard arrives. The others stand to attention as this new arrival takes control of the situation. He orders two of the junior guards to pick up Hans' body and carry him away. As they lift him up, Hans' right arm hangs limp and lifeless.

My legs won't hold me up any longer. I slide to the floor and sit, sobbing in the hallway. I am dead.

Dieter

The kitchen door flies open and crashes into the wall. Claudia is standing in the doorway, clutching a newspaper in her trembling hand. Tears are rolling down her face.

"Die Arschlöcher!" she shouts.

I jump to my feet and rush over to her. "Whatever's the matter? What's happened?" I went to bed at about three this morning. It's now eight o'clock and far too early for crashing doors and hysterics.

I lead her to the table. "Coffee please Werner. And make it strong."

"Coming right up," says Werner, trying to sound cheerful, but looking at me in alarm.

"Now tell me what's happened," I say to her.

She slams the newspaper down on the kitchen table and points to the front page. "Look at this!"

The headline, printed in large, bold letters, is *"Tot!"* Dead!

"He didn't stand a chance!" She spits the words out.

"Who didn't?" asks Werner, placing the mug of hot coffee on the table in front of her.

Claudia's chest heaves with sobs.

I put my hand on her arm. "Just take a deep breath and tell us."

She nods her head. "There was a shooting. Last night. At midnight."

Midnight, I think. I was so happy last night at midnight. But in another part of the city someone was being shot.

"Where was it?"

"At the Wall," Claudia says. She's more in control of herself now. "Near Checkpoint Charlie. A teenage boy. Just a kid. He made a run for it. Nearly got over too. But they gunned him down and he fell."

"*Scheisse!*" I say, taking hold of her hands. They are still trembling.

I glance at the picture on the front of the paper. It must have been taken by someone in the West, looking over the Wall. There's a figure lying on the ground, curled up on his side. In the background, a group of border guards are just standing there, like dummies.

This is nothing but cold-blooded murder and I can see why Claudia is so upset. I'm upset too, but it makes me want the tunnel to succeed even more.

I turn her face to look at me. "Listen," I say, "that's why we're doing this. That's why we have to keep digging the tunnel. We mustn't give up. That's why we have to get our friends and family out of East Berlin."

She looks at me, blinking away the tears. "I know. I know."

Sabine

I wake up. I'm back home in my own bed. For a split second I feel safe. And then the events of last night come rushing back to me: Hans, holding me in his arms, kissing me, running towards the Wall and then…I cry out at the awfulness of the memory. The door opens and Brigitta appears.

She runs over and hugs me tight. I hug her back. I don't ever want to let her go.

"I've been waiting for you to wake up," she says at last, pulling away from me and giving me a searching look.

"Thank you," I nod. I have a vague memory of returning home in a state of shock and screaming my head off for an hour or so.

"We gave you something to help you sleep," says Brigitta, pointing at a bottle on the chest of drawers.

"I see." My mouth is dry and I have a splitting headache. I'm not sure how coherent I was last night, so I ask Brigitta, "Did I explain what happened?"

Brigitta nods. "I'm so sorry."

I can feel the hot tears welling up in my eyes.

Brigitta leans forwards and whispers. "You've got a visitor."

"Who?" My first thought is that I was spotted last night near the scene and the Stasi have come after me.

"It's Astrid. She's heard the news."

"Oh." I'm surprised Astrid's heard about it so quickly but I suppose these things travel fast. She'll be worried about me, knowing how fond I was of Hans. I touch my fingers to my lips. Our first kiss. If only it hadn't been our last.

I ease myself out of bed. "I'd like to see Astrid. It will do me good." I throw on some clothes and go to the living room where Astrid is sitting, reading a copy of *Neues Deutschland.*

As soon as she sees me she lays the newspaper aside and rushes over, throwing her arms around me.

"Sabine, you poor thing. I'm so sorry about what happened to Hans."

She's smothering me and I can't talk for the moment.

"Here, drink this," she says, passing me a mug of tea. "Brigitta made it for me, but I hardly touched it."

I gulp the tea down. "Shall we go for a walk?" I say. I feel like I need some fresh air.

"Of course, if you'd like to," says Astrid picking up her newspaper and folding it under her arm.

I fetch my coat and we walk down the stairs and out into the street. Last night's snow has settled on the ground, covering the city in a sparkling layer of white, hiding the blood stains. I thrust my hands inside my coat pockets. I didn't think to bring a scarf.

We set off down *Stargarder Strasse* but I don't want to walk past Hans' building so I cross over and turn down *Pappelallee*. I lead the way, Astrid follows. Neither of us says anything.

Eventually we come to the small park with the nineteenth-century water tower, where Hans outlined his escape plans to me. I can still picture us both, sitting on the grass. There's an old wooden bench by the path. I'm too weary to walk any further so I wipe the snow off with my sleeve and sit down. Astrid perches on the edge of the bench, watching me with a worried expression on her face. I know she's waiting for me to speak.

"If only I could have stopped him," I say. This is the thought that has been nagging at me ever since I woke up. I should have done more.

"*Ach*, Sabine," she says coming closer and putting an arm around me. "You mustn't blame yourself for what happened."

I shake my head. "I tried to persuade him not to do it, but he couldn't wait."

"Well, why would he wait? He wanted to escape and no one else was going to help him."

"That's not true," I blurt out.

"What's not true?" asks Astrid looking puzzled.

I've said more than I intended to. I bite my lip.

"What's not true?" asks Astrid again.

"It's not true that no one was prepared to help Hans escape."

"Hang on," says Astrid, "that's too many double negatives. Are you saying Hans knew someone who could help him get out?"

I stare down at my feet and nod my head. What does it matter now?

"But who?" asks Astrid. I can hear the astonishment in her voice.

"Me." My voice sounds small and pathetic in this empty place.

"No kidding! But how?"

There's nothing for it, so I tell her about Dieter and the tunnel. I don't tell her where it is because I'm not entirely sure myself.

"That's amazing," says Astrid staring at me with her mouth open. "Just imagine digging a tunnel all the way under the border. Like real adventurers."

I feel she's taking the whole thing rather lightly. "They're taking a huge risk," I say. "It's not some game. If they get caught they'll go to prison."

"Of course," she says. "Still amazing though. It's very brave of Dieter. So why didn't Hans just wait for the tunnel to be ready?"

I shrug. "Lots of reasons." I haven't got the energy to explain to Astrid about the problem with the identity papers and Hans' fears that the Stasi were onto him. Fortunately Astrid doesn't press me for more details. She seems lost in thought.

A few flakes of snow start to fall. I think of Hans, running towards the Wall, jumping up to it, almost making it over the top and then lying at the bottom, shot and dying. I wonder if his mother has heard what happened. I feel so sorry for her. I promise myself that when I make it to West Berlin,

I'll find out where she is and go and see her. I want her to know that Hans died fighting.

Dieter

I go into the kitchen to grab something to eat before I start my digging shift and find Harry sitting at the table, drinking coffee with a man I've never seen before. Even though the stranger is sitting down I can see that he's tall. He's also very blond – the perfect example of a Teutonic male. There's a black, leather holdall on the floor at his feet.

"Dieter," says Harry, "this is Rolf."

Rolf stands up and comes over to shake my hand, all but crushing my fingers in his firm grip. "Pleased to meet you, Dieter."

"Hi," I say. I find myself a bit intimidated by his blue eyes which have a way of boring into me. I extract my hand from his. We've done our best to keep the tunnel project secret, so I'm wary about this newcomer. Harry, on the other hand, seems perfectly relaxed. Maybe they're old friends.

"Rolf was just telling me about his girlfriend who lives in *Prenzlauer Berg*," says Harry. "He's desperate to get her out of East Berlin. He wants to help with the tunnel."

"Really?" I ask, spooning a heaped teaspoon of coffee into the least dirty mug I can find. There's no denying another pair of hands would come in useful, but how do we know we can trust this guy?

As if he was reading my thoughts, Rolf turns to me and says, "I know I must look a bit suspicious, turning up here like this. But, believe me, I just want to get my girlfriend out of East Berlin. There's no future for her there. The Stasi are pigs."

"So how did you hear about us?" I ask.

"Oh, you know," he shrugs, "I've seen Harry around the place. You can't miss him really, can you? I got chatting to him in a bar the other night. I thought, someone like him must be involved with a group helping people escape and it turns out I was right."

Damn you, Harry, I think, *always swanning around in your American greatcoat. No wonder people notice you.*

I don't really have much choice but to accept Rolf's story. The fact is, he's here now and he knows we're building a tunnel, so we might as well make use of him, see what he's made of.

Harry finishes his coffee and stands up. "Maybe you could take Rolf down to the basement and show him the ropes? And whilst you're doing that, I've got something for your lovely sister." He tucks a white envelope inside his coat. "Off into the lion's den once more. I hope I bump into Sabine this time. It's boring just leaving envelopes in the post box."

I ignore his comments about Sabine. For a while after his panic attack in the tunnel Harry was unnaturally subdued but recently he's been back to his ebullient self. If anything his mood grows more exuberant with every centimetre the tunnel progresses. The last few days he's been exploring the area around *Schönholzer Strasse*, working out how he's going to get the escapees into the house. He told us last night he's found a café on *Ruppiner Strasse* where they can all gather. The plan is for him to be the courier, go into the café and give a secret sign to indicate that it's safe for people to make their way to the house on *Schönholzer Strasse*.

He checks he's got his American passport. *"Bis bald!"* he says slapping me on the back. See you soon!

As soon as Harry has gone, Rolf stands up, rubbing his enormous hands together. "Are you ready to show me the tunnel?" he asks.

Sabine

It occurs to me that I still have the key to Hans' apartment. I find it hiding in the corner of my coat pocket. Frau Winkler didn't want it back. I sit at the kitchen table for more than an hour, turning the key over between my finger and thumb, trying to decide what to do. I don't know if I'll be running a huge risk going back there, but in the end I decide I will.

I tell Mother and Brigitta that I'm just popping out for a bit of air, then I trudge through the snow to Hans' building. My biggest fear is that I'll run into the Stasi. They must have identified Hans' body by now and will have visited his apartment, expecting to find his mother. If there are Stasi men around, I'll have to feign surprise that Hans is not at home.

I climb the stairs to Hans' apartment and knock on the door, just in case. To my relief there is no sound from within, so I slip the key into the lock, open the door and go inside. The familiar smell of beeswax greets me and a hundred memories of Hans come rushing into my mind's eye. I lean against the door for a moment, screwing my eyes tight shut, unable to move. Then I remember that the Stasi could appear at any moment and I pull myself together, telling myself to get a move on.

I walk, shakily, into the living room. I can imagine Frau Fischer sitting in her chair, reading the newspaper. I want to find something to take to her in West Berlin. I look around the room and catch sight of the photographs of Hans and his father on the small table by the side of her favourite reading chair.

I go over to the table and pick up the picture of Hans. He grins back at me and I think my heart is going to break. His seventeenth birthday. I remember that day, back in June. We went to the cinema and saw some terrible film, but we still had fun.

Outside in the street a car door slams, making me jump. I have to get out of here. I hide the photograph of Hans and the one of his father in my coat pocket and head for the door.

On my way down the stairs I encounter two men in raincoats going up. I'm already on the second landing, so they can't know where I've just come from. I stare straight ahead, pretending not to mind them. They will be going to Hans' apartment to look for signs that he was in league with other potential escapees or groups in the West. I feel inordinately happy that I managed to retrieve the photographs before the Stasi got their dirty hands on them.

As I walk home, I feel a mixture of grief for Hans but also hope for the future. I keep trying to imagine how long the tunnel is and what it will be like crawling through it. When I reach our building I check the post box in the entrance hall. I haven't heard from Harry for a while. I'm excited when I see a white envelope just visible in the slot at the top.

I open the post box and take out the envelope. It's from Harry all right. I'd recognise that handwriting anywhere by now. I'm so lost in my own thoughts that I don't hear the footsteps until they are right behind me. I turn with a start to find Frau Lange close by. She is peering with undisguised interest at the envelope in my hand. I clutch it to my chest so she can't see the handwriting on it.

"*Guten Tag*, Frau Lange," I say. My voice sounds strained.

She makes a pretence of peering into her own post box.

"*Guten Tag*," she says as she walks past me, still staring at the letter in my trembling hand.

Dieter

By the afternoon, Andreas and Rolf are going great guns at the tunnel face. Werner calls me and Claudia over for an update meeting.

"It's nearly time to start digging up to the surface," says Werner. "The horizontal tunnel is now almost one hundred and ten metres long. If we dig for another couple of metres, then dig upwards at a thirty degree angle we should emerge in the basement of number seventeen *Schönholzer Strasse.*"

Werner seems confident, but I just hope his maths is right. The last thing we need after all this digging is to miss our target. I think back to geometry lessons in school where the worst that could happen, if you miscalculated an angle, was a cross in red ink. There were never any life and death consequences. If we get this wrong we could find ourselves tunnelling up under the feet of an East German border guard.

"Rolf is doing a great job," says Claudia. "We wouldn't have made such good progress today without him."

Although it pains me to admit it, Rolf does appear to have been a godsend to the team. He shifted a tonne of earth this morning and is handy at shoring up the sides and roof as he goes. He spent the lunch break telling us about his girlfriend in East Berlin and how much he misses her. I thought he might be tired after the hours he put in this morning, but he was keener than anyone to get back to work.

After months of digging, every pair of trousers I have with me is ripped so I think, with Rolf on board, this is a good opportunity to go back to *Kreuzberg* and pick up some more clothes. I tell Werner and Claudia I won't be long, then I slip out and head back to the apartment I used to share with Bernd and where I left most of my stuff.

It feels strange being back in *Kreuzberg* after months of being holed up in the bakery and most of that time underground in a narrow tunnel. The streets are bustling with people going about their daily business but I find myself wondering what's going on under their feet. I'm sure we can't be the only people digging a tunnel.

I reach the apartment and let myself in. It must be Bernd's day off because he's in the kitchen making breakfast. It's three o'clock in the afternoon. He's still in his pyjamas.

"Hey, Dieter," he says, looking up from a table strewn with unwashed plates and dishes. "How are things?"

"Great, thanks," I say, wondering how I could have shared an apartment with such a slob. "And you? Still busy at the hotel?"

He nods his head. "Same as ever. Herr Pohl is still trying to recruit more staff to replace the ones we lost from East Berlin. Want a coffee?"

I look at the pile of unwashed mugs by the sink. "No thanks. I just came to pick up a few things." I head towards my old room.

Bernd follows me and stands in the doorway

munching on a bread roll whilst I rummage in my wardrobe, pulling out old pairs of jeans.

Bernd mumbles something but his mouth is so full of bread I can't understand what he's saying.

"What was that?" I ask.

"I said, did your old school friend track you down?"

"What old school friend?"

Bernd is already chewing another mouthful and I have to wait for him to finish before he can speak.

"This guy came calling the other day," says Bernd. "Said he was an old school friend of yours."

I stop what I'm doing and look at Bernd. "How did he know to come here?"

"He got the address of this place from Herr Pohl at the hotel."

I can feel the hairs on the back of my neck standing up. I don't like the sound of this. "Did he say what his name was?"

Bernd frowns. "I can't remember."

"Come on," I say, "you must have some idea."

Bernd stares at the ceiling. "Hmmm, I think he said Robert...or Rudolf...or, no wait a minute, it was Rolf. Yes that's it, Rolf. He said you were at school together in *Prenzlauer Berg*. He was so disappointed when I said you weren't here that I told him where to find you."

"You *what?*"

"What's the matter? I thought you'd be pleased. I..."

"You fucking idiot!"

I throw the jeans aside, push past Bernd and hurry out of the apartment. Then I run towards the nearest *U-bahn* station. Rolf isn't someone who wants to get his girlfriend out of East Berlin. He's a spy.

Sabine

I take the envelope to my bedroom and open it with trembling hands. Frau Lange always unnerves me. Inside the envelope is a folded piece of paper which I take out and read. It's a short note which looks as if it was scribbled down in a hurry. It gives the name of a café, *Gasthof zur schwarzen Katze*, The Black Cat, in *Ruppiner Strasse* where everyone is to meet on the evening of the escape. The date of the escape is still to be confirmed, but, says the letter, it won't be long now. Then, if everything goes according to plan, we'll be free: free from Stasi surveillance, free from the risk of being locked up on suspicion of being an Enemy of the State, free to travel anywhere in the world. I can hardly imagine what that will be like.

I must inform my list of contacts of the meeting point and tell them to get ready.

I no longer have my notebook in which to hide the letter. In any case, I know I mustn't keep the letter longer than necessary. I commit the name and location of the café to memory and then throw the letter into the *Kachelofen*. I can't afford to take any more chances, not now the tunnel is almost finished.

Dieter

The tunnel is almost finished and now this has happened! What a fucking disaster. My only hope is that Andreas is still working Rolf hard at the tunnel face. If Rolf has been allowed to take a break then he could have informed the whole of the East German Politburo of our plans by now.

I sprint up *Bernauer Strasse* feeling as if my lungs are about to burst. When I reach the bakery I nearly go down to the cellar but change my mind and run up the stairs to the kitchen. The black, leather holdall is still by the table where Rolf left it. I yank open the zip and start pulling out items of clothing. Rolf has certainly come prepared to stay a long time – there are dozens of pairs of socks and underwear. Then at the bottom of the bag my hand touches something different. It's a leather book. I pull it out and recognise it immediately. It's Sabine's notebook. I turn to the page where she wrote down the number of the *Hotel Zoo* and find that the number has been circled in red ink. In the margin an unfamiliar hand has written, *traitor's brother.* That's how Rolf tracked me down to the hotel and then Herr Pohl, still worrying about his staff shortages no doubt, didn't think twice about giving Rolf my address in *Kreuzberg.* Bernd, of course, is an idiot.

I throw the book aside and head to the cellar. Werner, Andreas and Rolf are climbing out of the vertical shaft just as I open the cellar door. Claudia is standing at the foot of the stairs with a full bucket of rubble in each hand.

"You did a good shift there," says Andreas, slapping Rolf on the back.

"Oh, don't mention it," says Rolf, all cheery smiles. Then he turns to Werner and asks, almost casually, "When is the escape planned for?"

Before Werner has a chance to answer I hurtle down the cellar stairs, almost knocking Claudia over, and punch Rolf as hard as I can in the face.

Rolf staggers backwards, blood pouring from his nose. Claudia screams. The back of my hand stings.

"Dieter!" shouts Werner. "Have you lost your mind?"

Claudia drops the buckets and runs over to Rolf, always keen to help the wounded.

"Leave him!" I shout. "He's a spy."

Everyone looks at me in stunned silence. "What are you talking about?" asks Claudia. "He was working really hard this morning." She pulls a bunch of tissues from her pocket and starts dabbing Rolf's nose.

"He's not who he says he is," I say, nursing my knuckles which are smeared with blood. "He's going to betray us to the Stasi."

"That's nonsense," says Rolf, getting to his feet. "Look, I understand you're nervous about letting new people in at this stage in the project. It must be a tense time for you, being so close to finishing and all that. I forgive you. Let's shake hands on it." He holds out a hand covered in dirt from the tunnel.

"You're lying," I say. "Otherwise, how do you explain that you have my sister's notebook in your bag upstairs and you tracked me down by going to the hotel and then to my old apartment?"

"Is this true?" asks Werner.

Rolf doesn't answer but makes a run towards the steps.

"Catch him," I shout. "Don't let him out or he'll betray us."

Andreas is on him like a rocket propelled grenade. He grabs hold of Rolf's legs and brings him crashing down on the cellar floor but Rolf kicks him in the groin and Andreas rolls over, squealing. Rolf makes it to the steps but Claudia grabs one of the loaded buckets she was carrying earlier.

She runs after him. "Take that!" she cries, swinging the heavy bucket into Rolf's back. He falls forward onto the steps.

"Grab him!" I shout to Werner. We each take

hold of an arm and pin him down flat. Even though there are two of us holding him down, it's like trying to wrestle a crocodile. I'm worried that he'll break free of our grasp when Andreas hobbles over and whacks him on the back of the head with a sledgehammer. Rolf is out cold.

For a moment we are all too stunned to speak.

Rolf starts to groan and tries to move. I place my right foot on his back to prevent him getting up.

"What are we going to do with him?" asks Claudia.

I realise with some trepidation that the others are waiting for me to speak. At this precise moment I have become the one in charge.

"We're going to have to lock him up," I say. "Until we've got our friends and family out of East Berlin. We won't treat him badly, but we can't afford to let him go. Not now, when we're so close."

Sabine

I decide to visit everyone that very afternoon. I take the *U-bahn* to *Cottbusser Platz* and then walk the short distance to Marion Weber's block of flats where I drop a note into her post box. Then I travel to *Pankow-Heinersdorf* where I find Ingrid at home reading a story to her niece and nephew. She looks relieved to see me again.

In the evening I go to the *Theater am Schiffbauerdamm* where I slip, unnoticed, into the stage entrance and take a note directly to Manfred Heilmann in his dressing room. He is now appearing in a production of Brecht's *Caucasian Chalk Circle*, another play that satisfies the aesthetic and dramatic criteria of the Communist Party. He offers me a couple of tickets for tomorrow night but I decline his kind offer.

I take the S-bahn back to *Schönhauser Allee*. I'm looking forward to spending the evening at home with Brigitta and Mother. As I walk down *Stargarder Strasse* I become aware of the sound of a car engine behind me. I don't look back but increase my pace a little. The engine gets louder, the car is accelerating. I'm almost at the entrance to our building when a pale green Wartburg pulls up in front of me, its front wheel rising up onto the pavement. Two men jump out. I recognise them immediately.

8 PRISONER

Sabine

There's nowhere for me to hide. I'm less than ten metres from the door to my building, but I can't reach it.

Herr Stein and his driver are walking towards me, Herr Stein tall and upright, the driver short and stocky. Herr Stein is smiling to himself. He knows he's got me.

"*Guten Tag*, Fräulein Neumann," says Herr Stein. "We have a few questions we need to ask you."

"What about?" I say trying to sound defiant but just sounding scared.

"If you could step this way." During this exchange with Herr Stein the driver has come up beside me and taken hold of my arm. He's gripping it so tightly it hurts.

I fall silent, knowing that arguing won't help. The driver steers me towards the car. Herr Stein opens the rear door and the driver pushes me inside so that I fall onto the back seat. The door slams.

The two men jump into the front and the driver starts the engine. As we pull away from the curb I turn my head to look back at the building. Frau Lange is standing in the doorway, arms folded, watching.

I slump back in the seat and stare at my hands which are trembling. I ball my hands into fists to stop them shaking, the fingernails digging hard into my palms. I can't believe what's just happened. This is a disaster. The tunnel will be ready in a matter of days and here I am, arrested in broad daylight, being driven away. The only witness to my predicament is Frau Lange and I don't expect her to make a friendly call on Mother and Brigitta and pass on the news.

I stare, stupefied, out of the window as first *Dimitroffstrasse*, then *Frankfurter Allee* blur past. This time I know where they are taking me – back to Stasi HQ at *Normannenstrasse*.

The car pulls up outside the familiar complex of buildings which I had hoped never to see again. Herr Stein takes me inside and leads me to an interrogation room.

"Sit down," he says, indicating the chair in front of the desk.

I feel the anger rising up inside me. I want to pick up the cheap wooden chair and hurl it at the wall.

"Sit!" repeats Herr Stein.

There is no cloth on the chair this time. There's no need for it. They have already captured my scent should they need to track me down with a sniffer dog. I sit.

I stiffen at the sound of short, sharp footsteps in the corridor. Frau Biedermeier appears. She is even more heavily made up than last time, her eyebrows arching to ever greater heights, her lips a more vicious shade of red. I would have preferred anyone but her. The last time I was here I annoyed her by not agreeing to become an informer for the Stasi. She is not paid to forget things like that.

Frau Biedermeier takes her place at the desk, opposite me. I can hear the blood pumping in my ears. She presses the record button on the tape recorder, then fires her first statement. It's not a question.

"*Fräulein* Neumann, you are associated with a West Berlin terrorist organisation."

A what? I'm tempted to say she must have the wrong person, but I can see from the look on her face she is deadly serious. She stares at me waiting for a response.

"I'm sorry," I say. "I don't know what you are talking about."

Frau Biedermeier is not impressed. "Come on, you can do better than that. You know how long these things take if you don't co-operate. Does the name Harry Hofmann mean anything to you?"

Oh God, I think, *don't tell me she knows about Harry. I must deny all knowledge of him.*

"Well?" she says. "Do you know Harry Hofmann?"

"No."

"Have you ever met this man?"

"No"

"Have you ever received letters from this man?"

"No."

"What if I told you that Harry has been arrested?"

"I don't know who he is." My head is in a whirl. Harry arrested? Surely not? But if it's true, what is happening to the tunnel project? I only received his last letter this morning. Frau Lange saw me taking it from our post box. Did she also see him putting it there? Did she contact the Stasi? It's possible. The thought makes me go cold. Frau Biedermeier has asked me another question but I didn't hear it.

"I'm sorry," I say. "What was that?" I must try to concentrate harder or she'll realise I'm worried about something. She repeats her question.

"Have you ever tried to escape from the German Democratic Republic?"

"Of course not." It's a bare-faced lie but I do my best to brazen it out, forcing myself to look her straight in the eye. She looks away first, looking at her list of questions and I experience a tiny victory.

"Where is your brother, Dieter?" My moment of victory vanishes. What do I tell her? I decide she probably already knows where Dieter is so there is no point in lying.

"He's in West Berlin."

"Exactly." She looks pleased with herself. "And he is working with Harry Hofmann." It's a statement, not a question.

"I don't know," I say, trying to bluff my way out. I feel as if she is drawing me into a trap and I have to tread very carefully at each step otherwise she'll eat me alive.

"What can you tell us about a tunnel that is being built from West Berlin into the capital of the German Democratic Republic?"

My heart skips a beat. She knows about the tunnel. If they really have captured Harry as she claims, has he talked? Has he cracked under pressure and told them everything? He always seemed so strong and resourceful, I find it hard to believe that he would have told them anything, but who knows what trials they have put him through? I have no option but to carry on with my statements of denial.

"I don't know anything about a tunnel."

She glances at her list of questions. "You listen to Fascist radio which denigrates the socialist society of the German Democratic Republic." I was expecting her to pursue the tunnel question, so her statement about the radio takes me by surprise. I think she means the RIAS channel, Radio in the American Sector, which we listen to. Only Frau Lange could have informed them of this. Unless – and my stomach churns at the thought – they've secretly bugged the apartment and have been listening in to all our private conversations. Beads of perspiration break out on my upper lip and my palms feel clammy. She prompts me to confirm her statement about our radio listening habits.

"You listen to the radio from West Berlin, do you not?"

"Yes," I say in a voice that sounds choked.

"But that is illegal. You know that don't you?"

"Yes."

"So why do you listen to a radio station that is banned in the German Democratic Republic?"

What am I supposed to say? Because East German radio stations are all controlled by the government? Because they broadcast nothing but government propaganda about how well the factories are doing and how the Wall is protecting us from the evil Fascists in the West?

"Well?" she says leaning forward and frowning.

I shrug. "We just enjoy hearing the news from West Berlin."

"Why would you be interested in the news from West Berlin if you weren't intending to illegally leave the GDR?"

I stare at her blankly.

"*Fräulein* Neumann, are you in contact with a West Berlin terrorist organisation, yes or no?" She has returned to her opening line.

I can see we are going to go round in circles like this for hours. My mouth is dry and I can feel the beginnings of a pounding headache. Outside the light is fading to dusk.

After another round of questioning in which I do my best to give all the same answers as the first time, Frau Biedermeier presses her fingertips together, looks at me as if she's thinking hard about something and then appears to come to a decision. She presses one of the buttons on her telephone machine and waits.

Moments later the door opens and two guards appear.

"Take her away," says Frau Biedermeier.

The guards each take hold of an arm and drag me to my feet.

"Where am I going?" I ask.

"That is not for you to know," says Frau Biedermeier coldly.

Dieter

Rolf is locked in a storeroom in the bakery and Andreas is standing guard outside the door. Werner calls a crisis meeting with me and Claudia.

"How the hell did Rolf find us?" he asks.

I explain to them how Rolf tracked me down using the number of the hotel which was written in Sabine's notebook.

"But how did he have her notebook?" asks Claudia.

"I don't know," I say, "but it looks as if the Stasi must be on to Sabine for some reason, I can't think what." I feel nauseous at the thought of the Stasi invading my family's privacy. And what if they found the letters that Harry has been leaving for Sabine? I just hope she had the sense to destroy them.

"This is *Scheisse!*" mutters Werner. "We're so close to finishing the tunnel and now the damn Stasi have infiltrated us."

"Rolf swears he hasn't passed on any information yet," I say. I helped Andreas carry him to the storeroom and all the time Rolf insisted that he'd come straight here after speaking to Bernd. "He's adamant that his bosses in the East don't yet know the location of the tunnel."

"We can't trust him though," says Werner. "If we let him out he'll go straight back to East Berlin and tell them everything. He's got to stay where he is for the time being."

"And what do we do now?" I ask.

"We carry on digging," says Claudia. "What else can we do?"

So Werner and I return to the tunnel face and Claudia does her best removing the buckets of rubble. But we're dispirited and progress is slow. By the evening we've only dug another half a metre.

It's only then that we realise Harry hasn't returned from East Berlin.

Sabine

The guards march me out of the interrogation room. They are both armed with rifles. They take me outside. A van is parked nearby. I'm surprised to see it here at this time of the night because from the writing on the side I can see it's a bread delivery van. We go towards the vehicle and I wonder what is happening when the guards suddenly lift me up and push me through an open door in the side of the van.

It's dark in the van but there's just enough light from outside for me to see that this is no bread delivery vehicle. It has a narrow corridor down the middle and five tiny cells, three on one side, two on the other, each with its own door. Two of the doors are bolted shut. The guards shove me inside one of the empty cells and force me down onto a narrow wooden bench. There isn't room to stand up. They slam the door shut and bolt it on the outside. I'm in pitch blackness.

"*Nein!*" I scream, slamming my hands against the cell door.

"Be quiet!" shouts one of the guards.

I cower in my cell, too scared to move. Where the hell are they taking me? And who was in the other cells? I wonder if one of them is Harry.

Orders are shouted. Then the rear door of the van is slammed shut and the vehicle jerks into life as the engine is turned on. I grip the edge of the bench with my hands and shut my eyes. It's pitch dark in here anyway. The van lurches forward and I'm thrown to the side, banging my head on the metal wall. I have no idea where they are taking me.

After about twenty minutes of jolting and being thrown from side to side every time the van turns a corner we come to a stop. There are more shouts and orders. Then there is a grinding, clanking noise, like the sound of metal gates opening and the van lurches forward once more. The van turns sharply to the left and I put my hands out to try and brace myself. We stop, then the vehicle reverses a short distance. The engine is turned off.

I sit still and listen.

The other cells in the van are opened one at a time and the people in them are taken away.

I hold my breath.

There are footsteps outside my door. The bolt is slid across. Then the door to my cell opens and two pairs of strong hands pull me roughly to my feet. The guards push me out of the van. I try to see where they have brought me, but the van is parked in a loading bay inside a building and I have absolutely no idea what is outside. Somewhere a dog barks.

They take me down a long linoleum-floored corridor. On either side of the corridor are grey-painted, heavy-looking doors at roughly two metre intervals. I am taken to one of these doors. One of the guards opens it and the other pushes me inside. They lock the door behind them.

I am a prisoner.

Dieter

It's gone midnight and Harry still hasn't returned. Something is definitely wrong, I can see it in the faces of Werner and Claudia.

For all that Harry likes to put on a show of bravado and nonchalance, he always comes to tell us he's back safely and boast about his exploits. We're his audience and he seeks our applause. He always laughs, afterwards, at the pedantic checks carried out at Checkpoint Charlie by the po-faced border guards. But what if he crossed once too often for their liking, arousing their suspicions? Did someone follow him to *Stargarder Strasse*? Did someone see him speaking to Sabine? The more I think about it, the more my thoughts run away with me until I'm imagining all sorts of scenarios. How do I know if Sabine's all right? Anything could have happened to her.

"So what happens now?" I ask. I'm sitting at the kitchen table with Werner and Claudia. Werner is compulsively tapping his pencil on the table whilst supposedly going over the plans. His face is drawn in a tight frown and there are dark rings under his eyes. None of us has had much sleep lately. Claudia is staring at a half drunk mug of coffee and chewing her nails.

"We have to assume the worst," says Werner, pushing the plans to one side and throwing the pencil down.

"That he's been arrested and is being questioned by the Stasi?"

Werner nods. "If they've arrested him it's because they suspect him of trying to smuggle people out of East Berlin. It's the only thing they care about – keeping their citizens under lock and key. Rolf's appearance and Harry's disappearance must be connected in some way, but if Rolf's to be believed, the Stasi don't yet know where the tunnel is. No doubt they'll try and extract that information from Harry, but of course he'll deny any knowledge of a tunnel."

"But what will they do to him to try and extract the information, as you put it?" asks Claudia. She is close to tears.

"That, I wouldn't like to say," says Werner. "They're not known for their gentle methods."

"*Scheisse!*" says Claudia turning away.

This is a nightmare. We're so close to digging

through to the other side, so close to achieving our goal, but now everything could founder at the last minute.

I turn to Werner. "What do you suggest we do?"

"I say we keep digging, but take extra care. If the Stasi discover the location of the tunnel they'll swarm over *Bernauer Strasse* and *Schönholzer Strasse* like flies but we'll see them from the roof first."

Claudia turns back to face him, her eyes red and swollen. "Without Harry we don't have anyone who can cross legally into East Berlin through the checkpoints."

"No," says Werner. "From now on, our only access to East Berlin is through the tunnel. Assuming we manage to dig to the other side without being discovered, then one of us will need to go through the tunnel and meet the escapees on the other side."

Sabine

"*Nein!*" I scream, my voice echoing against the hard surfaces of the cell. I bang on the door with my fists, shouting, but no one comes. It's no use. I will stay here until I'm called to an interrogation.

"*Arschlöcher!*"

If they can hear me, they ignore me.

I turn away from the door. They can watch me, through the peephole, whenever they like, and if they see me becoming violent they'll stick me in a padded cell and leave me there to rot. So I take a deep breath and try to pull myself together.

Light is filtering through the glass brick window from the floodlights outside. There's a narrow wooden bench with a blanket, a toilet and sink. Grey paint is peeling off the walls.

I don't know where they have brought me, but it must be somewhere secure and hidden from ordinary people. I think of Matthias and Joachim, the boys who defaced the portraits in Herr Schmidt's classroom, and wonder if they wound up here. Maybe they are still here, shut away from the world.

And what if they never let me out?

My pulse quickens and I find myself gulping for air.

I'll miss the date for the escape to West Berlin.

I have a vision of myself, years from now, locked up and turned into a crazy old woman who can't remember anything. I start to pace the cell.

It's tiny.

I feel like a caged animal.

Stop! I stand still and try to calm myself down.

I focus on my breathing, consciously trying to slow it down. I think of Mother and Brigitta. For their sakes I have to try and stay sane. It's very late and I should try and get some sleep.

I walk over to the bench and tentatively sit on the edge. When no one shouts at me to stand up, I try lying down. It is the most uncomfortable thing I've ever lain on. But I'm dog-tired and need to rest if I'm going to handle any kind of interrogation. I pull the coarse woollen blanket over me and close my eyes, longing for the oblivion of sleep.

*

I am being hauled out of a deep, dark pit.

I try to resist but rough hands have hold of me. They pull me into a sitting position, then to my feet. My eyes blink in the harsh, bright light that has been switched on in the cell. It's still dark outside, not yet morning. I feel shivery and disorientated. The guards march me out of the cell and down corridors which all look the same to me.

They take me to an interrogation room and tell me to sit on a small wooden stool in the corner. The only other furniture in here is a large desk and comfortable chair where my interrogator will sit. I'm so tired I collapse onto the stool and lean forward with my arms on my knees. One of the guards shouts at me to sit up straight. Then the interrogator arrives.

This time it's not Frau Biedermeier. It's an old man, with thin grey hair combed back from his forehead and heavy black-rimmed glasses with lenses that magnify his eyes out of all proportion to the rest of his scrawny face. He smells of stale nicotine. One of the guards addresses him as Herr Schulz. He takes his place in the comfortable chair behind the desk and watches me through his thick lenses. When he opens his mouth to speak to me I see that his teeth are stained yellow and brown.

"Do you like the plays of Bertolt Brecht?" he asks in a voice abrasive from years of over smoking.

His question takes me by surprise. I wasn't expecting a discussion of German culture. I have enough sense of mind to remember that Brecht is popular with the Communist Party so I mumble something positive.

"Then why did you not stay in the theatre to watch the second half of the opening night of *Mutter Courage und ihre Kinder?*"

Ah, so that's what this is about. "I wasn't feeling well that night," I lie. "That's why I had to go home early. I was sorry to miss the second act."

"But you recovered from your illness to return to school on Monday and then take the train to *Biesdorf-Süd* where you met Marion Weber."

Scheisse, I think, *they know everything about me.* "Marion's an old friend," I say. I hope he doesn't start asking me questions about how long I've known her but, whether he believes me or not, he lets the matter drop.

"Talking of old friends," says Herr Schulz, leaning across the desk towards me so that the saggy flesh on his neck is stretched taut, "one of your friends was shot trying to escape across the Wall, isn't that correct?"

My eyes prick with tears at the mention of Hans and there's a lump in my throat. I look down at my hands, refusing to meet his gaze. I want to scream at this horrible man that he has no right to speak of Hans but my voice feels strangled and when I try to say something no sound comes out.

Herr Schulz carries on, regardless. "Never mind Hans Fischer. He's dead and is of no help to our enquiries. But we have reason to believe he was in contact with a group supplying false identities. We believe his mother escaped in this fashion. What do you know about this?"

I shake my head. A tear lands on my lap.

"Fräulein Neumann," persists Herr Schulz, "what do you know about the provision of false identity papers?" His voice has risen in pitch.

I force myself to look at him. "Nothing."

"Then what about a West Berlin terrorist organisation? Are you in contact with such a group?"

"No"

"Do you know Harry Hofmann?"

No."

"Is there a tunnel being dug from West Berlin to the capital of the German Democratic Republic?"

"No." I answer like an automaton.

"What was the nature of the illness that prevented you from staying to watch the second half of *Mutter Courage und ihre Kinder?*" We're back where we started.

I know from experience that these people are indefatigable. That was round one of questioning. Goodness knows how many more rounds there will be. My back aches from sitting on the stool and every so often my head nods forwards. I have to force my eyes to stay open.

Eventually I'm taken back to the cell. I collapse onto the bed in a daze and fall into a disturbed sleep. I dream I'm being chased down a black tunnel. Behind me is a border guard with a gun and a barking dog. At the end of the tunnel Herr Schulz and Frau Biedermeier are waiting to catch me. Hans calls to me. Then I'm falling, tumbling through black space and I hit the ground with a thud.

I wake up.

The light in the cell has come on, piercing my retinas. No one has come into the room so the light must be on an automatic timer. I screw my eyes shut and try to ignore the harsh light from the bare bulb, but then a guard bangs on the door and shouts at me to wake up. It's daytime.

I struggle into a sitting position. My head feels like it's full of bombed out rubble. Outside the window is the faint light of early morning. Breakfast arrives through the hatch in the cell door. It's a bread roll and a cup of water. I don't want them. I have never been more miserable in my life.

Dieter

I don't know if it's because of Harry's

disappearance or the risk from Rolf and the Stasi, but there's a renewed determination amongst the team when I join them in the cellar next morning.

"Be extra vigilant," says Werner to Claudia who is preparing to go up onto the roof. "Report any unusual manoeuvres by the border guards immediately. If you see anyone sniffing around *Schönholzer Strasse*, tell us."

"Will do," says Claudia, running up the cellar steps.

"Right," says Werner, turning to me, "I've sent Thomas out to buy a secure padlock so there's no chance of Rolf escaping from the storeroom. In the meantime, Andreas is guarding him, so it's just you and me in the tunnel this morning."

"That's fine," I say. I'm just relieved Rolf is still under lock and key and I don't feel at all guilty about it. It's not as if he's uncomfortable. He has a mattress and some blankets and enough food and water to keep him going for days. In fact, he's probably getting better food as our prisoner than he did as a citizen in East Berlin so he should think himself lucky.

"Do you want to dig or clear the rubble and shore up the tunnel?" asks Werner.

"I'll dig," I say, picking up a shovel and lowering myself over the edge of the shaft.

I climb down the ladder, jumping the last metre or so and make my way along the tunnel. I've done this journey so often I've got used to walking bent double. I've developed a technique of walking with my knees bent so there is less strain on my back. As I go I check the wooden shoring is holding up and there are no damp patches which would give us cause for concern. The floor has worn smooth with the constant to-ing and fro-ing of boots. I no longer mind the musty smell. The ventilation unit that Werner rigged up is doing its job. Once the tunnel is open at both ends there'll be better circulation of air which will make it safer for the escapees.

I reach the tunnel face and prepare to dig. I've found that lying down on my back and using my legs to push the spade into the earth is the easiest way to dig in this cramped space. In no time at all I've filled half a dozen buckets with soil.

Werner arrives with planks of wood and starts shoring up the newly dug stretch of tunnel. I push the spade into the soil and keep digging. Werner hammers in nails. We don't talk, but I know what he's thinking. The hard physical labour feels good. It helps put out of our minds the fact that Harry still isn't back yet. It feels like we're in control again.

At eleven o'clock we're joined by Thomas and Andreas. Andreas gives us the thumbs up to indicate that Rolf is securely under lock and key. No one is talking down here for fear of being heard by guards in the street above.

By midday we've made such good progress that Werner signals at us to take a break whilst he calculates the distance from the vertical shaft to the tunnel face. Werner has been measuring the tunnel as we've gone along, marking off the distances on the wooden planks used to shore up the roof and sides. He takes his tape measure out of his pocket and gives me the end to hold whilst he walks back down the tunnel to the hundred metre marker, unrolling the tape as he goes. When he comes back there's a huge grin on his face. We've dug one hundred and ten metres in a horizontal line. It's time to start digging upwards towards the surface.

Sabine

I wait for something to happen, but nothing does. I am left in solitary confinement. In the end I eat the bread and drink the water. I need to keep my strength up and it passes the time. Occasionally I hear the clank of a cell door down the corridor opening and closing, the thud of footsteps, the shout of voices. But no one comes to my cell except to bring food – a watery soup at midday and a potato stew in the evening. Only if I lie down to rest does someone bang on the door and tell me to get up. Eventually the lights go out and I take that as a sign that it's time for sleep. I lie down and close my eyes.

I don't know how long I sleep but it's not enough. Before I know it I'm being shaken awake and marched back to the interrogation room. Herr Schulz is already there waiting for me. I'm made to sit down on the stool and we go through the same performance as last night.

He repeats his questions about the Brecht play, about Marion Weber, about false identity papers and, most worryingly of all, about the tunnel.

I can't work out how much he already knows about the tunnel, whether he knows its location or whether he just has a hunch about it. I deny everything. But the lack of sleep is making me angry and depressed. Only when I fall off the stool and collapse onto the floor do they take me back to the cell and throw me onto the bench. I curl up in the foetal position and cry myself to sleep.

Dieter

I hack away at the earth, showering myself in stones and rubble. We're digging upwards at a thirty degree angle. If Werner has got the maths right, we should emerge in the cellar of *Schönholzer Strasse 17*. Even though I haven't had a break for nearly four hours, I keep working with renewed energy, spurred on by the thought of finally reaching the other side.

Werner and Claudia both return with empty buckets. They crouch at the bottom of the slope as I thrust the spade upwards. The blade cuts through the dry, sandy soil and suddenly the earth above me starts to shift.

"Watch out!" whispers Werner.

I press myself into the side of the chute and shield my face with my arms as a clod of earth breaks free from the surface and tumbles down the slope, spraying me in grit and dust. When the earth has settled I open my eyes and peer upwards. I can't believe what I'm seeing. There's a hole, about the size of a man's hand and, above it, empty space.

I look down to where Werner and Claudia are crouched at the bottom of the chute. No one speaks, but I can see the triumph in their eyes.

Werner scrambles up the slope to join me. With our bare hands we widen the hole until I'm able to poke my head through. We've emerged in the corner of a large vaulted cellar with coal bunkers along one wall, a stack of empty wooden crates and a staircase at the far end. There is a row of small barred windows, high up, at street level which let in just enough light to see by. There is no one around.

I lower my head back down and give the thumbs up sign to the others to indicate that all is clear. Then working as quietly as possible, we widen the hole until it is big enough to squeeze through. Werner goes first, then I help Claudia through and I follow last.

It feels strange to have finally made it to the other side, to be standing on enemy territory. We move around silently, taking care to stay away from the windows. We're not safe here in the East and we need to watch every step.

There's a sound outside the barred windows. Boots and voices. We creep into the shadows as two pairs of booted feet march past. Border guards are patrolling the street. They stop for a moment outside our building. I feel sure they must know we are here. I'm all ready to dive back down the tunnel, but then the soldiers move on. We each let out a sigh of relief.

Werner indicates by pointing his finger that he's going to climb the cellar steps and try the door at the top. He leads the way and we tiptoe up behind him. The wooden steps are old and rickety and one of the treads gives a loud warning creak that it's coming to the end of its life. Thankfully the door at the top isn't locked but opens into the entrance hall of the building. If we were in any doubt as to our location, the drab décor and linoleum floor are a sure sign that we are in the East.

We stop and listen for any signs of life. Upstairs a door closes, then there's silence. The building is still inhabited.

"Stay there," whispers Werner. He moves across the hallway towards the door that leads to the street. It's an old, heavy wooden double door with peeling paintwork and a wrought-iron handle. Werner presses down on the handle. It creaks loudly, drawing attention to itself. Werner opens the door a fraction, then closes it again. He gives us a thumbs up sign. The door isn't locked so the escapees will be able to access the building.

Werner hurries back to the cellar door. "We should go now."

Claudia and I both nod. There's nothing more we can do today. We return to the cellar and take some of the wooden crates to conceal the hole in the floor. Then we slip back into the chute, pulling the crates behind us as we go.

When we reach the bakery we're jubilant, even though we haven't rescued anyone yet. We climb the stairs to the kitchen, laughing and talking. I push open the kitchen door and stop dead.

There's a figure sitting on one of the chairs, slumped over the table, beer bottle in hand. At the sound of our voices the figure stirs and looks up.

It's Harry and he's unrecognisable.

Sabine

The light comes on and two guards pull me into a sitting position. Waves of tiredness wash over me. I screw my eyes shut and try to resist the guards but they drag me to my feet. They are not allowing me to sleep for more than two hours at a time.

"Noooo!" I moan. All I want to do is sleep.

One of the guards hits me across the face and I fall backwards, banging my head against the wall. I cry out in pain.

"That's what you get for being disobedient," he shouts at me.

I cower against the wall, covering my head with my arms.

"Get up!" shouts the other guard.

When I don't move they each grab hold of an

arm and pull me back to my feet. My head is spinning and I think I might throw up.

They march me out into the corridor. They're taking me back to the interrogation room. Even in my befuddled state it occurs to me that I never meet any other prisoners in the corridor. How I long to meet one other individual who is in the same position as me, someone with whom I could exchange a look of sympathy. But we are kept isolated from one another, alone and in a state of fear.

We arrive at the interrogation room and one of the guards tells me to sit down on a chair by the desk. *What luxury,* I think, *a chair instead of a stool in the corner.* I wait for Herr Schulz to appear.

I smell the stale nicotine before I see him. He walks into the room and takes his place opposite me. He doesn't look at me and I can't read his expression behind those impenetrable glasses.

I expect him to start with the usual round of questions, but instead he pushes a piece of paper towards me across the desk. My eyes are stinging and I can hardly hold my head up, but straightaway I recognise the words on the paper.

Inoffizielle Mitarbeiter.

He wants me to sign up as an unofficial collaborator.

Dieter

Claudia rushes over to Harry and throws her arms around him. He winces in pain and she pulls away.

"Sorry," she says. "I didn't mean to hurt you."

"What the hell happened?" asked Werner.

"We've been worried sick about you."

Harry looks at us with haunted eyes. He has a bruise on his left cheekbone and a swollen lip. His jaw is covered in stubble and his hair is matted. There's a nasty red welt on the back of his right hand. He doesn't seem to want to talk.

Claudia disappears off to one of the bedrooms and returns with a wad of cotton wool and a bottle of anti-septic lotion. She insists on dabbing it on his cuts and bruises even though he tries to brush her off. I put the kettle on and make us all some extra strong coffee.

The coffee helps loosen Harry's tongue but he still refuses to go into details. "Let me tell you, those guys have got interrogation facilities Hitler would have been proud of. They know how to drive a man to despair so you tell them anything they want to hear. But I didn't tell them anything!"

"That's good," I say. "But why did they arrest you in the first place?"

He shrugs. "Maybe I went through the checkpoint once too often and they got suspicious. First they accused me of being part of a network of Westerners providing false identity papers to their citizens. Then they tried to tell me they'd found the tunnel. I knew they were bluffing, trying to see if I would reveal anything about the tunnel's location. But they couldn't pin anything on me, so in the end they had to let me go. And most importantly I didn't tell them anything."

For a moment he looks triumphant. Then his face clouds over again. "But we've got a massive problem now." He leans forward, his forehead in his hand. "I can't ever go back there. If they catch me there again they'll lock me up and throw away the key. I can't go back and deliver the final instructions to Sabine and I can't act as the courier on the night of the escape. I've screwed everything up. I'm sorry."

We stare at Harry. He's a broken man, his dream of rescuing lots of people in shreds.

"What are you talking about?" I cry. "You haven't screwed anything up. Just because there's no-one who can cross at the checkpoint doesn't mean the game is up. Harry, look at me, we've dug the tunnel! We've made it to the other side. The courier will just have to go through the tunnel."

Harry looks at me with a dazed expression on his face as if he can't quite take in what I'm saying.

"When you came back," I tell him slowly, "we weren't here because we were in *Schönholzer Strasse*. Harry, we're going to rescue our friends and family from East Berlin and we're going to show the East German government that they can't keep their people imprisoned behind the Wall."

For the first time a smile crosses his lips. "Yes!" he says. "Yes! We'll beat those bastards yet."

Sabine

It would be so easy to sign. All I have to do is pick up a pen and write my signature on the bottom of the form. Herr Schulz speaks more gently than he's ever done before. If I sign I can go to sleep for as long as I want; I can be released; I can see my family again; don't I want to see my mother and sister? They must be so worried about me.

He pushes a pen across the desk towards me. It's a silver fountain pen with a shiny nib. It's beautiful. I would love to own such a pen. I want to touch it but my arm feels heavy and is slow to move.

Herr Schulz picks the pen up and places it in my right hand. Then he points to the paper and says, "Be a good girl and just sign here, will you? That's all you have to do."

I look at the pen in my hand, feeling its weight. It's a high quality instrument. It probably writes beautifully, the nib gliding across the paper, the ink flowing smoothly. Then I look at the piece of paper on the desk in front of me. I'm too tired to read everything it says. I see the words *friends and family* and my head starts to spin. I want to see my friends and family again. I want to see Brigitta and Mother and Astrid and…

I try to focus on the words in front of me. I've lost the place where it said *friends and family*. I search the document, looking for those reassuring words. Herr Schulz clears his throat. *Where are those words?*

"Don't worry about reading it all now," says Herr Schulz. "You can do that later. Just sign here." He points to the bottom of the page.

I keep looking for the words I saw a moment ago. Suddenly I see them. And now I see them in context. If I sign this paper I'm agreeing to *Inform on friends and family and report all findings to the Stasi.*

Herr Schulz pushes the paper towards me with one nicotine-stained finger. I look up at his black, heavy framed glasses. The lenses are so thick that his eyes appear distorted. I don't see a human soul behind those glasses. I can feel the pen in my hand. It is no longer a thing of beauty but a thing of evil; an instrument with which I nearly betrayed my friends. I lift my hand, raising it high into the air and throw the pen against the wall. Black ink sprays out splattering Herr Schulz on the top of his head.

A hand hits me from behind so that I fall off the chair and collapse onto the floor.

Dieter

It's time for me to go to East Berlin. I need to deliver the final instructions to Sabine about the date and time of the escape. Then she can pass the information on to the others. We've waited until it's dark outside, but I'm nervous about this mission. I have a letter from Harry hidden in an inside pocket. I'm waiting in the cellar with Werner and Claudia until Andreas, who is on the roof, gives me the all clear.

There's a crackle on the radio equipment and then Andreas' voice comes over the airwaves. "No unusual activity on the other side."

Great, I think, *just the usual border guards with rifles then. Nothing to worry about.*

I'm wearing black trousers and Werner hands me a black sweater which I pull on. I feel like a criminal about to break into someone else's house, but all I'm doing is crossing from one side of the city to the other. It just happens to be illegal and if I'm caught I'll be locked up, possibly even sentenced to death.

Claudia gives me a hug. "Look after yourself," she says.

"Don't worry," I say. "I intend to do just that."

It makes sense for me to do this job because I'm so familiar with the streets between *Schönholzer Strasse*, where the tunnel emerges, and *Stargarder Strasse*, where I grew up. I know all the back streets and which streets are best to avoid because they are busier. But I haven't been there for so long now. Not since the Wall went up. I'm apprehensive. Not just because of the border guards, but because of how the city will have changed.

I clamber down the vertical shaft to the mouth of the tunnel.

"Good luck," calls Werner when I reach the bottom.

I set off down the tunnel.

It takes about five minutes to reach the other end, walking bent over. I wish we could have made the tunnel higher, but we'd still be digging it now if we'd done that. I just hope that all the people who are hoping to come through it have some flexibility in their knees and backs.

I crawl up the slope at the end of the tunnel and push aside the crates that are covering the hole. Then I haul myself up into the cellar and replace the crates, trying not to make any sound.

I dust myself off, then check the street level windows, expecting to see a pair of black boots standing outside. But the street outside the house looks to be deserted. I climb the cellar steps and open the door that leads into the hallway. The building is quiet. I take my chance and slip outside into *Schönholzer Strasse*. To my left, no more than twenty metres away, is the wide avenue of *Brunnenstrasse*. As I stand there a truck carrying soldiers drives down *Brunnenstrasse* on its way to the Wall. I turn and walk quickly in the opposite direction, keeping my head down, and listening all the time for the sound of footsteps behind me.

I keep to the back streets, seeing no one except the occasional old man on his way home from the local *Kneipe*. A Trabant goes past. At the wide junction with *Schönhauser Allee* I wait for a Wartburg to pass before crossing. I resist the urge to run and do my best to appear like any normal, young East Berliner on his way home. But if a Stasi official stops me and asks for my identity card then I'm done for. I hurry up *Pappelallee* and turn onto *Stargarder Strasse*. Within minutes I'm standing outside the building in which I grew up. My home. But it doesn't feel like home any more. It feels like a very dangerous place to be because this is where I'm most likely to be recognised.

I go inside and am struck by how quiet the building is. The Mann family, of course, are no longer here. I start up the stairs, knowing I have to get past Frau Lange's door before she sees me. Herr Schiller, I can trust, but I've never trusted Frau Lange. There is no sound at all coming from Herr Schiller's apartment and I find that strange. He always liked to listen to the radio and fry cabbage, but I haven't got time to worry about that now. I run up the last few stairs to the top floor and knock on the door. I can't wait to see their faces when they see who it is.

The door opens and I find I'm looking at a woman I barely recognise.

Mother's hair has turned almost completely grey and she has dark rings under her eyes. Her mouth is drawn in a tight line and her skin looks pale and haggard.

It takes her a moment to recognise me too.

Then she clasps one hand to her mouth and with the other pulls me into the apartment. She doesn't give me a chance to speak but holds me to her and cries onto my chest.

I can do nothing except stand there and stroke her hair. I look over her shoulder and see Brigitta standing at the end of the corridor watching us. Then she runs forward and throws her arms around my waist. I'm thrilled to see them. *But where is Sabine?*

I disentangle myself from the arms of my mother and younger sister. Brigitta puts her finger to her lips to tell me that we must be quiet. Then she pulls me into the kitchen and turns on the radio very loud. It's an East German news channel. There's still no sign of Sabine.

The three of us sit down at the kitchen table and lean close together so that we can hear ourselves over the sound of the radio. Mother is too upset to talk, so Brigitta explains, "We think the apartment might be bugged so we have to put the radio on to drown out the sound of us talking."

"But why would they bug the apartment for God's sake? And where the hell is Sabine?"

Mother buries her face in her hands.

"We don't know where she is," says Brigitta. "We think she's been arrested by the Stasi."

"What!"

"She was arrested back in September because of some defaced portraits at school. Now we think it might be to do with her role as a contact for the tunnel."

Verdammt! Damn! This is a hammer blow to everything I've worked for over the last few months. The Stasi must have linked Sabine with Harry. Harry was a physical wreck after the Stasi had finished with him. I dread to think what those bastards are doing to Sabine.

Brigitta lays a hand on my arm. She's remarkably calm in the circumstances. "How did you get across the border?" she asks.

"I came through the tunnel," I say. I take Harry's letter from my pocket. "These are the final instructions about when and where to meet. The escape is planned for tomorrow night."

For the first time, Mother looks up. "We're not going anywhere without Sabine."

"Of course not," I say.

Brigitta takes the letter from me. "I'll see to this," she says. "Even if we can't escape, there's no reason why other people shouldn't get the chance."

I can't believe this is my little sister talking.

I wish there was something I could do for Sabine, but it's impossible. I can't make my presence here in East Berlin known. "I have to go back through the tunnel," I say. "There are people waiting for me on the other side. If I don't return they'll think I've been arrested and then the whole tunnel project will fail."

Mother nods. "We understand. And Dieter," she reaches across the table and takes my hand, "we're very, very proud of you."

It's nearly midnight by the time I emerge from the tunnel into the bakery in West Berlin. Werner and Claudia are still in the cellar waiting for me.

They pull me up out of the tunnel and I collapse onto the floor, my head resting on my knees.

"You're back," says Claudia. She sounds happy. "We were getting really worried about you. How did it go?"

I can't talk. I just sit there and shake my head. I should feel happy at the success of my mission but all I can feel is anger and sorrow that Sabine has been arrested. I dug this tunnel for Sabine, Brigitta and Mother, but now it looks like it was all in vain.

9 THE TUNNEL

Sabine

The light comes on and I sit up. My head throbs with pain and I put a hand to my face. The skin around my right eye feels swollen. Then I remember being hit and falling to the floor. I don't know what happened after that. I suppose I was brought back here, to my cell.

I know I have sealed my fate. By refusing to sign up as an informer I will probably spend the rest of my life here. Even though I'm so tired, I am aware of the irony of the situation. I was falsely arrested for defacing the portraits in school. Now I have sprayed ink over a real life Stasi official. Hans would be proud of me.

Outside in the corridor there's a stomping of boots, then a clanking of metal as the bolts are slid across. The door opens and I jump to my feet. Two guards enter and take hold of me. I assume they are taking me back to the interrogation room. But they march me in a different direction. *Mein Gott!* I think, *what torture have they planned for me this time?* Part of me is too tired to care, the other part of me is scared as hell.

To my alarm they take me to the loading area where the bread van which is really a prisoner transporter is parked. At the sight of that vehicle I react like a frightened animal. I shake my head from side to side and try to break free from the guards, shouting and crying, but I'm too weak and they are holding me too tight. They push me inside and I stumble on the steps, falling into the narrow corridor. This time all the cells are empty, their doors standing open.

One of the guards pushes me inside the nearest cell and closes the door on me. I collapse into the dark, airless space and shut my eyes. I'm defeated. The engine starts and I'm driven away, to God knows where.

I must have slept because the next thing I know is, the cell door opens and two pairs of hands haul me to my feet and throw me out of the van onto the hard ground. Then the van drives away.

I stay there, on the ground, stones digging into my palms. I'm waiting for someone to grab me by the arm, haul me to my feet and drag me off for further questioning. But nothing happens.

After a minute I look up and realise that I'm entirely on my own in some back street I don't recognise. It's not yet fully light. The first rays of a grey dawn are seeping through the darkness.

I stagger to my feet and look around. Most of the buildings here are bombed out shells. There's no one around. Slowly, it dawns on me that I have been dumped somewhere, but I am no longer in custody.

I'm so tired, it's tempting to lie down in the dust and fall asleep. But it's also freezing cold, and if I lie down I'll die. Maybe that's what the Stasi were hoping for, but I'm determined they won't get their wish. On shaky legs, I start walking towards the corner of the street. I keep looking to left and right, expecting to see a pale green Wartburg on the main road, or a windowless van, but there's nothing.

I try to work out where I am. There are more apartments and a small factory. I head towards the factory, thinking it must be near to a main road. I turn another corner and find myself on *Dimitroffstrasse*. I know my way home from here. It will be a terribly long walk, and I don't know if I've got the strength to do it. But I don't have any money for a train fare. So I put one foot in front of the other and stare straight ahead, the thought of seeing Mother and Brigitta again the only thing keeping me going.

Dieter

It's happening tonight; this is the culmination of months of digging; this is the day I've been waiting for. But without knowing where Sabine is, the tunnel seems to me a futile waste of effort. If I can't get my family out of East Berlin then I've thrown away months of my life underground. I should have tried to get them false passports. But now Sabine is in custody and it's too late. I've failed them.

The kitchen door opens and Claudia appears. "Hey, are you going to help us finalise the tunnel or are you going to spend the whole day up here moping?"

She looks pointedly at her watch. "It's already ten o'clock. We could really do with your help to get this ladder fixed into place." Werner was saying something this morning about installing a proper ladder in the vertical shaft to make it easier for the escapees to climb out. He also wants to install a slide at the tunnel entrance in *Schönholzer Strasse* to make it quicker and easier for people to enter the tunnel.

"Sorry," I say, "I'm just not up to much today. I'm too worried about Sabine."

Claudia comes over and sits beside me. "I know you are," she says taking my hand. "But there are lots of other people hoping to escape through the tunnel tonight. You have to ask yourself, what would Sabine want you to do right now?"

When Claudia puts it like that, I realise that I've been selfish, wallowing in my own misery. Sabine wouldn't want me to be sitting here doing nothing, she'd want me to be doing everything I can to get as many people out of East Berlin as possible.

"You're right," I say to Claudia. "I should come and help. What do you want me to do first?"

Claudia grins. "Any good with a hammer?"

Sabine

When I reach the apartment building I'm so tired that I almost collapse on the floor of the entrance hall. But the thought of being discovered by Frau Lange gives me the strength I need to drag myself up the stairs. When I reach the fourth floor I use what little strength I have left to bang on the apartment door. There are voices and hurried footsteps from inside. Then the door opens and I fall into the arms of Mother and Brigitta. I can't believe I'm home.

Mother insists on giving me some bread to eat and tea to drink, but I fall asleep at the kitchen table so Brigitta leads me to the bedroom and tucks me into bed.

*

I have strange, disturbing dreams where Frau Biedermeier and Herr Schulz morph into a single being - half witch, half devil. I'm trapped in the top of a tower with no way out. Dieter rides his horse through the forest to rescue me but the Biedermeier-Schulz monster casts a spell and he is turned to stone. Now the tower has become a dungeon and I'll never escape. The dungeon is filling with water and I'm going to drown...I can't breathe...I can't breathe...I can't...

I open my eyes. It takes me a moment to realise I'm not dead. I'm home in bed. Safe.

No, not safe.

Not safe at all. I'll never be safe so long as I continue to remain in this country. The Stasi have my name on file. They have a long list of charges against me. They will never erase those charges. They will never let me go.

And yet I'm here. I don't understand why I was released from the prison. I didn't sign up as an informer like they wanted me to. *So why did they let me go?*

The bedroom door opens and Brigitta walks in.

"You're awake," she says, running over and sitting on the edge of the bed.

I pull myself up to a sitting position. "What time is it?"

"Six o'clock in the evening."

Brigitta passes me a piece of paper. In big letters she has scrawled the words,

TUNNEL ESCAPE TONIGHT. DON'T TALK. APARTMENT MAY BE BUGGED.

I stare at her in astonishment and she nods her

head, grinning and mouthing the word, *tonight*.

The fact that she suspects the apartment of being bugged doesn't surprise me. The Stasi could easily have come in one day when Mother was at work and Brigitta and I were at school. They will have been listening in to every conversation, but since when? There's no point trying to find the bugging devices – there are probably loads of them and they'd soon know if we tried to destroy them. Then they'd arrest the whole lot of us.

I hand the piece of paper back to Brigitta and indicate, with sign language, that she should burn it in the *Kachelofen*. She crumples it up and runs into the living room. Then she comes back to the bedroom.

"Come and have something to eat," she says. "Then maybe we can…" she makes a walking motion with the two fingers of her right hand. I nod. If the apartment is bugged we can't talk here. We'll have to go for a walk if we want to say anything to each other, even though I'm terrified I'll be arrested again if I step outside. But I think of the tunnel and more than ever I'm determined to make it to West Berlin.

I eat a quick meal of bread and cheese, then we walk down *Stargarder Strasse* towards the *Ernst-Thälmann* park. I'm jumpy and I find myself looking out for anything suspicious, but we don't see anything except a few battered Trabants.

Once we're in the park I feel a little calmer. I used to come here to play with Dieter when I was small, it being one of the few bits of green space that wasn't a cemetery. There are benches in the park but I think it's safer to keep walking. There is a woman pushing a pram and a man sitting on a bench reading a newspaper.

"Everything is ready for tonight," says Brigitta under her breath. "I have made all the arrangements with Marion, Ingrid and Manfred."

That is the best news I've heard for a long time. "Well done," I say. I'd like to hear all the details but there isn't time now. We need to keep our conversation brief. But there is one thing I'd like to know.

"What would you have done if I hadn't come back?"

Brigitta doesn't hesitate with her answer. "I'd have made sure the others got out, but I wouldn't have gone without you."

"Listen," I say, turning to face her, "you must promise me one thing."

"What is it?"

"You must promise me that if anything happens to me, like it did before, that you will escape to West Berlin with Mother. Do you understand?"

She frowns. "But I can't go without you, Sabine."

"But if you have to, you should. Do you hear me? Dieter will be there to look after you when you get to the other side. If something goes wrong and I'm…caught, I couldn't bear it knowing that you and Mother are still here when you could have escaped. Will you promise me that you'll go when you get the chance?"

She takes a deep breath. "I promise."

"Thank you."

We do another lap of the park. The man with the newspaper folds it and stands up. Suddenly I want to be back in the relative safety of the apartment. We head home and wait for night to fall.

Dieter

"I'll go to the café and bring everyone to the tunnel," says Claudia.

"But that's the most dangerous job," I say. "You should let me do that."

"And what makes you think you'd be any better at it than me?"

"I'm not saying that, I'm just saying I don't want you taking such a big risk."

"You men!" says Claudia turning away in frustration and going to stare out of the kitchen window. We've been arguing about who should do what for the last twenty minutes.

"I think Claudia's right," says Harry. "She's unknown to the East Germans. They're less likely to suspect a woman. She can slip quickly from the house to the café. They won't give her a second glance."

"Thank you," says Claudia to Harry. She gives me a told-you-so look.

I'm cross that Harry has taken her side on this. It should have been Harry's job to bring the escapees to the house in *Schönholzer Strasse*, but since he can't enter East Berlin without being arrested, and can't go through the tunnel without having a panic attack, it has to be one of us. "And what do you want me to do?" I ask, aware of the sulky tone in my voice.

"You take this," says Harry leaning down to fetch something out of the holdall that's lying on the floor at his feet. He passes a rifle across to me.

"Scheisse," I say, holding the weapon in both hands. I've never held anything like this before. The metal is cold and heavy. "Where the *fuck* did you get this?"

"Don't ask," says Harry in a tone of voice that's

not to be questioned.

"But what do you expect me to do with it?"

"Guard the entrance to the cellar in *Schönholzer Strasse.*"

"But surely you don't expect me to shoot anyone?"

"That's up to you," says Harry coolly. "It depends on the situation. Werner?"

"Yes?"

"Will you stay in the tunnel and help people through? Some of them might be scared, being in such a confined space." There's a flicker of embarrassment in Harry's eyes.

"Sure," says Werner. "And what about you and Andreas?"

"Andreas can wait at the bottom of the vertical shaft for people to come through. If anyone is too weak or infirm to climb the ladder, he can give them a fireman's lift." Andreas grins at this. He's the only one of us who could possibly do such a thing. "I'll meet them at the top and have the beers ready. And when the last person is safely through, we can let Rolf go so he can go back to East Berlin and report on the success of our project and the failure of his mission. Everyone happy?"

I'm not at all happy, but everyone else nods in agreement so it's better I just shut up and go along with the plan.

"Right then," says Harry. "Everyone into position."

Sabine

This time there will be no bags or rucksacks. I don't even suggest that we wear extra layers of clothes because it seems like tempting fate and makes me think of the failed escape attempt with Herr Schiller. There's no point taking any money with us because *Ostmarks* are worthless in the West. The only thing I do is remove the photographs of Hans and his father from their frames and tuck them inside my sweater.

We spend the final hour in the apartment quietly. Mother is looking through the photograph album, saying her final farewells to Father and Oma. Brigitta is reading her book of fairy stories one last time. I sit and stare into open space, wondering what happened to Matthias and Joachim, wishing I could have said good-bye to Astrid but, most of all, thinking about Hans.

On the stroke of nine o'clock I rouse myself.

"It's time to go," I say.

Mother goes to her room and returns wearing her best dark coat. I want to say it will most likely get ruined in the tunnel, but what's the point?

We've agreed that Mother and Brigitta will go first and I will follow five minutes later. It looks less suspicious if we leave separately and the Stasi are more likely to follow me than them. I help Brigitta into her coat. Mother is in the hallway putting her shoes on. I kneel down to Brigitta and speak quietly so that Mother can't hear.

"Remember what you promised me?" I say.

Brigitta nods her head but doesn't say anything.

I want to say more, but Mother appears in the doorway.

"Off you go then," I say to Brigitta trying to keep my voice light. "I'll see you in the café."

Mother comes over to me. She looks pale and her hands are trembling. "Sabine," she says, her voice shaking. "I…"

We haven't got time for big emotional speeches and I would much rather Mother and Brigitta just got going. I give her a hug and push her gently towards the door. "Go. We mustn't be late. I'll follow in exactly five minutes."

She nods uncertainly. Brigitta comes to take her hand. I shoo them out of the door and am left on my own in the empty apartment.

I take one last tour of the apartment: saying good-bye to the bedroom where I shared a bunk bed with Brigitta, the bathroom with the clanking water pipes, the tiny kitchen where we ate our meals. Then I put on my coat and shoes, open the apartment door and step out onto the landing.

It's dark. I press the light switch and start to make my way down the stairs. The building is silent. I pass Herr Schiller's old door and pause for a moment to remember our friend who tried to save us. As I continue down the stairs I hear a door opening on the landing below. I was so hoping to leave without running into anybody, most of all Frau Lange. I consider for a moment turning back, but it's too late. She has appeared on the landing and has seen me coming down the stairs.

"*Guten Abend,*" I say as I continue down. Good Evening.

"*Guten Abend,*" she replies in her clipped, formal tones. "*Wo gehen Sie?*" Where are you going?

The question stops me in my tracks. Why is she asking me that? Suddenly all the pent up feelings of living in this closed, secretive society burst out of me.

"*Das hat nichts mit Ihnen zu tun!*" I say to her. That's got nothing to do with you!

She looks astonished but I don't apologise. I storm past her, not caring what she thinks anymore.

Whether our escape attempt succeeds or fails, I will never see her again.

Dieter

Andreas takes up his position at the bottom of the vertical shaft and Werner, Claudia and I make our way through the tunnel into East Berlin. Against my will I have the rifle slung over one shoulder.

We pass the spot where the roof collapsed and I remember how Claudia nearly died. At the border we pause for a moment. Werner marked the border between East and West Berlin with a line of white paint and in an idle moment Andreas scrawled the words, *Hier beginnt die Freiheit!* Freedom starts here! Then, without a word, we move on.

When we reach the wooden slide Werner puts his hand on my shoulder. "Dieter, I just want to say thank you for everything you've done in helping to dig this tunnel."

"Oh, it was nothing," I say. "It was all your idea. We couldn't have done it without your plans."

Werner shrugs. "Anyway, good luck."

"Thank you," I say.

Claudia throws her arms around him and gives him a big hug. There's no need to say anything else.

"Come on," she says to me.

We leave Werner at the bottom of the slide, and make our way up to the top.

The cellar in *Schönholzer Strasse* is silent. A little light, just enough to see by, filters in through the barred windows at street level. The cellar is just as we left it. There's no sign that anyone has been here.

Claudia moves into the shadows and quickly changes out of her dirty old jeans and into a skirt and coat. She doesn't want to go to the café looking like she's just crawled through an underground tunnel. When she's ready we make our way to the top of the cellar steps. This is where I have to stay. If any of the residents come to the cellar to fetch coal whilst the escape is in progress I'm under orders to keep them here and not let them go. If any of them want to come to West Berlin, that's fine, but we can't risk them going off and informing the Stasi that an escape is under way in their building.

We stop at the top of the steps. I don't want Claudia to go. She turns to me. I pull her towards me in the shadows and kiss her on the lips. She kisses me back. Then she pulls away from me and slips out into the hallway.

Sabine

I hurry along the dark streets, keeping to the shadows wherever possible. I can't shake off the feeling that someone is following me, but I tell myself it's just my imagination. But I do feel conspicuous as if I was carrying a sign that says, *I'm going to escape from East Berlin*. It's a cold night and there are not many people about. The busiest place is the *U-bahn* station at *Eberswalder Strasse* where a crowd of workers appear from the exit. But they are all keen to get home and no one pays me any attention.

As I approach the area close to the Wall, the streets become quieter and darker. I keep my head down as I pass by an army truck. I imagine it is filled with soldiers.

I find the café on *Ruppiner Strasse*. The shutters are pulled down but a thin strip of light is escaping around the edge.

I push open the door and go inside.

It is dark and smoky. The walls are painted brown and the only light comes from a low-wattage bulb in a red, glass shade. There's a sickly sweet smell of beer. I'm stunned by how many people there are.

Every small round table is occupied by three or four people. There must be at least thirty people here. Are they all planning to escape through the tunnel? A café with that many people in it should be full of noise: chatter and laughter. But everyone here is either silent or whispering quietly to their nearest neighbours.

I look around for Mother and Brigitta. I feel a hand brush against mine. I look around and see Ingrid Huber sitting at a table with her niece and nephew. She clutches my hand and gives it a squeeze. I nod at her and smile. As I move on through the café I recognise Manfred Heilmann, the actor. He is sitting with a small boy and a woman who is cradling a baby in her arms. There's another woman at their table who I can't place for a moment although I'm sure I've seen her somewhere before. Then I realise it's Elisabeth Borgmann who played Mother Courage. Now that she's not wearing a dirty old headscarf she looks beautiful. At another table I notice Marion Weber whispering animatedly to her neighbours.

I find Mother and Brigitta sitting at the back of the café, on their own. Mother looks tense and worried, but as soon as she sees me she relaxes a little.

"So far so good," I say to them as I sit down. Now all we have to do is wait.

Dieter

I've never felt more scared, standing at the top of the cellar steps, cradling the rifle in my arms.

All my senses are on high alert, listening for every little sound. I hear the main door to the building open and I jump to attention. There are footsteps in the hallway. They walk a few steps, then stop. Then walk some more. *Please don't come to the cellar*, I think, *please don't come to the cellar. I don't want to have to hold you here.*

Then the footsteps start to climb the stairs and eventually disappear. I breathe out.

I check my watch. It's been seven minutes since Claudia left. She must have reached the café by now. I wish she'd hurry up and bring the escapees to the tunnel. I'm going to go mad with nerves waiting here.

Sabine

The café door opens and a young woman walks in. She's dark haired and petite and is wearing a woollen coat. I hope this is Claudia. She glances around the room, and I see a little alarm in her eyes at the number of people here. I don't know how many she was expecting.

Dozens of pairs of eyes follow her as she walks to the bar where Herr Lindemann, the landlord, is polishing and re-polishing glasses with a tea-towel.

The café is silent as everyone waits for her to speak. She clears her throat and says to Herr Lindemann, *"Einen Kaffee bitte."* A coffee please.

This is the signal. Now I know this is definitely Claudia. No one in East Berlin would ask for a coffee because coffee isn't available here. The people in the café exchange knowing glances with one another. Claudia's Aunt, Ingrid Huber, looks close to tears. She is telling Claudia's brother and sister that they must keep very quiet.

Herr Lindemann puts down the glass he has been polishing for the last five minutes and replies in a shaking voice, *"Es gibt keinen Kaffee."* There is no coffee.

"Danke," says Claudia.

She leans over the bar and has a whispered conversation with Herr Lindemann. I think they're discussing the numbers. Then Claudia moves into the centre of the café and addresses everyone.

"I will take half of you now," she says. "Everyone sitting in the front half of the café come with me. I will come straight back for the rest of you."

The people in the front of the café all stand. There's a scraping of chairs and a buzz of children's voices. Parents tell them to be quiet.

"Quick!" says Claudia. "Stay close to me and keep quiet!"

She goes to the door and looks out, up and down the street. "Now!" she says looking over her shoulder.

The first group of escapees follow her into the street.

We wait for her to come back.

Dieter

It seems to me as if Claudia has been gone far too long. Surely, it can't take her all that time to reach the café and bring everyone back. I start to imagine all sorts of things that could have gone wrong: she's walked into a patrol of border guards; the café is swarming with Stasi officials; the escapees never made it to the café in the first place. My palms are sweating against the metal of the rifle. I strain my ears to try and catch any sound outside in the street. I hear a truck on *Brunnenstrasse*, delivering new border guards no doubt.

Suddenly there are footsteps in the hallway. Lots of them. Then there's a knock on the cellar door.

"Dieter, it's me." Claudia's voice is an urgent whisper. I open the door immediately and Claudia ushers about fifteen men, women and children, none of whom I recognise, into the cellar. "This is half of the group," she says.

Mein Gott, I think, *I wasn't expecting so many people.*

Some of them are old and I don't know how they are going to manage to crawl through the tunnel. One woman is carrying a small baby strapped to her chest. Many of them are wide-eyed with terror. I look in vain for Sabine, Mother and Brigitta but they are not there.

"This way," says Claudia leading them to the tunnel. "Hurry."

I continue to guard the door as Claudia shows them the tunnel. One by one they disappear down the chute. But it's taking far too long and I'm convinced we're going to be found out.

Once the escape is running smoothly Claudia runs back up the cellar steps. "Now for the rest," she says, disappearing once more into the night.

Sabine

With the first group gone, the atmosphere in the

café becomes even tenser. Herr Lindemann gives up the pretence of polishing glasses and stands by the door, listening for Claudia's return.

Mother looks pale and tired. I worry that she won't have the strength to crawl through a tunnel. I try to take her mind off the coming ordeal by talking.

"You know," I say, "I still can't believe that I'm here, that I'm not in prison. I thought they were going to keep me there forever and then they suddenly let me go. I can't understand what happened."

"But it's simple," says Brigitta, her eyes twinkling.

"What do you mean?"

Mother lays a hand on Brigitta's arm to stop her, but Brigitta is determined to tell me. "I went to Frau Lange and asked her to help us."

"You did what?" I ask. "But I thought you were terrified of Frau Lange."

Brigitta shrugs. "She's not so scary. I realised that the day we helped her with her coal bucket and she told us the story of her husband."

"But what did you say to her?"

"I told her that she had lost her husband but that we had lost our father, one to one regime and one to another. What happened to Frau Lange's husband was dreadful and wrong but two wrongs don't make a right. I told her that you had been arrested without any justification and she understood that. She didn't promise anything but she said she would see what she could do. She remembered the time we helped her with the coal. She knows we're not bad people."

I'm astounded that Brigitta had the courage to speak to Frau Lange. But most of all I'm shocked that Frau Lange responded so positively. I think of my last meeting with Frau Lange on the stairs, and feel bad that I was so rude to her. After all, she was just a lonely old woman who had lost her husband in terrible circumstances and was hoping that Communism would bring a better world.

At that moment the café door opens and Claudia returns. She must have delivered the first group safely to the tunnel.

Everyone gets to their feet. Mother has gone deathly pale. I grab her hands in mine. "It won't be long now. Just be brave."

We gather behind Claudia, and wait whilst she checks the street.

"Now," she whispers.

Our group snakes along *Ruppiner Strasse*, turning left into *Schönholzer Strasse*. Ahead of us is *Brunnenstrasse*.

It's very quiet in *Schönholzer Strasse*. The houses are silent and seem to offer some sort of protection. In places there are vacant lots where a building was hit during the war. I feel more exposed then, when there is no building in which to run and hide.

Suddenly from *Brunnenstrasse* there's the sound of a heavy vehicle manoeuvring. It's an army truck turning around and as it reverses and swings around, engine rumbling and gears clanking, its headlights suddenly shine down *Schönholzer Strasse*, illuminating the street like a pair of searchlights.

"Don't move!" hisses Claudia as we all press ourselves against the wall of the nearest building, wishing ourselves flat and invisible.

Please God, I think, *don't let the truck drive down here.*

I hold my breath as the gears grind and the engine revs. What if it breaks down with its lights shining on us? Or runs out of petrol? *Come on*, I think, *get a move on.*

The engine roars and the vehicle jolts forward and disappears back up *Brunnenstrasse.*

I breathe out.

Claudia waits a moment, then beckons us on with renewed urgency.

We reach the door of number seventeen and Claudia ushers us inside.

Dieter

At the sound of Claudia's voice I yank the door open and the second group makes its way down the cellar steps. I scan each of their faces. They are strangers to me, all of them. And then, at the back of the group I see Sabine, Brigitta and Mother, the three of them holding hands. I've never been happier to see them, but there's no time to talk now. Claudia is ushering people towards the tunnel. So far everything has gone according to plan, but we must get this group through the tunnel before the guards on *Brunnenstrasse* discover what is happening.

I abandon my post at the cellar door and follow the group down the steps. Claudia is helping people into the tunnel, showing them how to slide down safely and reassuring them that there's nothing to be frightened off. There's a family with three small children. The father says it's going to be an exciting adventure and they mustn't be scared. He slides into the tunnel first and persuades the children to follow him one by one. Then the mother disappears down the chute. Then Claudia helps an elderly couple who have difficulty bending down. *For God's sake,* I think, *hurry up.* We have to get out of here before we are found out. It occurs to me that we should have barricaded the door to the cellar, but it's too late now. The next few people are able-bodied and, to my relief, disappear down the chute in a matter of moments. At last the only people left are Mother, Brigitta, Sabine, Claudia and myself.

"You next," says Claudia to Mother.

But Mother is trembling from head to toe. "I can't do it," she says. "I can't go through the tunnel."

Sabine

"Mother, you have to," I say.

"I can't, I…"

"It's all right, Frau Neumann," says Claudia calmly. "It's really not so bad down there. There are people in the tunnel to help you."

Mother stares in terror at the hole in the ground. Her chest rises and falls erratically. She shakes her head from side to side. "*Nein, nein, nein.*"

"*Mein Gott!*" says Dieter, "what are we going to do now?"

"I want to go back home," whimpers Mother in the voice of a frightened child.

"You *can't* go back home," I say to her. "It's impossible. You'll be arrested." But it's no good, she's not listening.

"Come with me Mama," calls Brigitta who is sitting on the edge of the hole.

But Mother starts to move back towards the steps. "I have to get out of here. I have to get out of here."

Dieter looks at me in despair as Mother starts to climb the cellar steps. Then he throws the rifle aside and grabs hold of her from behind with both arms.

"Let me go!" she screams.

"Shut up!" cries Dieter, lifting her back into the cellar. "I dug this hole for you and you're going through it *now*."

"I can't," she wails.

"Be quiet," hisses Dieter, "or you'll give us all away."

She continues to struggle in Dieter's arms and suddenly I can't stand it any longer. Dieter has risked his life to dig this tunnel. We've all risked our lives to get here tonight. Eight years of pent up frustration explode inside me and before I know what I'm doing I run over to her and slap her hard across the face.

The sound ricochets off the empty cellar walls. Then silence.

My hand stings, but Mother has stopped struggling. She has gone limp in Dieter's arms.

Claudia comes over and helps him carry her to the tunnel. Brigitta slides down the chute. Then Dieter calls to Werner to help him and he lowers Mother's unresisting body into the hole. Dieter follows.

I'm still standing where I slapped Mother, too shocked to move. I can't believe I did what I did. I hope she'll understand and will forgive me.

Claudia comes over to me. "You did the right thing," she says. She takes hold of my hand. "Come on now." She leads me towards the tunnel.

We are almost there when the cellar door flies open and a bright light shines into the basement.

Dieter

Werner takes one look at Mother who is in a

state of mental and physical collapse and says, "You take her shoulders, I'll take her feet." Together we lift her up and start to carry her through the tunnel. Brigitta goes ahead of us.

It's impossibly slow and back-breaking. Every ten metres or so we have to put her down and readjust our hold on her.

"Run ahead," I say to Brigitta, "and ask for Andreas to come and help us."

Brigitta disappears down the tunnel, her small frame making it easier for her to move quickly in the confined space. Werner and I stagger on with our load.

A few minutes later Andreas appears.

"Give her to me," he says. He takes over from me and I watch as he and Werner continue down the tunnel. It's only then I realise that Sabine and Claudia haven't appeared. *Where the hell are they?* I stagger back down the tunnel towards East Berlin.

Sabine

The light dazzles me and I am caught like a frightened animal. I'm vaguely aware of Claudia pulling me by the hand but then a voice I recognise calls my name.

"Sabine."

"Astrid? Is that really you?"

Astrid lowers the torchlight and I see then her tall figure and unmistakable blond hair. She is standing at the top of the cellar steps. She puts a hand on the wooden banister and starts to make her way down the stairs. I let go of Claudia's hand and run towards her.

"What are you doing here?" I ask.

She pauses on the second step from the bottom. She is distracted. "I…I…followed you here tonight. I was hiding in a doorway in *Schönholzer Strasse*. I…" Her voice trails away.

"Do you want to come to West Berlin?" I ask. "Is that why you're here?" I never thought for one minute that she would want to leave her family and go to the West, so I'm both surprised and excited to see her. I make a move to take hold of her hand but she jerks it away from me.

"No!" she says. "That's not why I'm here."

"But why…"

She cuts me off. "Sabine, I didn't think you'd still be here." There's anxiety in her voice. She glances nervously up the stairs towards the cellar door. She looks at her watch. "Sabine, you should go, before…"

"Before what?"

She drops her voice and speaks in an urgent whisper. "Before someone comes."

Suddenly it's as if I'm seeing her for the first time and I don't recognise her as my friend. Fear is written all over her face, but I think it's not fear *for* me, it's fear *of* me, and the truth starts to dawn in my mind.

"It was you, wasn't it?" I say.

"What do you mean?"

I fix her with a stare and she doesn't dare look away. "You knew Matthias and Joachim had defaced the portraits because you saw them come out of the classroom whilst you were waiting for me. You reported them to the Stasi. That's why they're now in prison."

"But, Sabine, the Stasi released you when they knew it was Matthias and Joachim. I thought you'd be pleased."

"Pleased? That my friend would shop her own classmates to the Stasi? And what was your reward for informing on Matthias and Joachim? Tickets to the opening night of *Mutter Courage*?"

She stares at me wide-eyed. "How did you know…"

"I was *there*," I say. "I saw you, sitting in the best seats in the theatre. You and your family. But you never even mentioned it."

"Sabine, how could I? We were only there because my father's boss invited us. What would you have thought of me if you knew my father was a Stasi official? You don't know what it's like trying to live a double life."

"What do you mean, a *double life*? What has your father's job got to do with this? We're talking about you."

She clenches her hand into a fist and hits the banister. "You don't understand!" she cries. "It was so hard! I needed to be one person at school and another one at home. I tried to fit in at school by making fun of Herr Schmidt and all that, but at home I was expected to report on what was going on in the school."

"You mean you worked as an… *informer*?" I spit the word out in contempt, making her blink. I can't believe this. Twice I refused to become an informer for the Stasi, even when to do so would have given me back my freedom. Astrid seems to have done it just to make her parents happy. But there's one last thing I have to know.

"Astrid, tell me the truth. What did you tell the Stasi about me?"

"Nothing, I mean…"

"Why was I arrested a second time? You told them about the tunnel didn't you?"

She nods. "I'm sorry. But Sabine, you have to believe me," she grabs hold of my shoulders, "I don't want you to get hurt. You have to go *now*. I'm giving you this chance. They will be here any minute."

I stare at her in disbelief. She has betrayed the tunnel, but still wants me to be safe.

"Come *on*," says Claudia, pulling me by the arm. She starts to drag me towards the tunnel.

Suddenly there are pounding feet up above. The cellar door bursts open and a border guard appears at the top of the steps followed by two men in beige overcoats. One of them is Astrid's father. The other is Herr Stein. The Stasi men stand at the top of the steps whilst the border guard runs half way down, his rifle aimed squarely at me and Claudia.

"*Scheisse!*" mutters Astrid under her breath.

"Stay where you are!" shouts the guard from his vantage point half way up the steps.

Claudia and I freeze.

The guard descends a couple more steps.

At that moment, Dieter pokes his head up out of the tunnel entrance. "Sabine, where are...*what the hell?*"

The guard fires into the air, shattering the single bulb that hangs from the cellar ceiling. Crystals of glass shower down over Claudia and me. Astrid screams.

Herr Stein shines a torchlight into the cellar. Dieter pulls himself out of the tunnel and picks up the rifle which he had abandoned. He aims it at the guard.

"*Nein!*" I scream at him.

Claudia pushes me towards the hole.

The guard shouts a second warning. "Stay where you are or I shoot!"

Then he lifts his rifle, and aims it at me. In the split second that it takes him to pull the trigger, Astrid launches herself in front of me and the bullet finds its target in her breast. Claudia pushes me into the hole. The last thing I see as gravity pulls me down is Astrid's body flying through the air and landing with a thump on the cellar floor.

Dieter

The body of a young woman flies past me and lands in a tangled heap on the cellar floor.

Rage surges up inside me. I point my rifle at the border guard and pull back hard on the trigger.

Nothing happens.

I try again. Still nothing.

I don't believe it. The rifle's got no ammunition. Or it's a dud. Harry never expected me to fire it. It was just for show. I throw it away in disgust.

"ASTRID!" shouts a voice from the top of the cellar stairs.

It's only then that I become aware of the two men standing by the cellar door. One of them, with steel-grey hair, standing rigid, the other throwing his arms into the air and shouting Astrid's name in a voice wild with despair. This second man runs down the stairs, past the border guard, and throws himself at the prone figure lying on the floor.

"Meine Tochter ..." he sobs, lifting her into his arms. My daughter. I realise it must be Sabine's friend Astrid and her father. Sabine has talked about her.

I would go and help them, but she's already dead and the border guard still has me in his sights. If I move, he'll shoot.

"Stay where you are!" he says, walking down the steps towards me. "And you too!" he says to someone behind me.

It's only then that I realise Claudia is still in the cellar with me. I thought she had gone with Sabine.

The guard continues his way down the steps, the thump of his boots making the wood creak.

Suddenly, Astrid's father jumps to his feet. His eyes are wide and staring. He looks like a man deranged.

"No! *You* stay where you are," he shouts at the guard. Then, slowly and deliberately, he puts his hand inside his coat, pulls out a pistol, aims it at the guard and fires, hitting him square in the forehead.

The guard's body goes into a spasm, the rifle is ejected from his hands, then he falls forward and topples over the banister, landing with a sickening thud in front of my feet.

I grab hold of Claudia's hand and together we run for the tunnel. From the top of the cellar steps the grey-haired man shouts at us to stop. We ignore him and slide down the chute together.

We scramble to our feet and move as fast as we can through the tunnel. We've gone about ten metres when there's a thud behind us. I look over my shoulder and see the grey-haired man at the bottom of the slide.

"Keep moving," I say to Claudia. "Don't look back."

The man shouts at us. "Stop! Or I shoot!"

We keep going. I can hear the man's footsteps behind us.

We reach the white line painted on the shoring. At that point I turn and face our pursuer. He lifts his pistol to shoot. Claudia is crouched right behind me, breathing hard.

"You can't shoot us," I say to him. "Look. This is the border between East and West Berlin. We are in West Berlin now."

He looks in confusion at the words scrawled on the white paint. *Hier beginnt die Freiheit!*

"Go back to East Berlin," I say.

The hand holding the pistol falls to his side. He stares at us, speechless.

Then I take hold of Claudia's hand and together we walk into the West.

Sabine

As I cross the *Tiergarten* I notice that the first shoots of spring are starting to appear. It's one month now since we made our escape through the tunnel and so much has changed.

Mother has found a new job as a chamber maid at the *Hotel Zoo* and seems much more contented. Brigitta has started at a new school and is making friends. I will sit my *Abitur* in the summer and then I hope to go to university. Werner and Marion are going to be married in the summer and we are all invited to the wedding. Dieter and Claudia are very much in love. In fact, Harry has asked me out on a date. He's a great guy, but I'm not sure he's really my type.

Rolf was released from his captivity in the bakery storeroom once Dieter and Claudia had made it safely through the tunnel. At first, he was in a furious state, shouting that he would denounce the whole lot of us. But when he heard that Astrid had been killed, he broke down and wept. It seems they knew each other from their camping trips with the *Freie Deutsche Jugend*. Maybe it was even Astrid who told him about the tunnel. I don't know if Rolf returned to East Berlin. It would have been very difficult for him after the failure of his mission.

I've been making enquiries at the refugee centre in *Marienfelde*, asking after Frau Fischer. I still have the photos of Hans and his father. The administrator at *Marienfelde* was reluctant to divulge any details at first, in case I was a Stasi spy, but when I explained my own escape through the tunnel and showed her the picture of Hans, she relented. It seems Hans has become something of a martyr to West Berliners. There is talk of erecting a memorial to him, on the West side of the Wall, near where he died. Frau Fischer is living in a quiet corner of *Zehlendorf-Steglitz* in south-west Berlin. I have set aside today to pay her a visit.

I go into a flower shop and buy six red roses, each one a perfect specimen. Then I walk down to the River Spree which is part of the border between East and West Berlin. I can see the border guards on the other side. As I stand on the bank of the river I remember Herr Schiller, our friend who tried to save us; I remember Matthias and Joachim who took a stand and whose fate remains unknown; I remember Hans who was too impatient to get out; and I remember Astrid who gave her life to protect me. As I think about each one I toss a rose into the water and watch it float away on the current. I hope the border guards can see what I'm doing.

Then I take the sixth rose and make my way to Frau Fischer's.

~~~

POSTSCRIPT

The Berlin Wall stood for just over 28 years, from 13 August 1961 to 9 November 1989. During that time at least 136 people lost their lives trying to escape from East to West Berlin.

Initially it consisted of coils of barbed wire. Then it became a solid wall, topped with barbed wire. Its final reincarnation was as a 3.6 metre high concrete barrier with a cylindrical top, making it virtually impossible to scale. An "inner" wall was constructed on the east side and the ground between the two walls became known as the "death strip", a 100 metre wide stretch of land incorporating watchtowers, anti-tank defences, signal fencing, dogs and trip wires. It was raked with sand to make it easy to spot the footprints of any would-be escapees. Houses that lay within the death strip were demolished, such as those on the east side of *Bernauer Strasse*.

A large section of the Wall has been preserved at *Bernauer Strasse*. Part of the former death strip has been landscaped over and there is a memorial to those who died.

The Church of Reconciliation on *Bernauer Strasse* was blown up by the East Germans in 1985 because it obscured the border guards' view of the death strip. Today a new memorial church has been built in its place. You can still see the outline of the old church marked with metal strips on the ground. The bent iron cross of the old church also lies on the ground.

The former Stasi headquarters at *Normannenstrasse* is now a museum with detailed displays about life in the German Democratic Republic and the Stasi's spying methods. In the entrance hall is a prisoner transporter van, like the one Sabine is transported in. They were often disguised as delivery vans. The Stasi remand prison at *Hohenschönhausen* (where Sabine is taken, although she doesn't know where it is or what it is called) is now a memorial site with very moving and informative tours about the Stasi and its interrogation methods.

West Berliners were not allowed to visit East Berlin until Christmas 1963 when they were allowed to apply for a visa for a short visit. It was not until 1971 that West Berliners were allowed to apply for visas in the same way as West Germans. Permission for East Berliners to travel west was almost impossible to obtain and was only granted in a few circumstances, such as to the elderly, or to those participating in cultural and sporting activities.

By 1989 political changes were taking place in many Eastern Bloc countries. In August 1989 Hungary removed its physical border with Austria. As a result, thousands of East Germans escaped to Austria via Hungary. The Hungarians tried to prevent any more East Germans from crossing the border, but many East Germans took refuge in the

West German embassy in Budapest. Similar events occurred at the West German embassy in Prague. Peaceful, mass demonstrations broke out in East Germany, notably in Leipzig and Berlin.

To ease the situation, the East German Politburo decided to remove travel restrictions to West Berlin and West Germany. The new regulations were to take effect on 10th November, but at a press conference on 9th November Günter Schabowski, the spokesman for the party, who had not been fully briefed, announced that, as far as he was aware, the new regulations would come into force immediately. The press conference was broadcast on television. Thousands of East Berliners began gathering at the checkpoints along the wall. The guards, who were not aware of the broadcast, were confused. Thankfully no one fired a shot. The guard in charge at *Bornholmer Strasse* took the decision to open the crossing and thousands of East Berliners swarmed into West Berlin. The Berlin Wall was over.

ABOUT THE AUTHOR

Margarita Morris was born in Harrogate, North Yorkshire. She studied Modern Languages at Jesus College, Oxford and worked in computing for eleven years. She lives in Oxfordshire with her husband and two sons.

Connect with Margarita
Website: http://margaritamorris.com

OTHER BOOKS BY MARGARITA

The Sleeping Angel
Scarborough Fair
Scarborough Ball

Made in the USA
Lexington, KY
24 August 2019